Shortbread Cookie Princess

by

Zelda Benjamin

Highland Falls

Shortbread Cookie Princess

Cover Art by *Tina Lynn Stout*

The Wild Rose Press, Inc.
PO Box 708
Adams Basin, NY 14410-0708
Visit us at www.thewildrosepress.com

Publishing History
First Edition, 2022
Trade Paperback ISBN 978-1-5092-4593-2
Digital ISBN 978-1-5092-4594-9

Highland Falls
Published in the United States of America

"Who knows how many scraps of plaid have been preserved in mothballs and hidden away in family attics?"

His low voice held an edge of seduction. Sophia stepped closer. The underlying sensuality of his tone captivated her. In all the times she had dusted over the fabric, she never got close enough to inhale the faint scent of mothballs. She wrinkled her nose.

"You're very lucky to have it." Ian ran an index finger over a thin red line woven vertically down the plaid. "Highland dyers and weavers were highly skilled. It's evident in pieces like this. Run your fingers along this line. Do you feel the thickness? The fabric was mended many times, perhaps torn by a sword or knife thrust."

"Or it could have been caught on a rock." Sophia reached out and touched the coarse wool.

"It's possible." Ian laughed. "If we settle for the simple explanations, we might never learn the history of the people who owned these valuable pieces." He placed a hand over her fingers, guiding her touch along the uneven weave. "This can likely date back before the British banned the wearing of kilts."

"I never noticed the inconsistency in the red line." Sophia rubbed a finger to the end of the weave. The air around them became electrified. "How long ago were kilts banned?" She never had much interest in history, but Ian's enthusiasm intrigued her. No one ever reacted with such passion to the dusty fabric—especially not her. An awkward moment passed before Ian released her hand.

Praise for Zelda Benjamin

"Zelda Benjamin's stories are delightful with engaging characters and intriguing plot twists."

~Tara L. Ames, USA TODAY bestselling author

~*~

"Heartwarming stories, engaging characters, and descriptive settings that will make you a fan!"

~Nancy J. Cohen, award-winning author

~*~

"Zelda Benjamin's writing is a delightful treat for the senses."

~Alyssa Maxwell, mystery author

~*~

"A scrumptious confection for sure…flows smoothly with well-defined descriptions that are witty and utterly entertaining."

~InD'Tale Magazine

Dedication

To the memory of my mother, Florence Gottlieb Benezra, who taught me the joy of reading.

Chapter 1

What may be done at anytime, will be done at no time. Sophia Porter's father had been a wise man with a Scottish proverb for everything. Of all the things he taught her, the most important was that time was precious and shouldn't be wasted. Sadly, his untimely death proved that to be true.

Time-sucking mishaps and too many unexpected interruptions happened everywhere, but his sound advice helped her adjust to interrupted schedules and inevitable setbacks. "Thanks, Daddy," she whispered. "Today's schedule's tight, but I've got this." She stood in front of the counter and glanced at the dozens of kilt-shaped shortbread waiting to be precisely decorated to the specifications of each clan. Without any interruptions, she'd have them delivered to the Scottish Society hall on time for tonight's event.

"Did you say something, chef?" Alana asked from across the kitchen.

"Just thinking out loud." Sophia put her rolling pin on the counter and stared at her assistant's hair. "Cobalt blue suits you much better than last month's hot pink."

"Blue streaks are more appropriate for tonight's event." Alana stepped close. "We've been rolling and cutting since before dawn. How about a cup of tea?"

Sophia opened her mouth to speak.

"No excuses. We're ahead of schedule." Alana

gestured toward the cooling racks, and the perfectly defined little kilts waiting to be frosted.

"Okay. A tea break sounds perfect." Sophia stretched her fingers. Surely the author of her father's proverb wouldn't quibble over a quick cup of tea.

"It won't take long." Alana grabbed a box of teabags off the shelf. "Get off your feet and relax." She passed through the archway to the front of the bakeshop.

Sophia reached for a rag and cleaned a smudge of frosting off the glass partition separating the work area from the café. Every counter, window, and tabletop needed to be sparkling clean before the doors opened.

"I said relax." Alana looked back and shook her head.

"I am relaxing." Sophia scrunched her lips. She disliked it when Alana acted like a drill sergeant—even if it was for her own good. She tossed the rag to the side and turned her attention to the neat line of café tables and chairs along the front window. Rays of morning sun hit the window. Decorated shortbread in the window display exploded in a full array of fall colors.

If not for the Adirondack foothills surrounding the town, the scene outside could be a fall morning in her old Brooklyn Heights neighborhood. The tree-lined streets came to life. Shopkeepers opened for business, locals rushed off to work, and tourists braved the cold wind. That was where the similarities ended. Emptiness echoed in her heart for anonymous strolls along the streets of Manhattan, but anonymity was unheard of in Highland Falls, New York. In the three short months she lived here, everyone, right down to the endearing town drunk, knew the terms of her late Aunt Mary's will.

She looked over her shoulder at the trays of kilt-shaped shortbread and smiled. Tonight's event could give her the financial boost she needed to succeed. She had until the end of the year to prove herself. Mary's lawyers believed she had all the right ingredients to make the bakery a success. She was young, single, and a hard worker with no family obligations. Hard work didn't scare her, and failure wasn't an option. Either way, she'd never return to her boring job as an accountant, or the malevolent duplicity of living with her stepmother.

A hard rattle at the back door shook her from her thoughts. "Who's there?"

No one answered. Highland Falls was a safe town, but city life had taught her to be cautious. The other day, customers mentioned coyote sightings in the back alleys. Something or someone pushed against the door. Instinctively, she reached for her rolling pin.

The door opened. A tall, ginger-haired stranger stood framed in the doorway.

"Can I help you?" Sophia looked up at his piercing blue eyes, and raised the rolling pin between them.

He took a step forward.

"Wipe your boots." Alana rushed back with the box of teabags in her hand. "What are you doing sneaking in our back door?"

"*Ach*, lassies. I didn't mean to frighten you." He scraped the soles of his boots on the doormat. "You could do some damage with that." He nodded at the rolling pin.

"I wasn't expecting anyone. I thought you might be a coyote." Sophia clenched her fingers.

"A coyote?" His brows turned down. "Where?"

The stranger's voice was quiet with no hint of animosity. The soft sound was like people used in a library. She found it ridiculously sexy. "They've been spotted coming out of the hills." What a fool she must look like attempting to defend herself from a pointed tooth predator with a baking utensil.

"Aye, I heard it mentioned at the pub," he said. "No worries, lass. Coyotes are naturally afraid of humans."

"I didn't know that." After all, what did a city girl know about coyotes?

"Just a random fact I've stored away for an occasion like this." He smiled and raised his hands.

Sensing he meant no harm, she placed the rolling pin on the counter. "Is that butter from Fiona?" She pointed to the small, tightly wrapped package in his hand. A stickler for details, she noticed the fine stitching around the cuffs of his shirt. Except for his dirty boots, he was better dressed than Fiona's usual delivery people.

"*Aye.*" He placed the parcel on the counter.

"Where's Georgie, her regular delivery boy?" Alana asked.

"Excuse my manners," he said. "Georgie's sick today. My name is Ian."

"Thanks for delivering the butter, Ian." She handed the butter to Alana.

Alana reached for the package and read the label. "We won't be using lemon butter today. I'll put it in the freezer." Alana turned and returned to the café.

"I should get back to work, too." Sophia gestured toward the counter dusted with flour.

"Those are some tidy, *wee* cookies you've made." Ian pointed to the rows of trays.

"You're visiting from Edinburgh, aren't you?" Sophia detected a posh lilt to his Scottish accent.

"*Aye*, lass. I lived there for a while. You've got a *verra* good ear for accents. Most Americans can't tell an Irish accent from a Scottish. You have it pinpointed down to the city."

"The accent's familiar. My father lived in Edinburgh. Originally from Aberdeen, he received his medical education in Edinburgh. He had a similar accent."

"And you? Where are you from, lass? Your temperament doesn't quite fit this peaceful little town." He nodded at the rolling pin on the counter.

"Neither does yours." She sensed a hint of mystery blended with an intelligent sophistication.

"Let me take an educated guess where you're from." Stroking his chin, he studied her closely. "You were raised in New York; Brooklyn to be exact."

"A Brooklyn accent is easy to identify." Self-conscious of his close attention, she brushed flour off her apron.

"And your mother, was she a Scot like your father?" he asked.

"On her father's side." She got the impression he was searching for more than just the origin of her accent. The question seemed odd coming from someone she'd just met. From the corner of her eye, she noticed the rolling pin about to roll off the marble counter. She reached out to grab it.

Ian, an arm's length away, caught it first.

"Dark hair, dark eyes, and a quick temper, I'd say

you've got some dark-haired Irish in you. Most likely a descendant of the Spanish Armada." He hesitated before handing her the rolling pin.

"I don't know about a connection to the armada, but I've been told I have Irish ancestors somewhere along the line." She shrugged and placed the rolling pin securely behind a mixing bowl. "Do you always guess at someone's family history?"

"It's connected to what I do for a living." Ian shrugged.

"I'd like to hear all about it, but I've got cookies to bake and frost." In spite of his odd interest in her genetic background, he had a cosmopolitan air she found refreshing. She placed a tray of sugar cookies in the oven and set the timer for fifteen minutes. He was breaking her rhythm.

The bell over the front door announced an early customer. *Game over.* The timely interruption saved her from having to answer more personal questions. Ian already knew more about her than she would offer to a stranger.

On the other side of the partition, a lanky man with a tool belt slung over his shoulder whistled as he walked past the café tables.

"Hi, Tim. You're early today." Sophia joined Alana in the café.

"You here for Granny Ulster's usual?" Alana asked.

"It's too early for my granny's order. I'm looking for the doc," Tim said.

"I'm here, mate. What can I do for you?" Ian stepped through the archway.

"Fiona has some restoration work for me at the B

and B. My car wouldn't start. She said I might find you here. Can I hitch a ride, Doc?"

"No problem. I'd enjoy the company." Ian gave Tim a thumbs-up.

"Wow, those cookies look delicious." Tim turned his focus back to the display case.

The short conversation between Tim and Ian piqued Sophia's interest. Tim offered a bit of insight into the handsome stranger. *A doctor? Was he a medical doctor or maybe a PhD of genealogy?* That would explain his interest in her background. After a quick summary of all the years needed to become a doctor, Sophia guessed he was a few years older than her—maybe thirty-four, or thirty-five. For a young man, Ian had a charming old-world way about him— the type to be wearing patches on his sleeves. A man like that should have been more aware of tracking in dirt on his boots. What was he doing making deliveries for Fiona? Was he a guest at the B and B and seeing Fiona in a bind, he offered to help?

"Hey, Tim, how about some shortbread in exchange for fixing a loose hinge?" Sophia reached into the showcase and plated a few cookies for Tim

"Doesn't sound like a big problem. I'll take a look." Tim adjusted his tool belt and carried the cookies to the back.

"I'll bring you something to wash down the cookies." Alana followed with a cup of coffee.

Sophia thought of offering the mysterious deliveryman a taste, but his focus was on the side wall. She followed him to the wall where a coat of arms, and woven tartan tapestry decorated the wall. The display screamed ancient Scotland. Although precious to her aunt, and popular with the tourists, the heirlooms were dust collectors that needed her attention daily.

"This is an amazing piece of history." Ian placed a palm on the fabric. "It's MacLennan, isn't it?"

"Yes, it is." The faded dark green and black pattern was interesting, but the fabric was too harsh and dusty for her tastes. "It belonged to my mother's family." Sophia swallowed past the lump in her throat. "I've been told the clan had a dark history." She knew next to nothing and had little interest in learning about her family's past.

"Is the clan's dark history a fact or just hearsay?" He crossed his arms. "Where does your information come from—family or idle gossip?"

"Does it make a difference?" Sophia found his question very academic—like something a professor would ask a student. Did he forget about Tim?

"It does if you want the truth." He raised a brow. "Who told you about their dark history?"

"My stepmother…" A knot surfaced in the pit of her stomach. "Edna told me." She'd been six when her father married Edna Frost. From that day on, her stepmother, Mother Malevolent, lived by the creed— nice to Dad, mean to the kid. For too many years, Sophia tried to no avail to make her stepmother like her. Nothing she did worked, and she had learned to circumvent the woman's mean temperament. This stranger, however, could be right. Why should she believe anything that evil woman said?

"I heard your aunt Mary was a MacLennan before she married a Henderson." Ian cleared his throat—his focus was still on the tartan.

"Small town talk can be very informative. Is that

how you get your *facts*?" She raised a brow. He deserved a little push back. What gave this stranger the right to ask so many personal questions?

"Sometimes it has meaning. Most of the time it's gossip or embellished tales." He turned toward her with a half smile. "I'm sorry for your loss. Mary was a charming, bonnie woman."

"Yes, she was." Sophia would always be grateful to her aunt. She had given her a graceful way to separate from her stepmother. Before Sophia inherited the shop, her CPA work kept her busy and away from Edna's mean tirades. But it wasn't enough. The bittersweet goodbyes to her clients and colleagues were quickly forgotten when she packed her bags and boarded the first train out of Grand Central. "How well did you know my aunt?" She tucked a hand into her apron pocket.

"I met her last year when I came this way. Do you remember much about her?"

"I have some fond memories of visiting with my dad when I was younger. I remember how she always smelled like vanilla and butter." She shook her head, dismissing the thought, and hoping Ian had no more questions. That's where the fond memory ended. When she and her dad returned home, her stepmother always went into a rant. By the time Sophia was in her teens, the visits had ended.

"Your aunt had a fair knowledge of her clan's history. Do you remember any stories she might have shared?"

"If she did, I don't remember." She walked behind the counter, leaving Ian alone in front of the tartan.

"The cookies are done." Alana appeared in the

archway with Tim's empty cup and a tray of sugar cookies.

"I didn't hear the timer." Sophia had no excuse for this oversight. She reached for the tray. "Will we have enough for our early customers?" She glanced at the empty shelf in the display case.

"Another dozen should do it. They're in the oven, and the timer's set." Alana placed the dirty cup in a bin under the counter.

"I'll fill the case." Sophia reached for a spatula and moved the cookies from the tray to the empty shelf. She inhaled the fresh baked cookie smell, and she relaxed.

"Looks good." Alana peered at the display. "What do you think, Doc?"

"They smell delicious." Ian joined them. "I detect a strong scent of Madagascar vanilla."

"Our cookies are made with only the best ingredients." Sophia handed him an odd-shaped cookie that didn't make it into the display.

"I'm sorry I interrupted your work with so many questions." He bit into the cookie and smiled. "I'd like to explain, if you have a moment."

"Go ahead. I'm listening." She bit back a smile. He had already taken too much of her time—what were a few more minutes?

"I'm currently on a sabbatical from my position as Professor of Forensic Pathology at University of Albany." He wiped a crumb off the counter. "I recently received a grant from Edinburgh University to study the history of the Scots who settled this area of New York State."

"You're a professor and a medical doctor?" Alana handed him a napkin.

"That's an interesting combination of professions. Why would the people in your forensic studies care about their ancestry? Wouldn't they be dead?" *A perpetual student.* What was he doing delivering butter for Fiona?

"You lost me with studying dead people." Alana giggled. "You two talk about it. I'll watch the next batch of cookies." She carried the empty tray to the kitchen.

"Why ancestry?" Sophia asked. Perhaps she'd been a little too quick with her cheeky reply.

"Studying ancestry gives me the opportunity to explore genetic traits and lifestyle patterns." A muscle clenched along his jaw. "I teach my students to find a way around the silence of the dead. The job of a forensic investigator is to look for clues that will give the dead a voice. The answer to the simplest question can reveal a lot about someone, living or not. Look what we already know about each other." One eyebrow rose. "Everyone is an accumulation of not only their experiences, but of their ancestors as well."

What was he talking about? Smart could be sexy. This guy with his confident air, charming smile, and cornucopia of everything Scottish could hit the sexy mark if he weren't so serious and nosy.

"I see a lot of your aunt in you."

"How's that?" Sophia asked.

"The short time I spent with Mary left me with the impression she loved working here. I get the feeling that you're happy here too." He glanced at the case full of her artisan-designed shortbread. "You've done her memory well."

"Thank you." That was the kindest thing anyone

had said in the three months she'd been here. He didn't seem the type to pass out compliments so easily. Maybe he wasn't as stuffy as she'd first thought.

"What do you know about the history of the tartan?"

"Not much." She shrugged.

"Maybe I can be of some help." He raised a brow.

"It's not necessary." Sophia didn't have the time or interest to investigate her ancestors. She had little use for the past, liked her present, and needed to concentrate on her future. "There must be more interesting things to research than my family."

"Who knows how many scraps of plaid have been preserved in mothballs and hidden away in family attics?"

His low voice held an edge of seduction. Sophia stepped closer. The underlying sensuality of his tone captivated her. In all the times she had dusted over the fabric, she never got close enough to inhale the faint scent of mothballs. She wrinkled her nose.

"You're very lucky to have it." Ian ran an index finger over a thin red line woven vertically down the plaid. "Highland dyers and weavers were highly skilled. It's evident in pieces like this. Run your fingers along this line. Do you feel the thickness? The fabric was mended many times, perhaps torn by a sword or knife thrust."

"Or it could have been caught on a rock." Sophia reached out and touched the coarse wool.

"It's possible." Ian laughed. "If we settle for the simple explanations, we might never learn the history of the people who owned these valuable pieces." He placed a hand over her fingers, guiding her touch along the uneven weave. "This can likely date back before the British banned the wearing of kilts."

"I never noticed the inconsistency in the red line." Sophia rubbed a finger to the end of the weave. The air around them became electrified. "How long ago were kilts banned?" She never had much interest in history, but Ian's enthusiasm intrigued her. No one ever reacted with such passion to the dusty fabric—especially not her. An awkward moment passed before Ian released her hand.

"Kilts, bagpipes, any sign of Scottish culture were banned after 1749." The fact rolled easily off his tongue. He cleared his throat and stepped away. "You do know this entire region of New York state had a fairly impressive Scottish population?"

If this were a pop quiz, she would have failed. She had already missed the first two questions. The only information she had to offer was a well-known fact to everyone in the town. "My mom and Aunt Mary were born not far from Highland Falls. Their family settled here many years ago."

"I'm sure the MacLennan clan has a history to be proud of."

The words "MacLennan clan" slipped past his lips like a whisper. Her heart beat faster. She pressed her fingers against the uneven fabric. She remembered a photo of her parents. The picture was found hidden in her father's wallet. He wore a kilt, and her mother had a plaid similar to this one draped across her shoulder. When her father found her with the photo, he put a finger to his lips and recited one of his Scottish proverbs, "One for sorrow, two for joy. Three for a girl, four for a boy. Five for silver, six for gold. And seven for a secret that must never be told."

Even at a young age, she'd understood the consequences of her evil stepmother knowing her father still carried her mother's photo. The result would have been like pouring vinegar into a bowl of fine caster sugar.

Ian's close attention made her stomach quiver. She sensed he was seeing more than she wanted him to. A delicate thread had just connected her to her past. In the last three months, Sophia was too busy to think of her life before she'd come here. Out of the blue, this handsome stranger walked into her shop with questions that made her remember things she suppressed. Years passed before she'd realized her father remarried for her benefit. He had no way of knowing his new wife would be so heartless.

Ian followed her to the work area. "Are these *tidy, wee* kilts for tonight's celebration?" He turned his gaze to the cookies on her worktable.

"They are," Sophia said.

"Have you ever been to a Kirkin, lass?"

"It was a long time ago. I was six or seven. I don't remember much." What she did remember was not all pleasant. Her father had recently married Edna. They rode the subway into the city.

"So many Scots together, you must remember something," he said.

His gentle tone encouraged her to tell him what she remembered.

"There were pipers, friendly people, and lots of food." She hadn't thought of that day in years—with good reason. She took a cookie home in the pocket of her jacket. The next morning, Sophia searched her pocket for the cookie. She was too late, her stepmother had already removed the crumbled cookie. Edna scolded her for being careless, and said there would be no dessert after dinner. That evening her father was detained at the hospital. She'd cried herself to sleep.

"Tonight's event will be just as memorable."

"I'm not much for group events." Never feeling like she'd belonged, Sophia learned to appreciate her own company. "I'll have a lot of cleaning up to do." When the cookies were done, she'd have Alana deliver them to tonight's venue.

"I'd look forward to seeing you there."

I doubt it. Wasn't he listening? "Are you here to attend tonight's event for your research?"

"I never pass on an opportunity to meet a room full of Scots. They've got a knack for storytelling."

"I can attest to that. My father was a wonderful storyteller," she said. Even her stepmother listened when he told stories about growing up in Scotland. The rare occasions when they were all together left her envious of people from families who enjoyed each other's company. Without knowing much about Ian and putting aside his infatuation with dead people, she got the impression he was the product of a close family.

"Maybe you'll reconsider. It's an interesting event. All the local clans will be represented." Ian cocked his head in the direction of the backdoor where Tim turned the last screw into a new latch. "Unfortunately, I don't have the time to persuade you. I've got another delivery to make."

"We've all got work to do." Sophia pointed to the counter of half-dressed Scotsmen.

"Don't let me keep you any longer." Ian left

through the back door.

A cool Highland Falls breeze followed in his wake. As a rule, Sophia didn't share details of her personal life with strangers. She tried not to read deeper into his questions or comments—not to wonder if they were research-based or if he had another agenda.

She glanced at the tartan and coat of arms hanging on the wall. Her stepmother forced her to believe her mother's clan had a horrid history—maybe it wasn't true. She knew very little about her MacLennan ancestors. Mother Malevolent had made sure of that. Did she really want to know what this man from the land of whisky, kilts, and Highlanders could tell her about her family?

Chapter 2

Ian slammed on his brakes, barely missing the vehicle in front. "Damn tourists. They just can't park in the middle of the road."

"Driving's a hazard on nice days like today." Tim braced his hand on the dash and let out a long, slow whistle. "My dad says the fall leaf-seekers are good for business."

"I'm sorry." Ian apologized. The comment was out of place, but he hated when foolish people did foolish things. He'd rather be in Scotland, lost in a stack of old books, than sitting here waiting for the lady in the blue convertible to snap her endless photos. "Ma'am, there's a designated viewing spot up ahead. Do you mind moving your vehicle?" He shouted out the window, "I promise you'll get the same view." He regretted the sarcasm, but he wanted to get back to the B and B while Fiona had some down time. She could probably answer his questions about Sophia.

"No worries, Doc. If you stick around, you'll learn to tolerate a little inconvenience this time of year." Tim shrugged. "What'd you think of Sophia?" He leaned his head out the window. "Ain't she a burst of fresh air in this stale town?"

"That's one way of putting it." His research was off to a good start thanks to her late aunt's request to begin his research with the Clan MacLennan. Sophia's

Irish roots were discovered with just a simple statement directed at the color of her hair. But from which of her parents did she inherit that charmingly uneven tilt of her brow? The connection warranted further investigation.

The woman taking pictures returned to her convertible, and was hemmed in by other cars.

Horns blared.

"I'll be right back." Tim stepped out of the car. "Ma'am, can you pull your front end off the road?" He motioned for her to turn the wheel to the right.

Ian remained in the car. Meeting Sophia face-to-face caught him off guard. Except for a minor ptosis of her right eyelid, she had a classic beauty. The slight droop of her upper lid took away nothing from her natural prettiness—most people wouldn't notice it. From just a visual assessment, he determined Sophia was a healthy female in her late twenties.

"Okay, Doc, the road's clear." Tim slid into the passenger seat.

The cars ahead moved slowly.

"You here for a long visit this time?" Tim asked.

"Depends where my fact-finding takes me." Ian inched the truck into the oncoming flow of traffic. "My home in Albany is booked through a rental service. Fiona's offered me a room in the main house for as long as I need." In the last year, he applied himself to his research with purpose—searching old documents and following leads from people like Mary who supplied names and locations. Two hundred-plus years of MacLennan history led him from Edinburgh to Australia, and then back to the Adirondack region in New York.

"What kind of research are you doing?" Tim asked. "Another dead body? A cold case?"

"You might consider it a cold case, but it's not just one dead person I'm interested in. I'm exploring an entire clan." Ian shifted into low gear. "Mary suggested I investigate her family when she learned about my grant to study the Scots who settled here." The request intrigued him.

"Shame she passed away. Nice lady. You know she was a MacLennan before she married Mr. Henderson? I've seen both names on several lists in the town museum—lots of clan history there," Tim said.

"A visit to the museum is on my list." Ian liked Tim. He could be a bit chatty, but wasn't a gossip. "Geography and tourism trends can be helpful in my research. Other than the clans, I have limited knowledge of the area."

"There's not much to know," Tim said. "Highland Falls wasn't always an intentional destination. Now the seasons bring the tourists to the mountains and our quaint little town."

"I imagine the majority of visitors come for the poetic views of the fall foliage." Ian gestured toward the lady with the camera.

"Depending on the season." Tim shrugged. "Occasionally, someone asks about the falls, but they dried up decades ago. Lately, everyone is searching for their roots."

Not everyone. After meeting the sassy pastry chef, Ian was glad he'd chosen the MacLennan clan as the starting point for his research. She was ready to smack him with her rolling pin when he'd walked in, but she became courteous when he showed an interest in the artifacts hanging on the wall. However, her lack of knowledge of their story was disappointing.

"It was real nice of you to step in for Georgie and help Fiona."

"No big deal. That's what family does." Curiosity prompted his offer to make this morning's delivery for his sister.

Up ahead, traffic began to smooth. Ian turned off Oak Road and took the left fork. The view always impressed him. This morning was no exception. The house sat on several acres of what was once profitable farmland. Wrapped in pristine white siding with blueberry shutters, the restored, three-story farmhouse rested against the gray silhouette of the Adirondack foothills.

"Where'd all the cars come from?" Ian slipped the truck into a narrow spot between two vehicles with out-of-state plates. "Don't they have their own foliage in Connecticut?" More cars parked around the B and B than there were registered guests. "Why aren't Fiona's guests taking advantage of the scenery and hiking trails while there's still daylight?"

"Your sister's teatime is a very popular event in these parts. Her guests interrupt their sightseeing in order to be back in time," Tim said. "Did you read the article in the fancy travel magazine? They called the experience a true Highland tea. She's so busy at teatime, she added more days since the last time you were here."

"Aye, I did." Ian grunted. "The author took liberty when she referred to the tea as a *true* Highland tea." He folded his arms across his chest and shook his head. "You do know that historically Highlanders were too busy working during the day to indulge in the luxury of afternoon tea?"

"I get it…it's a tourist thing." Tim shrugged and walked toward the house.

Ian and Tim entered through the mudroom door. Comforting scents of lemon, mint, and lavender filled the air.

"No muddy boots in my kitchen." Fiona pointed to Ian's feet.

"My bad." Ian slipped off his boots. "Sorry. I should have changed shoes after my sunrise hike." He pulled a pair of worn loafers out of the box by the door. The soft leather yielded to his feet. For the second time today, someone had commented on his muddy boots.

"What took you so long? I'm just about ready to serve tea." The electric kettle whistled, the water at a rolling boil. Fiona reached for the handle and poured the steaming liquid over loose leaves.

"Traffic." Tim adjusted his tool belt. "Where do you want me to start?"

"Upstairs hallway, you'll see the trim at the head of the stairs." She pointed Tim toward the stairs.

Tim took the stairs two at time.

"Where's Cora?" Ian noticed Fiona's right hand girl was nowhere to be seen.

"She's out sick. Must be something going around." Fiona sighed. "Today of all days. It's a shame she'll miss this year's Kirkin."

"What can I do to help?" Ian looked around the cluttered kitchen.

"You can plate the cookies." Fiona pointed to the bakery box. "Alana delivered them last night."

He wasted no time in placing the cookies in neat

rows.

"Move it along." Fiona glanced at the half-filled plate. "You don't have to be so meticulous. Just get them on the plate." She rested the lid on the teapot and set the timer.

Ian cringed as he placed the remaining cookies in a haphazard design on the platter. When the menial task was completed, he followed Fiona into the dining area. He did a quick assessment of the room, the guests, and the Scottish decor. Plaid linen tablecloths covered all six tables. Fine china tea services like their granny's cream thistle pattern sat alongside heavy-duty Brown Betty teapots.

A young woman with hazy blue eyes met Ian's gaze and winked.

Ignoring the desire to diagnose the cause of the haze, he turned his focus to the window. Outside the flawless fall day mimicked a vibrant painting. Resisting a scientific explanation, he marveled at the autumn shades of red, orange, and dying yellow cascading down the mountains.

"Is this a Scottish tea?" a woman asked from the far corner of the room.

"No. The one at your table is an English Afternoon tea." Fiona reached for the Brown Betty on the table to her right. "If you prefer a heartier Scottish tea, you might want to try this one."

"What makes the teas different?" the woman asked.

"I'll let you answer that one." Fiona tapped Ian on the shoulder.

Loud, harsh voices, and hazy eyes—the room was a petri dish of aliments. Ian turned toward the group and answered the question from the lady with the harsh smoker's cough. "In the past, teas were blended to accommodate the condition of the water in the areas where they were marketed and consumed." He circled the room, interacting with the guests. "Scotland's soft water perhaps demanded a strong tea."

"And strong whisky." A robust man seated to Ian's left raised his teacup.

"If you're looking for some good whisky, I suggest you attend tonight's Kirkin." Ian laughed along with the guests.

"Is the event held in Scotland, too?" The question came from a sweet old lady in a sweater the color of cheap mint ice cream.

"The event is a Scottish-American creation started in the 1940s." Ian quickly corrected their misconception.

"Will there be bagpipes and men in kilts?" the heavy-voiced smoker asked.

"I can't imagine a Scottish event without a piper and bagpipes." Ian avoided the universal question of what's worn under a kilt. "If you give me a nod, I'll be happy to buy you a dram." Ian didn't wait for a response. He followed his sister back to the kitchen.

"That was a pretty impressive impromptu lecture. Maybe I should consider making you work for your keep." Fiona placed an empty cup in front of Ian. "English, herbal, or Scottish tea?"

Ian reached for the pot of strong, malty Scottish tea and poured himself a cup. He took a slow, meditative sip before returning the cup to the saucer.

"Any problem with the deliveries this morning?" Fiona asked.

"No problems." Teatime was the perfect time to engage his sister in conversation.

"And Sophia—was she what you expected?"

"*Aye*, more or less. She's a sassy lass." He suppressed a laugh. "I got the impression she doesn't like to be interrupted when she's working."

"Did you do something to offend her?" Fiona sighed. "You've got a lot to learn when it comes to women."

"Dirty boots, I guess." He rocked back on the chair legs. "She implied she wasn't close with her aunt." He leaned forward, leveling the legs. "Do you know the cause of Mary's death?"

"Heart disease. It's sad Sophia didn't get to see her aunt before she passed." Fiona mixed milk into her tea and stared into the cup. "It's a long story."

"I've got nothing but time, but keep it to straight facts. No rumors or hearsay." Ian leaned back. On the outside, he was a man who lived by facts and precise information. With Fiona, it was different—she knew his secrets.

"Facts can be so boring." Fiona gave him a dismissing wave. "I know you better than that. Your fondness for tales of ancient heroes and mythical creatures makes you a romantic at heart."

"Try not to get too far off track," he said.

"Well, she's an only child. Her father, Doctor Porter, passed away last year." Fiona's voice wavered. "I don't think she has any living relatives."

"What a sad life." He watched his sister's face. The concept of being an only child and having no relatives was foreign to them. He and Fiona got their strength and spirited ingenuity from being the youngest of their three other siblings. With three older brothers and more cousins than they could count, they had to be strong and determined to accomplish anything. "No family eliminates the problem of someone contesting the will."

"It's still not so clear and free." Fiona stirred her tea. "The terms to Mary's will are explicit to the success of her shop. In order to inherit the shop, Sophia has to spend one year in Highland Falls and show a profit at the end of the year."

"I don't like gossip, but I got a good bit of information about Sophia at each delivery stop," Ian said. "Most of the merchants seem to like her. I suspect some businessmen would like to see her fail."

"Her shop is located on one of the best spots in town. I don't doubt they're interested in the location." Fiona watched him over the rim of her cup. "You're fishing for something specific, aren't you?"

"What do you know about the plaid hanging in the shop?" The tartan seemed the most convenient place to start.

"Sophia thinks it's nothing but a dust collector."

"An item like that is an irreplaceable piece of history. Everyone should be able to have the privilege of seeing it." He rapidly drummed his fingers on the table.

"Don't worry. She has a lot of business sense for someone with no merchandising background. The tourists like the Scottish memorabilia." She gestured toward the dining room.

"Memorabilia?" Since they were kids, Fiona had a knack for getting him all riled up. "Maybe there's a different reason Sophia doesn't remove the tartan. I pointed out an imperfection in the fabric." He knew better than to keep something from Fiona. They held no secrets between them. "Sophia had a strange reaction when she touched it—almost like it evoked a memory. Maybe something she didn't want to remember."

"I thought you were studying genealogy—not psychology or fashion." Fiona raised a brow. "What did she say when you told her you're my brother?"

"It didn't come up." Ian reached for a shortbread cookie.

"Didn't you introduce yourself?" She pulled away the plate.

"I told her my name." Ian shrugged. "I was delivering butter. She didn't ask for references or my genealogical chart." The conversation wasn't going the way he thought it would. He could sure use a dram of whisky in his tea.

"After seeing that tartan, I'm surprised you didn't chart her lineage right there and then." With a long sigh, Fiona drained the last bit of tea in her cup.

"I was able to attain some basic information about her." The disagreeable look on his sister's face amused him. "She's not much of a historian when it comes to her family."

"And what did you notice?"

"She's a pretty lass." He couldn't fool his sister. He never walked into a room without focusing on something—a minor deformity or an obvious genetic trait. In Sophia's case, it was the uneven tilt of her brow when he'd asked about her family history.

"You academics are all the same." Fiona flipped her braid. "Your heads are full of information, but you're lacking in social graces. And you..." She pointed a finger. "You're the worst, studying dead people all the time."

"*Dinna fash*, Fiona. I'm not going to turn into a vampire." He winked.

"*Beir buaidh*, brother. The best of luck," Fiona said. "I told you, Sophia doesn't view the plaid or coat of arms as anything other than frills to attract tourists."

"Nothing that old should be considered a useless ornament. The possibilities of connecting them to her family history are infinite."

"I'm not going to let you make her one of your research projects. Maybe she has no interest in the past."

"That's the impression I got." Ian ran his hand along his jaw. "I wonder if there's a way to change her mind." Important artifacts were often found in the possession of unsuspecting people like Sophia.

"Why are you so interested in her?" Fiona pushed the plate of cookies toward him.

They smelled sweet and buttery, like Sophia's shop. "It's not what you think." He placed a cookie on his saucer. "Mary asked me to see what I could find out about her ancestry. The names and locations she gave me led back here."

"What's your timeline for all this research? How far along are you in finding out about the Scots who settled here?" Fiona asked.

"My sabbatical allows me all the time I need."

"It's a credit to your prominence in your field that the University of Edinburgh gave you such a generous grant to study out of field," Fiona said. "When do you plan to publish?"

"My deadline is sometime after the New Year." His hard-earned paid leave provided more than enough time to accomplish his goal.

"If your sabbatical is indefinite, this must be a self-imposed deadline." Fiona refilled her cup. "Don't be hard on yourself."

"I've encountered some unexpected wrinkles," he said. "Mary's untimely death being one—the other could be Sophia. She gave me the impression she has no interest in her family history." Ian broke a cookie in two. He ate one half, placed the other on the table, and stared at the crumbs.

"What?" Fiona watched him. "Don't tell me there's some clue to Sophia's past in those crumbs."

"Maybe." Leads often came to him from far-out connections. Some played out, but many didn't. "Not only her past, but maybe her present, too." The cookies, her shop, and the tartan were all leads. "You said she has no family."

"None that she's aware of," Fiona said.

"The facts led me here for a reason. It's possible she's not the only remaining descendent of the MacLennan clan."

"What if it's more than facts? It could be Mary's ghost or an Adirondack red stag channeling the spirit of an ancient clansman," Fiona teased.

"No, it was fact. I found the name of a MacLennan clansman on a ship manifest that dates to before the revolutionary war." He was attracted to more than the tartan this morning. "An historical event, not a romantic notion, brought me here." He took a bite of the cookie and chewed slowly, waiting for the delicate buttery taste to assault his palate.

"I'd like to sit and chat, but I've got work to do." Fiona gave his shoulder a squeeze. "Do you have time to slice my veggies for tomorrow's breakfast casserole?" She removed bags of onions and potatoes from the refrigerator.

"Julienne or diced?" He smiled.

"Slice the onions thin, and dice the potatoes in small cubes." She handed him a knife.

He accepted the handle and weighed the knife in his palm. Heavier and fuller than a scalpel, it would do for this menial chore. He'd approach the task scientifically—peel first and slice thin. He made the first cut. The blade was duller than he preferred. Chilling the onions in the fridge was a good decision. *No tears.* The cold retarded most of the onion's noxious chemical response.

Precision slicing brought him back to the days he spent in a sterile forensic lab. Emotions were left at the door. Genealogy was different. His research to this point dealt with lifeless people from the past. Today, a simple inanimate cloth touched the life of a living ancestor. He couldn't ignore this emotional component to his research. Sophia's reaction to the tartan carried a warning; he was now playing in a field where emotions could affect logic and judgment.

Chapter 3

By mid-afternoon, Sophia needed another break. Ian's unexpected visit had thrown her off schedule, leaving her with unsettled thoughts of ancient clans floating around in her head. To clear her mind, she diligently frosted and striped dozens of cookies in record time. Out front, the shop was busy. She put down her pastry bag and joined Alana. Sophia stepped behind the counter and waited on the next customer. Pointy nose Judy, the mayor's secretary, stood in front of her.

"Looks busy back there." Judy glanced past Sophia toward the work area and then returned her focus to the showcase. "Before you ring up my order, add two cranberry shortbread."

"Can I put them in a bag?" Sophia asked. The mayor's order of one dozen-lemon shortbread cookies was already boxed and tied.

"I'd prefer everything in the same box," Judy said. "I noticed you had a visitor early this morning."

"If you mean Tim, he stopped by earlier than usual." Sophia forced a smile. She untied the box, added two more cookies, and pulled the string tighter than necessary.

"Not Tim." Judy's pointy features looked down at Sophia.

"Who then? The only other person in the shop

before we opened was Ian. He stepped in for Georgie." She pushed the box across the counter.

"Yes, that handsome redhead, Ian Campbell, Fiona's charming brother." Judy stared over the rim of her glasses. "Didn't he tell you?"

"I was busy, and he had another delivery." Sophia turned away. She had no time for this game.

"Really? It looked like Professor Campbell was here for a while." Judy leaned a hand on the counter.

"He told me he's a professor and was doing research here in town." This gossipmonger didn't miss a beat. "His relationship to Fiona never came up." *He had every opportunity to mention he was Fiona's brother.*

"Nice man, finding time in his busy schedule to help his sister," Judy said. "I heard Georgie is under the weather."

What don't you hear or see? With the view of Main Street from her office window, Judy saw all the comings and goings in town, and was quick to offer her opinion. Her silly blathering never took a day off.

"Ian must like this shop." Judy picked up the box. "Did he mention how often he stopped by on his last visit to Highland Falls?"

"Matter of fact, he did."

"And…" Judy waited.

"And nothing else." Sophia wasn't about to give Judy anything to bring back to her gossip circle. "You already know he delivered my butter. I had no idea he was Fiona's brother."

"I wonder why he didn't tell you. I hope you weren't uncivil toward him." Judy raised her brows. "No worry, dear, you can apologize for anything

31

offensive you said later tonight at the Kirkin." She curled her lips. "Do you think he'll wear a kilt?"

How would I know what he's wearing tonight? "Lots of men will be in kilts," Sophia said. Ian looked pretty good in his jeans and fancy shirt. It never crossed her mind to imagine him in a kilt. Why should she think of him at all? He hadn't thought enough of her to mention he was Fiona's brother.

The rest of the afternoon was slow, allowing Sophia and Alana more than enough time to complete decorating the shortbread. "Done." Sophia tossed the empty pastry bag in the trash.

Next to her, Alana piped the last blue stripe on the last kilt. The stripe matched the blue streaks in her hair.

"Seems like everyone's home preparing for tonight's event," Alana said. "I don't think we'll have many customers the rest of the day."

"Why don't you take advantage of the lull, and go home?" Sophia suggested.

"Are you sure you'll be okay?"

"Absolutely." Sophia gestured to the counter covered with trays of frosted cookies.

"Okay, then see you later." Alana left through the back door.

Sophia remained on the stool in front of the counter. The kilt shapes were perfect. The frosting was smooth and even. The black lines she added along the stripes were a good decision. They worked well to enhance the checkered pattern against the undercoat of white royal icing. But something was missing. Tonight's guests would be pipers, dancers, and a whole lot of people who spent more time in a kilt than the average person. They would appreciate an extra touch.

What had Judy asked about Ian and a kilt? On a whim, she let go and imagined Ian in a kilt. The image worked too well. She forced her eyes open. The image quickly faded, but before it vanished, she saw a black sporran hanging below his waist.

A sporran. Yes, the perfect touch. She reached for a thin tube of black frosting and piped a small circle with two lines connecting the circle to the top of the kilt. The tiny purse-like sporrans were exactly what had been missing. Satisfied that they were perfect, she snapped a picture with her phone. She reached for the bottle of Fiona's homemade, currant berry liqueur and poured a celebratory drink. She lifted the glass and reflected on enormity of what she and Alana had accomplished. "Here's to the biggest shortbread cookie order since I arrived in Highland Falls." Half the profit from tonight's sales would be donated to the Scottish Society, and the other half could make today her most profitable.

Sophia was on her second glass when Alana returned. "Wow, you look fantastic. I love how you paired the slinky dress with lace-up boots." Sophia attempted a whistle, but only a hiss of air passed her lips. She laughed, topped off her drink, and poured one for her assistant.

"Here's to a job well done. The sporrans are the perfect touch." Alana clinked her glass in a congratulatory salute.

"The frosting should be dry by now. Let's get them boxed." Sophia drained the last drop from the bottle, sharing it evenly between them.

The cookies were boxed and tied in record time.

"Let's get them in the van." Sophia picked up a

short stack of bakery boxes.

When the van was packed, they took a breather on the bench in front of the shop. Sophia stared at the small letters under the Just Baked Cookies logo, *Founded in 1870 by Marjorie MacLennan.* "Ever wonder what possessed a woman of that time to venture into a business?" She sighed.

"I do." Alana echoed her sigh. "What do you know about your great-great-grandmother, Marjorie?"

"Thanks to my wicked stepmother, I don't know much." The liqueur loosened her tongue. "My father told me a bedtime story about a cookie train. I loved hearing how Marjorie sold her shortbread cookies to railroad passengers on their way to Albany."

"It is curious, isn't it?" Alana asked. "I'm sure there's more to her story."

We might never find out." Sophia glanced over her shoulder at the tartan hanging in her shop.

Just before five, Tim, dressed to the nines in a purple-and-black plaid kilt, passed by on his way to the hall.

"Look at you, all spiffed up." Alana walked around him. "Nice, verrrry nice." She focused on the leather and fur sporran hanging below his waist.

Tim blushed.

Sophia laughed. Alana often joked about knowing Tim since they were in preschool and insisted they were nothing more than good friends.

"I stopped by to let you know that I'll be carrying the MacLennan Tartan tonight. It's the least I can do to honor your aunt Mary. She was a good woman," Tim said.

"That's wonderful," Alana said. "Sophia, your clan

has a long history with this town, so the family should be represented."

"Thank you, Tim." Sophia wished she had known her aunt as well as Tim and the other people in Highland Falls.

"My pleasure." Tim turned to the boxes piled into the back of the van. "Looks like you ladies could use some assistance in transporting those cookies."

"That would be great. You can pull up in front of the hall. I'll help carry them in." Alana tossed Tim the keys to the delivery truck. "Sophia, are you sure we can't convince you to come with us?"

"No thanks. It's not my thing. You two have fun." Sophia waited until the van disappeared down the street. She stopped at the door to her shop—did someone just call her name?

"Hey, lass. I thought I'd stop by and see if I could change your mind." Ian dressed for the occasion.

He was dressed to the tens—if there were such a thing. Of course, he had all the bells and whistles. From the flying plaid draped over his shoulder, down to his kilt hose and flashers, his appearance not only surprised her, it took her breath away.

"Do you dress like this often?" Sophia turned her attention to a passing car before she made a fool of herself.

"Weddings, bar mitzvahs, and an occasional christening." He did an awkward two-step.

The driver honked.

"Cute, but not funny." This morning, he'd been in serious teacher mode—interested only in facts. Was this the same man?

"Not even a smile. Did I do something to offend

you?"

"Why didn't you tell me you were Fiona's brother?" Since he'd broached the subject, she had no reason to keep her disappointment bottled up.

"Would it have mattered?" He pressed his lips together in a sly smile.

"I guess not."

"My apologies, lass. I meant no offense."

Rude, no, more likely socially inept.

"Ian Campbell, Fiona's favorite brother." He extended a hand.

It was getting late. Around them, the streetlights came on. A gust of wind rocketed off the mountain. The tailwind caught Sophia off guard, pushing her a step closer to Ian. Losing her balance so easily was unusual. She inhaled a woodsy outdoor scent. Was it his soap or cologne? Either way the scent suited him.

Ian reached out to steady her. His hands rested on her waist. "Now that we're properly introduced, will you accompany me to tonight's gala?" He released her and bowed. "I'd like to prove I'm not as rude as your first impression led you to believe."

Family events were out of her comfort zone, but how could she refuse such a charming invitation. She considered her options—another lonely bottle of liqueur, or an evening in a room full of men in kilts. Was there really a choice? "Only if you promise not to talk about dead people or dusty tartans," she conceded.

"You drive a hard bargain, but I'll try my best." He placed a hand over his heart. "You sound a lot like Fiona."

"How's that?"

"She's not a fan of conversations about dead

folks." He smiled.

"I'll give it a try." How could she refuse his intoxicating smile?

"Is that a yes?" He reached in his sporran and removed his car keys. "Would you like me to drive you home?"

"Drive me home?" She followed his gaze to her flour-stained apron and baggy chef's pants. "You're right. I should change."

"Not that you don't look bonnie in your work clothes…" He massaged along his jaw and over his mouth.

"It's not necessary." Sophia refrained from smiling. She let him fumble before offering some relief. "I live above the store." She pointed to the windows.

At the curb, the bakery truck came to a screeching halt.

Why were Alana and Tim back?

"We're missing two dozen cookies." Alana jumped out of the van. She grabbed Sophia by the arm, pulling her toward the door. "The Buchanan and Wallace cookies are missing."

"I'm sure it's just an oversight. We had a lot going on." She glanced at Alana and winked. Perhaps they had done a bit too much celebrating.

"Yeah, right." Alana released her hold.

Ian held the door and let everyone enter. Inside the shop, they went in opposite directions.

"Found them," Sophia said. They were exactly where she expected them to be—on the counter hidden under a large roll of parchment paper. In their rush to get the cookies to the hall on time, she had overlooked the empty liqueur bottle sitting off to the side. Should she even try to explain?

"A bit too much?" Ian wiggled a brow and pointed to an empty cordial glass. "I thought you lassies would have celebrated with a dram of good Scottish whisky."

"I'm not a fan." Sophia reached for the glasses and moved them to the sink.

"It's an acquired taste." He glanced at his watch. "It's getting late. Tim and I'll bring the cookies to the hall. Alana should stay and help you dress. Don't take too long or you'll miss the opening ceremony."

"She's going to the Kirkin?" Alana opened her eyes wide. "You convinced her?"

"*Aye*, I did."

"See you in a while." Sophia shoved the boxes at Ian.

"I'm looking forward to it." Ian placed the boxes in the back of the van and climbed into the passenger seat.

Sophia watched the van disappear. When it was gone, she led the way up to her apartment and stopped in the living room.

"What's wrong?" Alana asked.

"Wish we had time for a cup of tea." She might not be in a rush to get there, but Alana was looking forward to the evening.

"We don't, not if we want to get there in time for the ceremony." Alana crossed the living room, walked down the short hallway, and entered the larger of the two bedrooms.

Sophia's only choice was to follow through with this. The evening might turn out to be more pleasant than she expected.

"I'm going to dress you up and get you ready for your date with Hot Scot." Alana tossed aside the magazines scattered on the bed.

"It's not a date." Sophia couldn't remember the last time she wore anything but chef pants and an apron. It might feel good to clean up and have some place to go.

"Whatever." Alana headed straight for the closet. "Where did all these adorable clothes come from?"

"I brought them from New York." Shopping had offered temporary relief from spending the entire evening berated by her stepmother.

"Where do you think you'll ever wear those clothes in the sticks?" Right down to the day Sophia left, Mother Malevolent had something nasty to say.

"To a party with men in kilts, you witch." Sophia slipped out of her chef pants and tossed them in the hamper.

"Did you just say something about men in kilts?" Alana tilted her head to the side. "And witches?"

"Just thinking out loud."

"I'm getting used to hearing you talk to yourself." Alana stepped into the tight rack of clothes and reappeared with a navy blue lace dress. "This is perfect." She placed it on the bed.

"Isn't it a little cool for short sleeves?" The dress was one of Sophia's favorite bargains. She loved the way the hem flowed just below her knees.

"You get cleaned up. I've got this." Alana pointed to the dusting of flour in Sophia's hair. "I'm a big fan of streaks, but this makes you look like a sack of flour."

The warm pulsating shower relaxed Sophia's stiff muscles and joints. She shampooed twice. A zesty lemon scent filled the bathroom. One more rinse and her hair felt squeaky clean. She reached for a towel and stepped out onto the cushioned bath mat. The surface yielded to the contour of her feet.

"Hurry up in there." Alana knocked on the door.

Sophia glanced at the watch on the vanity. No time remained for a proper blow dry. Good thing sloppy buns were in style. Why did she ever agree to attend the event? Everything so far shouted bad idea. Her fairy godmother nearly emptied the closet.

Alana placed a plaid wool shawl on the bed. The muted fall shades blended well with the blue dress.

"These are perfect." Alana tossed a boot to Sophia. "Put them on and let's go. I don't want to be late."

****

Sophia kept pace with Alana as she rushed the short distance to the event hall. The weather was perfect for walking, and Sophia was tempted to continue on to the edge of town.

"Here we are." Alana stepped inside.

"There aren't many seats left." Sophia cringed. Customers told her that, before last year, Kirkins were held in the old Presbyterian Church at the end of Main Street. With the increase in the number of tourists attending, town officials decided to move the event to the great room of Scottish Society hall. From where she stood, it looked like they would need a larger venue next year.

"There are two seats at the front, next to Ian." Alana grabbed her hand, urging her forward.

"You go ahead. It's too stuffy. I see a seat near the open window." Sophia preferred the back—inconspicuous and close to the exit.

"Are you sure?" Alana asked over her shoulder.

"Positive," Sophia said. "You better hurry before someone takes the seat." She removed her shawl and hung it over the back of the vacant aisle seat in the last row. She had a good view, in spite of the huge crowd.

Mr. Gordon led the way down the center aisle. He rhythmically squeezed and filled the pipes, creating a popular Scottish melody. In front of the stage, he faced the congregation and waited for the tartan carriers to assemble. A burst of plaid in almost every color flanked the side aisles.

"Welcome to our annual *Kirkin'o'th'Tartans*." A minister took the stage. "A Kirk is the Scottish name for a church. The ceremony, however, is an American creation started in the 1940s at the New York Avenue Presbyterian Church in Washington, D.C. Today the Kirkin ceremony is conducted in churches of many denominations throughout the United States."

Boring. Way too much history. Sophia tapped her foot. How would she ever last through this evening? She glanced at the exit sign in case she needed a quick escape.

"We have eighteen tartans representing the fifty families in our community who have a tartan as part of their family history." The speaker pointed to the men flanking the side aisles—each carried a pole with a tartan the size of a tablecloth attached.

Sophia looked for Tim and the MacLennan tartan. She spotted the green, red, and blue plaid lost in the flood of colors.

"Each plaid weave is the symbol for a particular Scottish clan." The speaker went on about the tartans.

Even Sophia, with her limited knowledge of history, knew that much. She glanced around the room, observing the different kilts. Although the color combinations were interesting, some of the weaves had aged and lost their intensity. Ian's short lecture this morning on the skill of Highland weavers left her thinking about the tartan on the wall in her shop.

"Today plaids can represent nations, states, organizations, businesses, societies, and even individuals. But foremost, the tartan is a symbol of a family," the speaker concluded.

An unexpected twinge of pride surged through her. The faded plaid on the wall of her shop had a history. It wasn't a modern plaid created to represent a company or organization. For a moment, she envied the proud men in their family kilts and the multi-generations of family sitting alongside. Was this strange emotion what people felt when they had the security of loving relatives and a true home? The dusty old tartan hanging in her shop never entered her thoughts, until this morning. The plaid had history behind it, but without a family, what significance did it have for her?

The light nasal hum of Mr. Gordon's pipes drew her attention back to the procession. Each carrier placed their tartan pole into the stand and left the stage. She kept her gaze on Tim and the MacLennan plaid. After placing his pole, he remained on stage to assist with the placement of the other tartans. The last tartan, the American Saint Andrew's tartan, was placed into the position of honor. While the names of the clans were read, the leader recited the Blessing of the Tartans.

"Those of you not of Scottish descent please join us with a blessing for your family too." He looked out at the group and smiled.

This was her cue to leave, but something made her stay. *"Go Beannai Dia Duit."* She remembered the words her father taught her and joined the crowd in

saying, "May God's Blessing be on you."
****

Ian rushed to the back of the room. People moved through the crowd greeting friends.

"Can I buy you a drink, lad?" A guest from the B and B stopped him.

"It's on me. I left an open tab at the bar for anyone who mentions Fiona's B and B." He was anxious to find Sophia while her thoughts on the evening were still fresh in her mind.

"Thanks, mate. I'll get you next time." The man headed toward the bar.

Ian worked his way through the swarm of men in kilts. *Damn, I'm too late.* The chair by the window was empty. Her orange shawl hung over the back of an empty chair. *She can't be far.* He searched through the crowd, but there was no sign of Sophia. "Did you see where the woman who left this shawl went?" he asked the older woman seated to the right.

"What did she look like?" The woman squinted.

What was the best way to describe Sophia to the farsighted lady? The telltale droop of Sophia's eyelid was obvious to him, but he doubted the woman with hyperopia would have noticed such a close detail. "She's a pretty little lass wearing a blue dress."

"She left, young man." The woman pointed to the exit. "It's chilly out there. You might want to bring her the shawl."

Ian clenched the shawl in his hand. A rush of vanilla and cinnamon surrounded him. Outside, the smell of cigarette smoke offended his senses. Past the haze of the smokers, he caught a glimpse of Sophia. She stood against the wall of the building.

A tall man wearing a Logan plaid shielded her from the wind.

Should he intrude? He had no claim on who she spoke to.

The man said something, and she laughed.

He envied the easy way she smiled at the Logan clansman.

"Ian." Sophia waved. "You found my shawl. I was just going back to get it."

He held out the wool wrap, noting the tiny goose bumps covering her arms. The man in the Logan kilt took the shawl and placed it with a bit too much familiarity across her shoulders. An irrational pang of jealousy shot through Ian.

"I'm glad you're here." She hugged the shawl close. "John was just telling me the MacLennan clan was without a chief for over three hundred years. They just recently chose a new chief."

"*Ach*, that's true." Ian had discovered that bit of information when researching the clan for Mary. He would have told her the fact if he thought she was interested. He assessed his rival. Just a tad bit taller with a scar along his jaw—women might consider him good looking. "Are you a genealogist?" His objective wasn't to discredit the man. He needed to level the playing field.

"Me, no." John laughed. "I only recently jumped on the ancestor bandwagon."

"What's your interest in the MacLennan clan?" An amateur wouldn't come across such a little-known fact. "Wouldn't your research lean toward the Logan clan?" Ian pointed to the flying plaid draped over John's shoulder.

"I wouldn't call what I do research. It was just something I read while helping my grandfather with some leads he was investigating for an article." John leaned back against the wall and crossed his arms. "What about you? You seem to know a few things about the clans. Are you a history buff or something like that?"

"Aye, something like that. Who's your grandfather?" John piqued Ian's curiosity.

"Judge Logan," John said. "He and my grandmother live outside of town on Acorn Road."

"I didn't see him in the hall." Sophia looked at John. "Are he and your grandmother here?"

"No, they couldn't make it tonight. My grandfather injured his foot last week. The doctor suggested he avoid crowded places."

"I'm sorry to hear that. What happened?" Sophia asked.

"He tripped in the paddock. The horses were acting up the other evening. He thought it might be a coyote." John removed a cigarette from his sporran.

Ian stepped back. "You lighting up?" He nodded at the smoke in John's hand.

"Don't worry. I'm trying to quit." He slipped the cigarette behind his ear.

"It's a good habit to break." Ian nodded.

"Are the coyotes as leery of horses as they are people?" Sophia glanced at Ian.

"Aye, lass they know better than to start with such a large animal." Her teasing smile was the distraction he needed.

"Still it's better to be cautious." Sophia turned her attention back to John. "I'll have to bring your grandfather a box of his favorite lemon shortbread while he's recuperating."

"Grandfather would enjoy that. He loves sweets and a pretty delivery girl." John winked.

"*Ach*, who doesn't?" Ian folded his arms across his chest.

Sophia placed an open palm on his chest.

"What exactly is your grandfather researching?" Ian felt her gentle but persuasive touch. The muscles beneath his linen shirt quivered. Competing desires warred inside him; his need to know more about Judge Logan's research battled with wanting to get Sophia away from this bloke.

"All the commotion in the paddock turned over some old rocks. My grandfather hired someone to dig them up. They discovered they weren't just random stones, but part of an old wall."

"An old wall?" A discovery like this could be the local connection Ian needed. "Anyone investigating?"

"My grandfather contacted a friend at the state university. When the weather warms up, they'll be out here digging," John said. "In the meantime, he's doing some investigating of his own."

"I'd like to see what he's got so far." A discovery like this could validate his findings. If he could connect it to the MacLennan clan, it could be objective evidence to support their settling here.

"You should talk to my grandfather. He's retired with a lot of time on his hands."

"I've got a great idea." Sophia moved her hand to Ian's arm. "I can't go this weekend, but my shop is closed on Mondays. If you can wait until then, we can go together."

"My grandfather would enjoy the visit." John adjusted the collar of his jacket. "Dress warm. They're predicting flurries."

"Will you be there?" Ian liked the idea of spending the morning with Sophia as long as it didn't include John.

"I'm afraid not. I've got to get back on the job. I'm a detective at the sixty-fifth precinct in Brooklyn." John handed him his card. "Give me a call if you ever need my assistance. I'm getting pretty good at this ancestry thing."

"Brooklyn? Did you two know each other back in the city?" Another pang of possessiveness shot through Ian.

"We just met this evening." John offered Sophia his arm. "Ready to go back inside?"

"You go ahead. I'm staying out here. I need to ask Ian a few things."

"If you're ever back in Brooklyn, give me a call." John departed with a two-finger salute.

"Do you think all the families here tonight can trace their roots back to the Scots who settled here?" Sophia focused on a family leaving the building. "Maybe the stones belong to a house one of their ancestors built."

Her questions were unexpected but welcomed. "Most of them might have a descendent or two who settled here," he said. "An official dig can turn up personal items to help identify ownership."

"Interesting." She pulled her shawl closer. "I'll meet you at the farm Monday at nine. Is that okay?"

"Works for me." Ian was never at a loss when it came to understanding someone's actions. His study of dead people taught him a lot about the living. Sophia didn't fit any of his neat little categories.

"Remember to dress warm." She smiled over her shoulder.

He watched her walk away—unsure how to interpret her sudden interest. The sexy sway of her hem around her knees muffled his thinking. He inhaled the cold night air and got back on track. Tonight, thanks to Tim, the MacLennan tartan hung proudly along with all the others. Did Sophia feel something when she saw the plaid? *Stay focused. Research is not based on feelings or sentiment.*

He could visit without her, but he appreciated any excuse to see her again. No living being came close to arousing his curiosity and senses like this in a long time. She challenged, tested, and teased him without even knowing.

Chapter 4

John was right about the weather forecast. By Sunday night, the weather turned cold enough to snow. A light dusting of white powder fell overnight. Dressed in a puffy jacket, a hat, and boots, Sophia arrived at Judge Logan's farm a little after nine on Monday. She angled her red vintage roadster along the side of the house.

A box of lemon shortbread balanced preciously against her right forearm. She reached for the doorbell with her other. *Darn* The box of cookies tilted to the right. She secured the box between her side and the door.

"Don't move an inch. We can't have you dropping those delicious cookies," Judge Logan called from the far end of the driveway. "Let's help the lady," he said to the Irish setters heeling on each side.

"Thank you." She breathed a sigh of relief and followed the man with rosy cheeks and Santa Claus smile into the foyer.

"My grandson mentioned you might stop by today." He signaled for the dogs to sit. "Your friend is already here charming my wife with his knowledge of everything Scottish."

The dogs stayed on her heels until she reached the archway to a bright atrium. On the far side of the doorjamb, the dogs sat without a command.

"Impressive," she said.

The well-behaved dogs acknowledged her compliment with wagging tails.

"What a beautiful view." From every angle, a one-eighty view of the fields, Adirondack foothills, and blue sky wrapped around the room.

"It's nice any time of the year. Lily and I like to take our meals in here." The judge stood next to her.

Inside the glass enclosed room, Ian and Lily were unaware they were being observed.

Sophia caught his last remark.

"It was nice to see so many clans represented, especially the MacLennan clan," Ian said.

A twinge of annoyance stiffened her muscles. She rarely heard the clan mentioned by anyone in Highland Falls.

"I think it's wonderful you're researching the clan for Sophia. Everyone should know his or her roots," Lily said.

Why would she think his research was for me? Her stepmother had done a stellar job assuring her nothing good would come from knowing about her ancestors. Sophia couldn't make it any clearer—she had no intention of pursing her past. Next to her, one of the dogs whined. Did he sense her tension?

The whimper drew Lily's attention. "Come in and sit." Lily gestured for Sophia to take the seat next to Ian.

"Hope you're enjoying your day off, lass." Ian pulled out the chair.

She acknowledged his impeccable manners with a nod and took her seat.

"Did you have a busy weekend?" He rested a palm

on her shoulder.

"You know what they say about men in kilts." Her shoulder tingled. "The kilt cookies were a big hit. The tourists loved them. Alana and I took dozens of orders."

"Aye, lass, but did your *wee* cookies reveal the secret of the kilt?" Ian laughed and sat.

"Don't worry, the secret is safe," she teased.

"Oh, yes. Kilts are definitely a popular topic among the ladies," Lily said. "I've been meaning to pick up some of the judge's favorite cookies, but a few days without them won't hurt him."

The judge managed a *yes, dear* expression without saying a word.

"I'll make some fresh tea, and Ian can finish telling us about the clans." Lily reached for the teapot. "He's an endless source of information. Isn't he, dear?"

"Yes, he is," Sophia said. Whatever possessed her to suggest this expedition? Seeing Ian all decked out in his kilt must have altered her sensibility. Anything done because of a handsome Scot in a kilt was just foolish. Where was her intelligence and logic?

"Sorry I missed the event. This darn injury was acting up." The judge passed the plate of cookies to Ian. "I've walked that field a thousand times and never saw a hint of those stones until last week."

"The wet weather and the horses' activity most likely churned up the ground," Ian said.

"You're probably right. Since the discovery, we've been bringing the horses into the barn at night." The judge bit into a cookie and smiled. "Have you heard about the coyote sightings?"

"Sophia and I were discussing them the other day."

"I was told by a reliable source they're naturally

afraid of humans and avoid horses," Sophia said.

"No worries then." The judge dismissed the subject with a wave of his hand. "Whatever brought those stones to the surface after so many years has definitely piqued everyone's curiosity. Don't you agree, young lady?"

"I'm intrigued." Sophia nodded. "It's not something the average person encounters in their backyard very often."

"You'd be surprised how often discoveries like this are made," Ian said. "Unfortunately, many are never reported."

"Enough about the stones." Lily returned with a fresh pot of tea. "It's remarkable how Sophia looks like her mother. Just like Laura when she was a girl." She filled Sophia's cup first. "Do you remember much about her?"

"No. I was very young when she passed away." Sophia fidgeted with the napkin on her lap. A vague memory of looking into an open oven surfaced. No face or body was present—only a soft voice warning her not to reach inside. She looked up. Ian was watching her. With a shake of her head, she cleared the thought and reached for the milk creamer. Milk spilled onto the saucer.

At a young age, her father told her never to bring up her mother's name in the presence of Edna. The words were hurtful, but in the end, his advice spared her from hearing Mother Malevolent destroy all the memories she had of her mother. Except for a delicate clink of china, and soft sipping sounds, everyone was quiet. Next to her, Ian placed his cup on the saucer and stared out across the field. It must be difficult for him to keep his curious nature in check. He must have hundreds of questions for Lily about Laura MacLennan Porter.

"Did you see much of my mother and Aunt Mary when they were young?" Sophia saw no harm in talking to these kind people about her mother. Never in a million years would she have asked such a question in her stepmother's presence.

"Not often enough. They were lovely girls." Lily sighed. "Most of the time when the judge served in the state court, we lived in Albany. We purchased this property when our girls were young and spent weekends here. Your grandparents, Sophia and Finn, were our good friends. Sometimes Laura and Mary would come out and ride the horses. Those MacLennan girls were excellent riders. Your aunt was the more aggressive of the two, but your mother had a special bond with the horses." Lily paused. "But you must already know that."

Sophia gave a sideways nod. She tightened her hands around her napkin. *Her mother rode horses.* As a child she had two possibilities in dealing with the loss of her mother. She couldn't be both a happy, brave little girl, and sad, too. She accepted the reality her father created and pushed the loss of her mother to the back of her mind. Sophia glanced at Ian. Did he see every little fact as a lead for his research? Surprisingly, he didn't say a word.

The judge's wife passed around a plate with homemade biscuits.

Sophia reached for one. "The biscuits are perfect," she said. The bread was delicious, warm and yeasty with just the right amount of butter.

"So are your cookies. Aren't they, Lily?" The judge took another bite. "Were you professionally trained, or is your baking talent an inherited skill?"

"I'm self-taught," Sophia said. Her stepmother never berated her baking talent. She gave her free range in her kitchen and willingly served her cookies and cakes to friends. She often took credit for the delectable desserts. *A dash of cayenne or some other unpleasant ingredient would've taught her a lesson.*

"You might look like your mother, but it's your aunt's talent you inherited," Lily said. "Would you like my biscuit recipe?"

"That will have to wait, my dear. We've kept these two long enough. They're here for a purpose, to see the stones." He signaled for the dogs to wait by the front door. "I'll get my walking stick and show you where the first stone was discovered."

Sophia and Ian followed the judge down a gravel road.

He stopped at a fenced-in field. Two blanketed horses greeted them at the gate.

"Do they seem to enjoy this weather?" Sophia removed her glove and rubbed the gray stripe along the thoroughbred's nose. He looked older than his companion, a slender-legged Arabian.

"Except for the havoc the mud does to their hooves, they're better off out here than in their stalls." The judge nodded at the muddy ground. "It's been wetter than usual until this week. When the temperature dropped last night, it was the first time this year we blanketed them."

A silly thought crossed Sophia's mind—could either of these horses be offspring of the horses her mother rode? She always liked horses and envied her friends who took lessons at the Prospect Park Stable. Her stepmother said it was a foolish expense. Until three months ago, when she'd walked into Aunt Mary's shop, the shadow of her mother was nothing more than a vague memory. And now, she stood in the same paddock where her mother and Aunt Mary rode horses. The awareness of her mother living and laughing with friends led her away from the fence. She needed to refocus and listen to what Ian and the judge were discussing.

Shielding her eyes from the sun, she looked across the vast field. Warmer weather this morning melted most of the snow from last night's flurries. What must have been a postcard-perfect view was now a slick layer of mud. All that remained was an accumulation around the posts of the fence. A light breeze created a powdery swirl around her feet. She reached down and cleared the snow away from the tops of her boots. The thoroughbred poked his neck through the lower rail and nuzzled her jacket. "Mind your manners," Sophia said.

The horse followed her command and cleared away from the gate.

"You have a way with animals," the judge said. "The pups warmed up to you instantly. Did you have many pets when you were growing up?"

Sophia shook her head.

"A dog, a cat, a bird?" the judge asked.

A cat. She suppressed a laugh. A malicious Persian with the evil toothy grin of her stepmother would have been an appropriate choice.

"Not even a pet fish?" Ian raised a brow.

"I had a goldfish once." Years had passed since she

thought about the fish. "He didn't last very long." She won the fish at a school fair, but the next day it was gone—no explanation. That evening, something stuffed the plumbing. When the unfortunate goldfish floated to the top of the toilet bowl, Sophia went to her room and cried herself to sleep. The poor fish would have been better off if someone else won the prize. Only on a rare occasion did her father confront Mother Malevolent, but that night she heard them arguing. To prevent her father from being subjected to Edna's harsh tongue, Sophia never brought up the fish's demise. And she never tried to win another fish.

"No pets?" Ian asked again.

"None." She gazed into his blue eyes. What she saw was far more intimate than she expected— understanding and compassion. She wasn't used to being on the receiving end of either of those emotions. "How far out are these stones? We better get started before the weather changes again."

"Good idea." The judge pointed toward the hills. "Sorry you have to tramp through the mud, but the stones are in the far north end of the field. There's no other way out to the site. I had John fence off the area. I don't want hikers tripping over them."

The dogs ran in circles, barking at the horses until they cleared away from the gate.

"Hikers? Isn't this private property?" Ian asked.

"It is, but it leads to a trail on a list of historical Adirondack sites. I don't mind hikers crossing the field, as long as they're mindful of the animals and close the gate." The judge adjusted the collar of his jacket.

"Did you hike the trail before your injury?" Ian pointed in the direction of the foothills at the end of the paddock.

"Lily and I prefer to walk the hills when all the tourists are gone. We haven't been up there in a while." The judge tapped his cane on the sole of his shoe and looked at the sky. "Doesn't seem like the sun is going to stay out long. Maybe you'll get a chance to hike the trail a bit. It forks about two hundred feet up, and then leads south."

"If we go that way, it sounds like a long trek back down." Sophia hadn't planned on spending the entire day out here, especially if the weather would be bad. "We'd have to hike to your farm to pick up our vehicles." Behind her, she heard the rhythmic sloshing of the horses' hooves as they hit the mud. She turned and watched them run across the paddock. The pounding of their hooves wreaked havoc on the already messed-up ground. Mud flew in every direction.

"If we decide to complete that path, we can always get a ride out to the farm and collect our cars." Ian glanced across the field.

She shrugged, not wanting to commit. Her day was free to spend as she pleased. She'd wait and see how far they got before the weather turned.

"Was the town always situated in its current location?" Ian opened the gate.

If she could keep her family's past out of the equation, she was not against learning a little about the town. It would make interesting conversation for her customers.

"For a few decades, it centered around a mill at the bottom of that hill." The judge pointed south. "But the falls dried up in the mid 1800s."

The hill was a good distance away. It would take

even longer to reach if they decided to hike the trail. Sophia hiked many of the surrounding paths on her days off. She liked being alone in the woods. She'd convince Ian to save the trek for another day—without her.

"Must have been a blow to the town's economy," Ian said.

"It was. Lots of townspeople were forced to move to Fulton County and work in the glove factories."

"I always imagined the settlers were farmers or loggers, not glove makers," Sophia said. Where did her family fit into this bit of information?

"Most settlers were farmers." Ian nodded "Glove manufacturing was a big industry here for many decades. It goes back before the American Revolution when a general in the British Army needed gloves for his troops. He brought over a skilled group of Scottish Highlanders. With their closely-guarded guild techniques, they helped the troops keep their hands warm through the bitter winters."

"Get ready for a history lesson." Sophia rolled her eyes and patted the horse's neck. A brief answer was all she needed.

"I don't think the young lady is interested in all this history." The judge winked at Sophia.

Had he seen her eye roll?

"You two should get started if you plan to investigate the stones and hike the trail." He stepped outside the paddock and closed the gate. "When you have the time, I suggest you visit the town's historical museum. There's a nice collection of manuscripts with accounts written by the early settlers—mostly Scots and Irish transported here in the eighteenth century."

"Tim mentioned the museum. It's on my list."

What else was on that list? Sophia spent many Christmases on Mother Malevolent's naughty list. It would be nice to be on someone's good list. A few steps into the paddock, her boot heels sank into the mud. She wiggled to get free.

"Take my hand." Ian removed his glove.

Her palm fit nicely in his. A strong grasp provided the leverage she needed. She stepped forward.

He tightened his hold. An invisible spark of energy flowed from his fingertips.

"Static electricity." Ian released her hand.

"Of course." She adjusted the fingers of her glove.

No doubt he would have a scientific explanation. The fiery look on his face, however, was not the kind she'd expect from a man thinking about electrical charges.

Ian rubbed his palms together, turned, and started toward the stones.

Sophia waved goodbye to the judge and followed Ian. The farther out in the field they walked, the murkier the ground became. Her legs ached. Walking through mud was not basic hiking. Each step was like a large suction cup pulling her to the ground. By imitating Ian's style of walking on the balls of her feet, she kept her heels from planting in the mud. Somehow it prevented suction from forming between the mud and the bottom of her boots. Without complaining, she pushed herself to keep pace with Ian.

He strode ahead with a steady gait.

Was it his curious determination or Highland breeding that kept him moving?

Roped poles marked a spot covered with rocks and

stones. Is this what she hiked through the mud to see? The least she could do was pretend to be interested. "Do you think the stones were part of a house?"

"They look more like stones used for the border wall. Without a proper excavation team, it's hard to say." Ian placed his hands on his hips and looked around.

"Do you see something?" She stepped next to him.

"Over there." He pointed beyond the stones. "Some kind of fabric is sticking out of the mud. It might not have been visible the other day when the ground was more solid."

"Why not check it out? If the weather changes, it might be covered again." Her suggestion got an *A+ good idea* look from the professor.

The darkening skies and dropping temperature didn't seem to bother Ian. He removed his jacket and picked up a flat stick. The stick became an impromptu shovel. He used it to loosen dirt around what looked like some kind of leather. Sophia looked around for another piece of wood similar in size and shape. *If he needs my help, he'll ask.* She gave up the search, took a seat on a boulder, and enjoyed the view. The speed and accuracy of each move intrigued her. Under his polished veneer was a ruggedness that compelled her to keep watching; a sexy energy manifested in the way he dug deeper and deeper. She moved her gaze away from his hands to his strong wrists and forearms. The fabric of his shirt tightened with each toss of dirt.

Saved by the vibration of her phone—her thoughts were about to take a dangerous turn. She checked the screen. Fiona had sent her a text.

—Local beekeeper canceled. Need a speaker for

afternoon tea today. Group of seniors from Albany. Could you talk about shortbread?—

—I've got you covered.—

A warm fire and hot tea sounded more inviting than braving the cold on the hiking path. "What time does your sister serve afternoon tea?" Sophia shouted.

"What?" Ian concentrated on a rectangular object protruding from the ground.

"Teatime, at Fiona's, what time does she serve?" Sophia walked toward Ian.

"Two." He tossed his digging tool to the side. "Grab the other end."

She pocketed her phone, grabbed the hide, and braced her feet at the edge of the hole.

"We'll pull on three." Ian counted, "One, two…"

"Three." She tugged against the pressure of his strong grasp on the other end. Layers of dirt fell away, exposing a well-preserved secret. "What is it?" Sophia watched Ian unfold a tightly tied skin.

"Let's find out." He dusted off the dirt and unwrapped the hide.

"Why would someone bury a box out here, in the middle of nowhere?" Sophia stared at a well-preserved, wooden box the size of a loaf pan.

"If the stones"—he pointed to the marked-off corners—"are all that remain of someone's home, this wasn't the middle of nowhere back then. They might have meant to return for it."

"Do you know who lived out here before the Logans?" Sophia couldn't imagine the land without the road or fence.

"The farm ownership must go back further than the previous owners," Ian said. "Lily told us she and the judge purchased this property when their girls were young. I'll check with the judge. He might have old deeds to the property." He tightened his hold. "The land could have belonged to a Fraser, a MacKay or even a MacLennan. They all settled here."

A MacLennan. She shivered. She had a secret box when she was young. Odd shaped- or exaggerated-sized objects always intrigued her. They were her only physical possession Mother Malevolent never knew about. "Aren't you curious about what's inside?" She moved closer for a better look.

"Anything found on private property belongs to the owner of that property. It's the judge's choice to open the box or not." Ian gave her a slow nod. "I'm sure you know what they say about curiosity."

"It killed the cat." Her father's proverbs surfaced at the most unexpected times. "No doubt the cat learned something, making it a noble death."

"Interesting twist on an old proverb."

"My father lived by them," she said. "Are you suggesting we wait for the judge to open it? I would have thought your inquisitive nature couldn't stand the suspense."

"Giving this to the judge is the right standard of procedure." He tucked the box under his arm.

"If it's not locked, why not take a peek inside." Sophia ran her fingers over the surface. The wood was cold and had no telltale markings. An odd tingle teased her fingertips, sending a chill up her arm. "You're right. We should let the judge open it." Disturbed by the strange sensation, she pulled away.

How did he do it—separate any personal feelings from the things he discovered?

Chapter 5

Dark gray, low-lying clouds swept in from the hills. Sophia adjusted her collar, quickened her steps, and caught up with Ian. The contents of the box jingled. Pushing her hands deeper in her pockets, she resisted the urge to quiet the curious rumble. Had they disturbed something that was happier where it had been?

She never questioned another person's actions. Ian was right. The box was found on the judge's property; he should be the one to get the first glimpse inside. The decision was his to do whatever he wished with the contents. Still, all her reasoning could not suppress the sense of suspense.

The Logan house was warm and offered shelter from the wind. Inside the foyer, Sophia took a breath. The cozy atmosphere settled the anxious butterflies in her stomach.

"Back already?" The judge greeted them.

"It appears the stone wall was not the only thing buried in the paddock." Ian showed him the box.

"Bring it along. I'm sure Lily would love to see it." The judge glanced at the box.

When their jackets were neatly hung on the hall rack, and their boots scraped clean, they followed the judge to a comfortable looking room.

"Back so soon?" Lily left her cozy chair in front of the crackling wood fire.

Sophia looked around the room. Downturned books rested on the armchairs by the fire. They obviously interrupted the Logans' quiet afternoon, though neither seemed the least bit put out.

"They made another discovery, my dear." The judge pointed to the box.

"Do you have any idea what's inside?" Lilly clasped her hands to her lips. "How will you open it?"

Good question. Would Ian open the box? Sophia shifted.

"It's not complicated." Ian placed the dirt-covered box on top of a magazine, creating a barrier between the dirty box and the antique desk. With a finger, he drew an imaginary perimeter of the circle of stones. "These are the stones." He placed a book on one corner of the desk. "This is where we found the box. It was buried directly along what was most likely the outside wall of a main structure."

Sophia watched Ian use objects on the desk to imitate the discovery site. A ruler defined the north border of the site, a coaster represented the first stone, and a notepad denoted the box. He might be a stuffy professor, but he sure knew how to teach.

"What do we do with the contents once we open it?" Judge Logan crossed his arms.

"The box and whatever we find inside is yours to do with as you please," Ian said. "However, I would suggest caution when we open it."

"Caution?" Expecting a hoard of some ancient insect, Sophia inched back. How could something the size of a pound cake send a shiver of uneasy curiosity through a group of educated adults? She took a breath. The anticipation left a heavy feeling in her chest.

"No worries. I'm more concerned for the integrity of the objects than worried there's something harmful inside." Ian ran a finger along the sealed edges. "I doubt anything crawled in." He reached for Sophia's hand. "Come closer."

"No thanks." Sophia took another step back, putting distance between her, the box, and the man with the ability to make her tingle with anticipation. She clenched her hands at her side. She had no reason to be on edge, it was just an old box. Whatever trinkets were inside would mean nothing to her. If something were important to Ian's research, the judge would, without doubt, let him have the item.

"Let's do this," the judge said.

"Why don't you do the honors, sir?" Ian moved aside.

"We're all waiting." Lily placed a hand on her husband's shoulder.

The latch opened easily. The lid popped with a faint squeak. A thick layer of sheepskin covered the contents.

"Someone went to great lengths to protect what they put in here." The judge turned to Ian. "I think you're better equipped to continue just in case it's valuable."

"Cotton gloves would be ideal, but these will do." Ian tugged a pair of woolen gloves from his pocket. "It'll keep the oils on my skin from making contact with the surface of the objects."

Clever. Sophia inhaled deeply. The interior of the box smelled of rusty metal and dry earth. She leaned in for a closer look. Several objects were inside—a tarnished crest, an old pen, and two keys.

"It's a Victorian mechanical pencil." The judge used a tissue to pick up the pen. He rolled it between his fingers. With another tissue, he rubbed off a layer of dirt. A glimmer of metal peeked through. "There's a rose gold case hidden beneath all this dirt. I wouldn't be surprised if the pencil still works. I'd bet the original lead is inside."

What looked like a pen was really a pencil. This was just the kind of find Sophia was hoping for. She itched to hold the slender pencil with its ornate design.

"I don't think we'll do any harm to these objects if we handle them." Ian removed his gloves and reached for the crest. "This is a brooch a clansmen would have worn on his plaid. The motto could help us discover who buried the box."

"Can I hold it?" Sophia picked up the silver brooch. It rested with familiarity against her palm. She closed her fingers around the edges. "It has some weight." It should have felt cold after being buried in the frozen ground, but it didn't. It felt warm—too warm. She quickly returned it to Ian. The effect was similar to when she'd touched the tartan. Only, today it wasn't a picture of her parents; the image in her mind was an old photo of Sophia and Finn MacLennan—her mother's parents. Their clothes suggested the picture was taken in the 1950s—one of them wore a similar brooch. She tried to recall the details of the photo but couldn't remember who wore the brooch. A voice snapped her out of her dreamlike stupor. The memory faded as quickly as it appeared. Chilled, she wrapped her arms around her waist.

"I think we can all use a celebratory drink," Lily said. "And something to calm our nerves." She walked over to the tiered bar cart and poured four glasses of whisky.

"Oh, no thanks." Sophia looked at the clock—it wasn't even noon. She never drank this early, and never whisky.

"My grandfather loved to educate people to the beauty of drinking good Scottish whisky." Ian winked at Sophia. "Give it a try."

Sophia imitated the way he held his glass at chin level, waved it side to side, and inhaled through both his mouth and nose. "Ugh." The pungent, peaty scent offended her senses.

"If you get more nose, it will change the aroma a bit, making it less powerful when you take a sip." He sniffed again before bringing the glass to his lips.

She took the smallest taste, detecting a hint of sherry, and some other notes she didn't take time to decipher. "It burns." The warm liquid hit straight into her bloodstream. She cleared her throat, put down the glass, and looked at Ian. "I don't think it's for me."

"We'll make a Scotch drinker out of you yet." He smiled.

"I don't think so." Her queasy stomach did a flip. She turned away, hoping the activity at the desk would distract her from the sick feeling.

"Is it okay to clean some of the tarnish off the pencil and brooch?" Lily asked.

"No reason why we can't." Ian put his empty glass on the tray. "The box and its contents are yours to do with as you please. All we need is some baking soda and water."

"I'll get some," Lily said.

"Silver tarnishes faster in warm humid air." Ian

handled the brooch by the edges. He held it to the light and gently turned it over. "The moderate temperatures in this area, as well as the sheepskin, and cool ground kept the contents in fairly good condition."

Lily returned with a clean cloth, a box of baking soda, and a bottle of water.

"This is definitely a clan crest." Ian rubbed the tarnish with the cloth. "The words are most likely the clan motto."

"Do you think it's an authentic period piece?" Lily asked.

"It's difficult to say. Finding a silversmith's mark would be helpful. Today, many reproductions are made with the same weight of silver and quality workmanship as older pieces." He rubbed off the powdery cleaner with a dry cloth.

"Can you determine the exact date it was produced?" The judge watched over his shoulder. "Mr. Paisley, the curator at our local museum, might be able to help you."

"If it's okay with you, I'd like to show it to a colleague at the university." Ian held the brooch in his palm. "He's an expert in silver objects and the smiths who produced them."

"Then we must send it to him," Lily said.

After her reaction to touching the brooch, Sophia did not share everyone's enthusiasm. She eyed the pencil. It seemed less daunting.

When all the letters were visible, Ian signaled for Sophia to come closer.

Forgetting the pencil, she took an uneasy step forward. *Hoc majorum virtus.* She knew those words. The glass of Scotch sat on the table next to her. This time she didn't wait for her senses to orient to the scent and flavor. She took a quick sip.

"Can you read it?" The judge directed his question to Ian.

"This is for the valor of my ancestors." Before she realized what she was saying, Sophia translated the words. A dull ache hummed along her forehead. Had to be the Scotch, she reasoned. Another memory surfaced in a disconnected rumble. She looked over at Ian. He was the catalyst that brought all this to the surface. His lips moved, but she didn't hear what he was saying. Everyone was speaking, but all she heard was a buzz in her ears. Through a hazy fog, she saw Ian rush toward her.

"Are you okay, lass?" He caught her and the glass before they hit the carpet.

"The drink made me a little dizzy." She forced a calming breath into her lungs, but it didn't work.

Ian eased her into the nearest armchair. He nodded.

But his eyes said he wasn't buying her excuse. Just like the other day, he was seeing more than she wanted him to.

Lily offered her a glass of water.

It went down easier than the Scotch and revived her.

"That's a perfect translation." Ian ran a finger over the words. "I didn't realize you had such a vast knowledge of Gaelic."

"I don't. What I know is mostly proverbs from my father, but…this is different." She sank deeper into the chair. "I've seen those words before."

"The oddest things can evoke a memory, dear." Lily stood at her side. "Do you think it's a MacLennan crest?"

"I'm sure it is." Sophia tucked her hands along the sides of the chair cushions, refusing to touch the brooch. "My mother had one just like it."

"Do you have it?" Ian gripped the back of the chair.

His voice was gentle with a rasp of excitement. "No." Sophia shook her head. Her stepmother made sure her mother's possessions were removed from the house. "It's with my grandfather somewhere in Scotland. When my mother died, he retired to the family estate in Scotland."

"Do you know where the estate is?" Lily asked.

"I remember seeing one or two photos but can't recall the name of the town." She pressed a finger to her temple. The house was a beautiful, fairy tale-like structure surrounded by lush green hills.

"No worries, dear." Lilly patted her hand.

"I'd like you to bring this to your colleague." The judge wrapped the brooch in the sheepskin and handed it to Ian. "See if he can validate the authenticity." He placed everything else in the box.

"I plan on driving to Albany tomorrow," Ian said.

Sophia refrained from asking when he would return. It might be good to put some distance between them. Suppressed memories started to surface the first day they met—too many in a short period of time. She needed time to digest what they discovered without the risk of learning more. The sudden revelation of secrets buried for years proved her mother's clan had a strong connection to this area. Mother Malevolent's mean words, *their shady past destroyed them*, created turmoil in her mind. If her ancestors buried this box, did something terrible cause them to leave their precious keepsakes behind? Where did they go? She rubbed her forehead. Was she ready for the truth? She stood on shaky legs, and followed Ian to the door.

"I think it's best if you drive Sophia back to town." Lily straightened the collar on Sophia's jacket.

"I'm not going back to town. I have to speak at Fiona's tea." Sophia zipped her jacket.

"You'll stay with her, won't you?" Lily asked Ian.

"You have my word," Ian said. "We're headed in the same direction so there's no need for two cars. I'll drive her to Fiona's."

"I'm feeling much better. There's no need for you to be inconvenienced." Sophia opened the door.

"Lily wants me to see you to your front door. I'm a man of my word." Ian followed her out.

****

"Wow is that what you drive when you're not making deliveries?" He stopped short. She constantly surprised him. "It's a vintage roadster."

"My father inherited the car from his father." She sighed. "My stepmother asked me to get rid of it, but I couldn't sell it. The car meant too much to my father. I paid her blue book value and shipped the car here."

"You could have gotten a pretty penny for a car like this." Ian ran a hand over the exterior. "It's in excellent condition. Do you know what year it is?"

"My father kept it garaged most of the time. This is one of the last models the company manufactured back in the 1980s." She placed a hand on the hood and smiled. "On weekends, we would sneak away and take a ride."

"My uncle was a road racer and owned a similar

vehicle. I haven't seen one like this in years. Did your father race?"

"In his younger days, back in Scotland." She walked around the car.

"How does it drive?" he asked.

"In the city, shifting at every stoplight was a hassle." She glanced over her shoulder at the road. "Country lanes were made for driving a car like this."

"I'd love to give it a try."

"Do you think you'll fit?" She tossed him the keys and slipped into the passenger seat.

"It'll be worth the squeeze." He caught the keys midair, opened the door, and maneuvered into the driver's seat. He started the car and shifted into Reverse. "Sounds like a *tidy* little engine."

"Tidy?" She raised a brow.

"It's a nice Scottish word. It can describe a *wee tidy scran* like your cookies…" He paused, not sure he should go there just yet. "Or a pure, *tidy* lass."

"If this is a compliment, thank you." She smiled.

A blush of amusement appeared in her smile—similar to the look Fiona gave him when his academic mind produced a compliment. An unusually warm feeling surrounded him. The people involved in his forensic work never evoked such an emotion. How could they—they were dead cold? Even the best mortuary cosmetologist couldn't capture Sophia's animated beauty. Would she appreciate his pathology humor? His sister didn't. He suppressed a laugh and backed out of the driveway.

Fiona would be proud. He could hear her saying, *a nod's as guid as a wink tae a blind horse*. He was off to a good start. Endless articles were written about the skills needed to develop a romantic relationship. You had to progress from one step to the next and keep it there. Social skills were not his forte, but even he understood compliments were necessary to develop more than a fact-finding relationship.

Chapter 6

Ian angled the car alongside a van.

A group of silver-haired ladies disembarked and made their way to the front door.

Sophia eased out of the car. "It's better if we enter through the kitchen." She preferred meeting the ladies for the first time in the dining room, after Fiona explained why they would hear about shortbread instead of bees.

"Lead the way." He placed a hand on the small of her back.

She glanced sideways. Ian's hair was tousled by the wind, and a day-old scruff covered his face. He looked more like an ancient highlander than someone who spent hours in a pathology lab or library. She didn't know which she found more appealing—his rugged appearance, or his sharp intellect?

Sophia felt at home in the kitchen bustling with activity and the essence of fresh-baked scones. What waited on the other side of the kitchen door had her a little nervous. Standing in front of strangers, talking about anything other than tax laws or profits and losses, was definitely a new experience.

"Fi's in the dining room." Fiona's assistant, Cora, waved a long oven mitt.

At the end of the counter, a pair of long, skinny

legs stuck out from under the sink.

"Is that you, Tim?" Sophia leaned forward for a better view.

"Look what the wind blew in." Tim let out a long, slow whistle. He wiped a wet palm on his jeans. "Did you two come together?" He stepped between Ian and Sophia.

"We were out at the Logans' house when Fiona called," Ian said.

"You went to see the stones *together*?" Tim opened his eyes wide and stared.

"I met Ian at the farm." Sophia looked sideways at Tim, warning him not to go there. Along with his talents as a handyman, Tim had a reputation as the town matchmaker.

"Something wrong with the sink?" Ian bent to take a look.

"All fixed—just a clog." Tim gathered his tools. In the doorway, Tim passed Fiona and whispered in her ear.

"Together?" Fiona dismissed it with a wave of her hand. "I'm much too busy to hear the details."

"What can I do to help?" Sophia tucked her hair behind her ears and reached for an apron. She needed a distraction. What would she say if Fiona asked about her feelings for her brother?

"You can plate the shortbread." Fiona handed her a serving plate. "And you, brother, can help me with the tea."

Sophia could tell which of her cookies were in which box without even looking. She opened the first box and inhaled the scents of coffee and hazelnut. A subtle scent of whisky permeated the other box. She laid out a nice sampling, including enough notched-edged traditional shortbread to make all Fiona's guests happy.

At the far counter, Ian and Fiona filled an assortment of tea strainers with loose tea leaves. He laughed over something his sister said. The bond they shared was more than a biological connection. No doubt, Ian could quote from numerous studies on the subject. Fiona was lucky to have an older brother close by who cared for her so much.

"All set." Ian crossed the kitchen with a teapot in each hand.

Always the gentleman, Ian let the ladies pass through the door first. Sophia maneuvered the long tray to fit the space between them. In contrast to the buttery shortbread, Ian smelled like wind and tea. She brushed past him, unable to avoid the back of her arm from sweeping across his chest. His hard, strong chest was the kind you wanted to rest on. Heat raced through her.

"Don't let them eat all the whisky cookies." He winked.

Fine laugh lines crinkled around the corners of his eyes. His intoxicating blue eyes electrified the space between them.

"I'll bake you a fresh batch if they're all gone." Avoiding temptation, she rushed into the dining room. Fiona's guests and the Albany seniors filled every seat. "Wow, a full house." Too late to turn back. In spite of her uneasiness, the room, with its explosion of color, drew her in. She studied the intricate overlay on a cherry red cup and saucer. This week, her bakery showcases were filled with fall designs: pumpkins, leaves, and autumn wreaths. Inspired by the designs of

Fiona's décor, she'd take a different approach when the season changed.

"Watch your step," Fiona warned. "The corner of the carpet is loose."

Sophia stepped over the edge of the carpet and carried the tray to the buffet. What an introduction—the guest speaker facedown with crumbling shortbread all over the pretty rug.

"They all look so good." A lady wearing a sweater the color of pink rose buds approached the sideboard.

"Let Sophia choose for you," Fiona said.

"Try a whisky cookie," Sophia suggested.

"That would be my choice, too." Ian stood at the long end of the table and watched the lady in the pink sweater.

Sophia didn't notice anything unusual about her appearance, but Ian must have. Was he *assessing her medically*? Sophia laughed aloud.

He turned in her direction and grinned.

"Did I miss something?" Fiona placed the teapots on the buffet.

"I think Ian is doing a medical assessment of your guests."

"Oh, no doubt he is." Fiona's mouth twitched. "He's a quick study, and you've got his number."

"Are you two finding something funny at my expense?" Ian asked.

"Me?" Fiona gave her brother a playful smile. She linked her arm through Sophia's and led her to the front of the room.

Sophia looked over the small group of silver-tops. On the way here, Ian offered suggestions for her presentation. What was it he told her to say to keep her audience interested? His suggestions to make it personal, be funny, and engage the audience sounded easy when they were alone in her car. "Are any of you bakers?" Personal and engaging was a good place to start. An audience with some basic knowledge of grating butter, creaming sugar, and regulating oven temperatures would give her their full attention.

Several ladies nodded in response to the question.

"I'll take that as a yes." She was off to a good start. What would the professor do now—a history lesson, or perhaps quote a study? *Why not?* She knew everything about shortbread and had an overabundance of facts the group might enjoy. "Does anyone know how long people have been baking shortbread?" Without waiting for a response, she reached for a fluted-edged cookie. "These treats are a descendent of the old Scottish Yule bannock and can be traced to the twelfth century." The idea that even her cookies had an ancestry was like a private joke between her and Ian. "It was a luxury for ordinary people and only eaten at Christmas and Hogmanay, the Scottish New Year's Eve. The traditional notched edges ensured good fortune and were symbolic of the winter solstice."

"That's one busy little cookie."

The comment came from the lady sitting directly in front of Sophia. Her face was so tight from a cosmetic injection, Sophia couldn't tell if her lips were actually moving. "It's the butter that makes it so delicious." She moved her gaze away from the lady's lips. "Butter was very expensive in the past, which is why they were only eaten for special occasions." *Did Marjorie churn butter every day?* "We take for granted how easy it is today to make such a simple cookie."

"Ooh, the best part of the cookie. What kind of butter do you use?" a lady with cheeks like a pillowy pastry asked.

"Before I came to Highland Falls, I experimented with different commercial brands. They worked well enough to get the dry crumble you expect in a shortbread." Sophia forced herself not to watch the stiff-lipped lady sip her tea. "Now I use only the fresh local kind. Your hostess supplies me with homemade herb butters for my more savory flavors."

"Where's the name shortbread come from?" Stiff Lips asked.

Didn't anyone else have a question? Sophia didn't want to be rude, but she couldn't look at the woman's motionless upper lip. "The high proportion of butter is what makes shortbread short. The term short means crumbly, like shortbread should be. If you prefer a softer cookie, you can bake them until set, but I wouldn't suggest dunking those."

Filled with hot tea and cookies, everyone laughed.

She survived.

From the back of the room Ian signaled with a thumbs-up.

She took advantage of the levity and ended her talk by opening the floor to questions.

Most of the women asked about baking, cooling techniques, and her favorite savory flavor.

"What's your boyfriend's favorite?" Stiff Lips nodded toward the back of the room.

"Oh, no. We're not together like that." Sophia was flustered by the question and said the first thing that came to mind.

"Listen, dear, in my day I dated more than my

share of handsome Scots. You can always tell by the way a man looks at you that he's interested. Trust me, I've been watching, and he's interested." She tossed a nod over her shoulder. "Those two old cougars sitting in the back would rather take a bite out of that delicious man than any of your delectable treats. I suggest you rescue him."

"He seems to be doing fine on his own." A flash of heat warmed her cheeks. She glanced at Ian. He wasn't the least bit uncomfortable. The women's flirty smiles and heavy fluttering eyelids said a lot about what they were thinking. No doubt he was charming them with his accent and maybe even a fact or two on some obscure subject.

Whatever Ian said resulted in high-pitched squeals and giggles that caused a few heads to turn.

Fiona came to his side and suggested he assist the ladies on board the bus.

Sophia watched him help his admirers on with their coats.

He offered an arm to each of the ladies and escorted them to the front door.

The ladies glided by locked onto his arms.

"What a lovely day." The lady hooked on Ian's right fluttered her eyelashes.

"Today's tea was more than I expected." The lady on his left flashed a toothy smile.

Sophia agreed. Putting aside her little discomfort after downing a shot of whisky, today was quite an adventure and unlike any day off since she arrived in Highland Falls.

"Wow, look at the time." Fiona hurried into the kitchen. "I've got late guests arriving soon. I've got to check the rooms."

"I'll clean up," Sophia insisted.

"Count me in," Ian offered.

Sophia hand-washed the delicate teapots and cups.

"It's been a long day." He scraped the last plate and placed it in the dishwasher. "All done." He leaned back against the counter with his arms crossed.

"Are all your days like this?" Sophia shut off the faucet and glanced out the window. Fiona's kitchen window was the perfect spot for viewing fall sunsets.

"Only the good days." Ian stepped behind her and massaged her shoulders. "The days I spent in libraries never had views like this."

His clean outdoor scent invaded her space. "I can't remember the last time I went to a library." Sophia stepped to the side, placed a teapot on a drying pad, and searched for a dishtowel. "Time to dry."

"Here you go." Ian handed her a towel.

"I'm surprised at how well you know your way around a kitchen," she said.

"Don't be impressed. It's my obsessive-compulsive personality. I operate my lab like a well-run kitchen. Everything needs to be neat, clean, and organized." He picked up a saucer.

She watched his strong hands move the dishcloth in a soft, circular motion around the outer gold rim and work their way toward the center with mechanical precision. He moved with a sensual motion—every stroke precise and calculated.

He handed her the dry saucer.

Her fingers gripped the edges. On the underside of the small plate, their forefingers touched. The light caress ignited her entire body.

"We make a good team." He stepped closer.

"Let's put these where they belong before I leave." Overcome by his closeness, she reached for the matching cup and placed it in the cabinet. She glanced around the kitchen. Except for the soft hum of the dishwasher, the room was quiet.

"I promised Lily I'd see you safely to your door." Ian tossed the dirty towels into a hamper in the mudroom.

"I'm fine now. All that tea flushed the last bit of whisky clear out of me."

"Why don't we compromise? I'd like another shot at your dad's car." The corner of his mouth twitched. "We'll drive back to the Logans together. I'll get my car and follow you to town."

His face was serious again—tender and a shade worried.

****

Monday nights were an early night for most of Highland Falls' businesses—the bakery was no exception. Sophia parked in front of the bakery and watched Ian back his truck into a space across the street. He was kind enough to follow her home. She would be rude, if she let him turn around and drive back to his sister's.

"If you're not in a hurry…" She fidgeted with her keys. "I know you might want an early start to Albany tomorrow…" She wasn't sure how to go about inviting a man to her apartment. "But if you have the time, one of my suppliers sent me some samples of sipping chocolate. I could use your unbiased opinion on the product." She smiled. "I might even have a whisky cookie or two in a tin upstairs. I tried my best to save one earlier, but the ladies loved them. I even got a few orders." She was babbling now.

"Who knew those old girls would devour them?" he said.

His words were precise and calm, unlike her nervous chatter. "My cookies weren't the only things they wanted to devour." She imitated their fluttering eyelids.

"*Ach*, I was sure they were going to drag me back to Albany." He flashed a charming smile. "It was an interesting group."

"As a group, they were pleasant." Sophia pictured the woman with the motionless lips and laughed out loud. "I'm sure you saw the lady who was cosmetically injected."

"Hard to miss. Must have been recently injected. She'll loosen up in a few days."

A playful sparkle glimmered in his blue eyes. He followed her upstairs.

Other than Alana, and occasionally handyman Tim, she never invited anyone to the apartment. She unlocked the door and stepped into the foyer. She rushed into the living room to see if she had forgotten to put away her personal items with the clean laundry. Except for a tin of rejected shortbread, the room was neat and uncluttered. She opened the tin and handed it to Ian. "We're experimenting with our winter cookie designs. The shapes are a little off, but they're only rejects in design, not taste. The cookies that make it into the showcase have to be perfect. You'll find some decent-size pieces of whisky shortbread in the tin."

"Didn't you tell the ladies, it's all about the buttery flavor, not the design?" He reached for a snowman without a head.

"Make yourself comfortable. I'll be right back." She left him in the living room and disappeared into the kitchen. The best sipping chocolate was made from rich, dark chocolate and prepared the French way. After one sip, she would know if these sample bars hit the mark. The Parisian process was simple but shouldn't be rushed. Tonight, however, a little help from the microwave would be acceptable.

Sophia measured two demitasse cups of milk and heated the liquid while she chopped the chocolate. The microwave *dinged*. She poured the milk in to a saucepan and whisked in the chocolate bits. Rushing never saved time. The drink had to be perfect. In a few moments, the ingredients melted together into a luxurious cup of sipping chocolate. The small kitchen filled with a rich chocolate aroma. Satisfied with the result she poured the mixture into two cups and gazed at the results. The presentation lacked a finishing touch. *Voilà*. She placed a delicate pink marshmallow on each saucer before returning to the living room.

"I've got something to show you." Ian looked up from his phone and tapped the cushion next to him. "Take a seat."

Sophia placed the tray with cups of steaming dark chocolate on the coffee table. Careful not to let their thighs touch, she sunk into the opposite corner of the overstuffed sofa. She reached for her cup and stirred the thick liquid while she listened.

"Before we left, Lily told me she knows of some antique pencil aficionados who live in the surrounding area." Ian stretched an arm over the back of the sofa. "They actually have an antique pencil club. Lily took a photo of the one we discovered and put it out there."

"Strange the things people find interesting," Sophia said.

"You'd be surprised," Ian said. "Lily said the group is obsessed with old pens and pencils. Her friends didn't take long to identify the pencil. They dated it back to the 1800s."

"You should think about recruiting the pencil ladies. They might be helpful with your research."

"Don't think the idea hasn't crossed my mind," he said. "That's not the only thing they found. They also collect writing samples from the time period. Another of Lily's friends found a well-preserved receipt signed by your great-great-grandmother, Marjorie MacLennan. The receipt is for six dozen cookies to be delivered to a Mr. O'Neil at Schenectady Station."

She reached for the phone. "Did you notice the date—August 8, 1868?" Uneasiness shivered over her. "The date is two years before the shop opened."

"It wasn't uncommon for women to help subsidize the family with income by taking in sewing or laundry. In Marjorie's case, she baked and sold cookies."

"Sweet shortbread is the easiest cookie to make and transport, but I'm not so sure with crude utensils it was less taxing than washing clothes."

"That's an interesting thought and a venue worth investigating." He reached for a cup of chocolate drink.

Competent intelligence surrounded him in appealing waves.

"The box, the pen, and the receipt with names and dates…" She placed the phone on the table and rubbed her temple. "All this information is too much to take in at once."

He brought the cup to his lips and inhaled. "It's like tasting a new whisky. The scent can tell you a lot about what's in the cup."

"Not exactly. There's no need to foreshadow with your nose. Drinking chocolate is about the sensuous first sip." She waited for him to take a sip.

"Wow, it hits you hard—like a liquid chocolate freight train." He arched a brow and licked his upper lip.

"Says a lot about the product. Is the chocolate too rich for your taste?" She preferred to continue discussing the chocolate rather than the box. So many unanswered questions filled her head. Was the motto enough proof that the crest belonged to the MacLennan clan? What did a buried box full of cherished possessions imply—a hasty departure? What if her stepmother's insinuations turned out to be more than just evil words from a bitter woman?

"A shot of good Scottish whisky would tone the flavor a bit." Ian placed his cup on the table.

"I don't have a liquor license for my shop, but there's always a bottle of whisky around for baking." She gave him a sideways glance. "You're serious, aren't you?"

"Have you ever met a Scot who joked about his whisky?"

"Give me a minute. I'll run downstairs and get a bottle." Before he could object, she was out the apartment door and down the stairs. The streetlamp illuminated the shop with an eerier burst of light. She grabbed the bottle of whisky and rushed upstairs.

Ian stood by the fireplace mantel, studying Aunt Mary's *tchotchkes*.

"Find anything interesting?" She poured whisky into Ian's cup and a dribble into her own.

"Just this old photo." He removed a black-and-white photo from the mantel. "I recognize your aunt Mary. Who are the two other women?"

"My mother, Laura, and my grandmother, Sophia." An unexpected feeling of nostalgia washed over her.

"Good Scotch tradition—naming the firstborn daughter after her maternal grandmother." He exchanged the picture for a cup of sipping chocolate and took a sip. "The whisky's the perfect addition to the drink."

"Are you complimenting the chocolate or the Scotch?" She did her own taste test. "I'm a chocolate purist, but you're right, the bitter notes of the Scotch balance well with the rich, dark chocolate." The sip of whisky warmed her from head to toe, relaxing her tired body with a warm sense of comfort. "Blended with chocolate, whisky is definitely a more pleasant drink."

"I'll keep that in mind next time I offer you a dram."

"Doesn't it make you dizzy trying to put the generations in order?" she asked.

"It can be uneventful at times, but the end result is always rewarding." Ian returned to the sofa.

"So many pieces are still missing." She avoided the sofa and sat on the chair across from him. She watched him shift comfortably into the corner of the sofa. A contained hint of excitement shadowed his features. Perhaps he was just cautious. From the moment she met Ian, she suspected he was either very good at what he did or else he was the kind of person who always appeared in the right place at the right time. "Was the pencil so valuable it was buried with the brooch?" The last thing she wanted to discover was a lead that would prove Mother Malevolent right. She had suppressed most memories from the past. Finding these tangible items gave life to her mother's clan. Imagining anyone dishonoring the memory of the women in the photo hurt.

"The pencil could have emotional value to whoever put it in the box. Today, finding a pencil in such good condition is a collector's dream. One of the pen club ladies told me it could sell for over a grand."

"And the brooch?" What was it about this Highlander that drew you into his world? The tea ladies, Lily and the judge, and now the pen club ladies were all under his spell.

"The brooch is priceless." He removed it from his pocket and put it on the table.

"Do you really think you can pinpoint the date of origin?" She glanced at the brooch then turned away. Seeing and touching the old object perplexed her. Excitement and uncertainty left a knot in her stomach.

"I'm taking it to my colleague at the university tomorrow. Want to join me?" he asked.

Did he really want her to go to Albany? His question sounded tentative. Was he testing the idea? "Too many orders to fill." She shook her head regretfully. "Maybe next time." It would be interesting to see his world. "Will you accomplish everything on your list in one day?"

"I have to check some facts. I'm hoping my colleague will have an answer about the origins of the crest before I leave." He put the brooch back in his pocket. "If not, he'll have to email me his findings. I'd like to return as soon as possible. Everything I need to explore is right here in Highland Falls." He smiled with a flicker at the corner of his lips "The little stories you remember are instrumental in filling in the blanks in my research."

"I hope you won't be disappointed if no more memories surface." From the first day he walked into her shop, and guided her hand along the tartan, she experienced one memory after another.

"I don't think that's the end," he said. "This afternoon at the Logans', you blurted out the meaning of the Gaelic words on the MacLennan badge without blinking an eye."

"I don't have your appreciation or interest in old stuff." *And don't want to.* Memories of her mother were guarded and deeply hidden. "Does it really matter who buried the box?"

"It could be important." He focused on the photos on the mantel. "I don't have the answers. Hopefully, my trip to Albany will help fill in the blanks."

"Other than the origins of the brooch, what else will you be looking for in Albany?" She fidgeted with the ragged cover on the arm of the chair.

"The judge suggested I check old property laws while I'm in the capitol. Land leases were popular in the past. It could tell me a lot about your ancestors. They might have lived on the land, but they didn't own it."

"Land leases?" Her stomach tightened. She never considered a land lease on the bakeshop property—until now. She crossed the small room toward the window. The pink letters on her delivery truck, *Founded in 1870 by Marjorie MacLennan* stood out sharp and clear in the glow of the streetlight.

"What's bothering you?" Ian came behind her.

"Aunt Mary owned the building free and clear, but what if there was a financial arrangement regarding the land?" She watched the headlights of passing cars flicker off Marjorie's name. "It's possible, even today, land and structure could be owned independently. You just said the same thing about the farm."

"Why the sudden interest in land leases?" Ian put his hands on her shoulders and turned her toward him.

"When you mentioned the possibility of a land lease, a bell went off in my head." She searched his face. "How long is a typical land lease?"

"They're long, usually fifty to ninety-nine years."

Not long enough. She did some quick calculations. "A ninety-nine year lease would have meant the original lease on this property ended years ago. Someone could have bought it. Have you ever seen the terms of a lease extended?"

"I've seen twenty to fifty year options." Ian guided her back to the sofa. "Why are you asking? Do you think it's possible this building sits on a land lease? It wouldn't be uncommon in a town founded so many years ago."

"I never really thought about it, until now." She sighed and sank onto the cushion. "I don't remember the subject coming up at the reading of my aunt's will. The lawyers transferred the deed for the building. I accepted the conditions of the will and never questioned if the land was in that deed. If it wasn't, and the land is still leased, why am I not paying rent? With hindsight, I should have asked more questions." She recalled the shock of finding out she'd inherited a bakery.

"Many land leases set provisions for allowances in rent. If so, and rent wasn't paid by a previous owner, nobody had reason to suspect that a land lease existed." Ian stepped in front of the sofa and stared. "I could check it out while I'm in Albany if you'd like."

"Wouldn't I be better off searching through the hall of records in town?" She looked up. The sincerity of his understanding expression did little to relieve her apprehension.

"The judge mentioned a fire at the turn of the century. Town records before nineteen hundred were destroyed. While I'm in Albany, I'll have the opportunity to examine official records kept by the state. I might have better luck locating the original lease for your property. Judge Logan referred me to a court clerk for assistance."

"It's not necessary. If a lease on the land exists, it should be on record somewhere in Highland Falls," she said. "This contract has nothing to do with your research. I'll find a way to solve the problem."

"That might not be true. The original lease might have everything to do with my research." Seeing her concern, he handed her his card. "See what you find locally. I'm available if you have any questions or just want to talk."

What did she get herself into? She looked at the card—Dr. Ian Campbell. Was he asking her to call because *he* wanted to talk, or was his reason purely academic?

"Do you know much about the different types of land leases?" Ian asked.

"What I recall from my accounting days could fit in a teaspoon."

"Why do I doubt that?" He raised a brow and laughed.

"I'm more familiar with government and non-profit land leases compared to private agreements, which don't provide tax deductions for the landowners. They have a high risk of not renewing."

"It's highly unlikely your shop is situated on either a government or non-profit," Ian said. "You would know."

"A private land lease can be complicated." She reached for her drink. Thick, gooey chocolate was just what she needed. She scooped the sticky chocolate off the bottom of the cup and paused with the spoon in midair. "The language of the lease is set by the landowners to maximize their profit. If that's the case, I could be in trouble when it expires."

"You need to find an original copy of a deed, or a lease, before jumping to any conclusion." Ian squeezed her arm.

"If a land lease exists, and I choose to stay, all my hard work could be for nothing." She licked the chocolate off the spoon. The way he watched her lick the spoon made her forget for a second what they were discussing.

"Check with city hall—something might show up."

His words were a passionate challenge. He understood her, even when she didn't express her full thoughts. Maybe, he learned how to hear silent thoughts from people who could no longer speak. No way was his trip to Albany going to be overnight. He would need time to prove or disprove the local tales, facts, and speculation he gathered. She would count the days until he returned.

Chapter 7

When Ian didn't return by the following Thursday, Sophia talked herself into believing he found something important to keep him away. After all, he had colleagues, an apartment, and a life in Albany. Her father's words came to her. "The hardest person to be honest with was yourself." At a young age, she learned she couldn't control anyone's comings and goings. Ian might end up being just another person who passed through her life. Some made an impact, and some didn't. He fell into the first category. Unlike her mother, her father, or her aunt Mary, Ian's departure was inevitable.

Mother Malevolent had a few catch phrases of her own. "To be honest and naive makes you an idiot."

I'd rather be honest and naive than cunning like you. She dismissed the memories and concentrated on today's schedule. She took an elastic band out of the drawer by the register, pulled her hair into a ponytail, and positioned her new toque over her hair. First on her list were the dozens of snowflake petticoat tails that had cooled overnight. The pie-like shortbread needed to be securely packed in bubble wrap, and boxed before they could be shipped to a customer in the city.

"I packed an extra petticoat for you to drop off at the mayor's office." Alana stepped behind the counter.

"I can't believe Judy's taken such an interest in your search for the lease renewal." She raised a brow. "Do you think she's up to something?"

"I don't think so. She's nosy but not guileless. Maybe she's just doing it for the free cookies." Sophia popped the bubble wrap. "Whatever her reason, I'm grateful for her introduction to the clerk in charge of the town archives. The woman looks old enough to have filed the first document, but her memory's sharp, and she remembered a box of documents that survived the fire."

"Did you get the answers you were hoping for?"

"It doesn't look good." Sophia shook her head, and the loose toque flipped off. "I didn't find the original lease. The clerk found papers of transfer from Marjorie to the next owner, Marjorie's daughter-in-law, my great-grandmother, Amelia MacLennan. If the original lease was a ninety-nine year land lease, she was okay." She placed the toque on the shelf.

"Any idea what happened when the ninety-nine years were up?" Alana asked.

"The original lease expired. We didn't find the first lease, but we did find a copy for a fifty-year additional option. It covered my grandmother and Aunt Mary," Sophia answered with a quick, half-confident reply.

"That would mean the extended grant should expire under your ownership." Alana tapped her fingers on the counter.

"I've done the math, too. I have less than a year left on the fifty-year extension." No reason to worry Alana with the details. It wouldn't be a sound financial decision to keep running a shop on land she might eventually have to rent. Her other option wasn't much better. She would have to find the money to purchase the land. With the current tourist boom, it could result in an expensive bidding war.

"Doesn't sound good," Alana said. "It would be nice if Hot Scot were here to guide you through this mess. All this ancestor stuff is so confusing. What are you going to do next?"

"He was supposed to be back last week. Who knows when he'll return?" Sophia shrugged. "I have an appointment with Aunt Mary's lawyer at two. The firm was around back in 1800s when Marjorie opened the shop. Maybe they can dig up something."

"Good for you. Hanging out with Hot Scot has worked out." Alana raised a brow. "Right?"

"He taught me a few tricks." Sophia placed the boxes in a shopping bag and grabbed her jacket.

"Take advantage of your time away from the shop." Alana walked her to the door. "Do something frivolous before you meet the lawyer."

Outside the cozy warmth of the shop, the weather was bitter cold. Sophia stopped at City Hall first, then the post office. The clock outside the post office struck twelve. Two hours was a lot of time to spend being frivolous. A visit to the local history museum was on Sophia's mind since the day the ancient clerk suggested checking the newspaper archives. This was as good a time as any. Small-town newspapers were notorious for airing dirty laundry. Gossip and society columns were popular back in Marjorie's day. It was worth a visit.

If Ian taught her anything, it was how one fact led to another. Maybe she'd find something in the archives she could offer to Mary's lawyer—something to help them find Marjorie's original lease.

"Enjoying the weather, Miss Porter?" Outside the hardware store, Mr. Durand tossed a shovel of snow off to the side.

"I'm adjusting."

"My grandda had a saying I'm sure you've heard. It's not the weather that gets to you." He glanced at her stylish boots. "It's not wearing the proper clothes. Those things waterproof?"

"Warm and dry on the inside." She tipped the thick, salt-stained rubber sole of her boot. "This morning, the weather lady said to expect more snow."

"It's not a bad thing around these parts. Cold weather and snow means a good ski season. That's good for everyone's business." He leaned on his snow shovel and glanced at the clouds. "Too cold to snow now."

"Does a correlation between temperature and snowfall exist?" She wondered out loud.

"Can't answer that one, but I do know I've never seen snow in the summer." Mr. Durand laughed. "You have a good day and stay warm."

She adjusted her earmuffs and headed into the wind. The museum was an inconspicuous structure on a street east of Main. The location off the beaten track hid the building from tourists, which was a shame. She often heard Tim remark that the exhibits were quite impressive for a local museum.

At the front door, she hesitated. Perhaps she should have called ahead and arranged an appointment with the curator, Mr. Paisley. *Too late to worry about that now.* Anyway, the place didn't appear to be overrun with visitors. With one foot in the door, she stopped and turned. Someone called her name. She shielded her eyes from the sun. She took a moment to adjust to the bright light and recognized the figure walking toward her. Ian was back.

He rushed toward her in a straight line. "We did it, lass." He wrapped his arms around her waist and pulled her close to his chest.

The air squished out of her jacket. Standing in full view of the town felt a little awkward, but she made no effort to pull away. "Did what?" She glanced at Ian. He wore a fur-lined cap with the flaps folded up. A blue plaid scarf hung from his neck. He hadn't bothered to button his jacket. He should know better seeing that he's a doctor. On the other hand, he lived in Edinburgh and descended from a long line of Scots with a tolerance for cold, wet, and wind.

"I found a lease for the property where the Logans' paddock is now. Marjorie and Ross MacLennan owned the farm. The brooch is authentic and…" He stopped and placed his hands on her cheeks. "Your interpretation of the motto was spot on." With his hands still on her face, he leaned down and kissed her.

The move was quick, excited, and impulsive.

The kiss warmed her like a pat of butter melting on a heated slice of toast. She took in a frozen breath. "Did your friend identify the silversmith's mark?" The sensation of the kiss lingered on her lips.

"Yes. The crest is authentic from the mid 1800s."

His enthusiasm was contagious.

"And the box?" A sensuous charge passed between them. "Could they date the box?"

"I left the box and the cloth with a colleague in the archeology department. They'll use carbon dating to help determine the age of both articles."

Tim cleared his throat.

Ian released her.

"Why don't I give you two a chance to catch up?" Tim shuffled his feet. "I'll go on in and give Mr. Paisley a heads-up about what you found."

"Give him my notes." Ian took an envelope from his pocket and handed it to Tim. "I want to share what I learned with Sophia."

"See you guys later." Tim disappeared behind the unremarkable doors.

"Can I buy you a cup of coffee?" Ian rubbed his bare hands.

"How about I make you a cup of coffee?" In spite of the frigid cold, she felt a rush of heat. "I've got some freshly baked lavender honey shortbread cooling. And, I've done some research. You'll be surprised with what I've discovered."

"I've been looking forward to a decent shortbread all week."

Was he thinking about her, too—even if it was her shortbread? She glanced at the brass museum clock over the door. She had plenty of time until her appointment. What would Alana say when she arrived back so soon—and with Hot Scot?

In front of her shop, she considered sneaking up to her apartment to avoid an embarrassing I told you so from Alana. The decision was made for her when Judy waved from outside City Hall. The news would spread fast if any of the townspeople saw Ian's greeting outside the museum. The last thing she wanted was to be the subject of gossip about a budding romance with the handsome doctor.

"Sit and warm up. "Alana met them at the door.

Alana didn't seem at all surprised to see them come into the shop. The gossip train sure worked fast in this town.

Sophia entered the empty shop and tossed her jacket over the back of a chair.

"Coffee or tea?" Alana directed Ian to the corner table. With a gentle nudge, she encouraged Sophia to join her behind the counter. "If you don't mind serving yourself, I'll finish boxing the weekend orders."

"No problem." She preferred serving Ian without Alana hovering over them with goo-goo eyes.

"If it gets busy out front, just call. I'll be in the back." Alana grabbed a spool of bakery twine.

Sophia filled a carafe with hot coffee, placed it on a tray next to the cream and sugar, and set out two mugs. She took the seat sat across from Ian. Inside, the shop was quiet without a peep from Alana. Outside, the sound of a snowplow distracted them.

"*Ach*, lass, you're going to get plowed in." Ian nodded at her bakery van about to be wedged in with a mound of snow. "If you have deliveries, I can drive you wherever you need to go. I'm parked in the municipal lot."

"No worry. My roadster is parked in the alley." She might have to take him up on his offer. From where she was sitting, she couldn't see where the plow would drop the next pile. Nothing she could do about it now. "What's in the notes you gave Tim?" She rested her elbows on the table.

"That can wait. I'm anxious to hear what you found." He poured coffee into each mug, leaving enough room for cream

"You were right about a fifty-year extension on the

lease." Sophia inhaled the fresh brew and added a dab of cream. "It was granted to my grandmother, Sophie."

"I'm assuming you didn't have any luck finding the original lease?" His eyes narrowed.

She shook her head.

"What's your next step?" he asked.

He sounded like a teacher encouraging a student. "I see my aunt's lawyer at two. Would you like to join me?" She forced a smile in an attempt to hide her ongoing internal debate. The terms of the lease could tip the scales in her decision to sell or stay.

"I'm free the rest of the day." He reached across the table and squeezed her hand. "Are you sure you don't mind me tagging along?"

"I wouldn't have asked you if I did." The tenderness of the gesture was far from professor like. It comforted and tempted her. "Tell me about your visit to Albany. What did you find out about Marjorie and Ross?"

"First step was to prove their existence and establish a place they called home." Ian released her hand and leaned back with his fingers locked behind his head.

"Was the farm profitable?" She wanted to know if her two-times great-grandparents had lived a good life. It might be enough to prove her stepmother wrong.

"From what I can tell, Marjorie and Ross made a living. They owned the land. They were descendants of Highlanders and not afraid of hard work. Records show sales of eggs, dairy products, and apples. The files were inconclusive, but there's a good chance they owned more than the land inside the paddock."

"An old apple orchard is just east of the Logans'

farm. Do you think their property extended that far?" She watched him lift his mug to his lips, then look away. "Why leave such a profitable farm?" she asked, unsure if she really wanted to know the answer.

"I have my suspicions, but no concrete proof. Learning why they left is the next step." He placed his mug on the table and rubbed the back of his neck. "Are you still interested?"

"I can handle the next step."

"I don't doubt it for a minute, lass." He nodded. "I could stop by in the evenings. You wouldn't have to give up your time in the shop."

Her mind wasn't on those details. The memory of his quick kiss excited her. She imagined his lips pressing against hers. Next time, she wanted his kiss to be slow and hungry. The thrill of the possibility made her shiver.

"Are you cold, lass?" He refilled her mug with hot coffee.

She shook her head and watched him over the rim of her cup. His expression was eager but tender. Would it ever be possible to have a relationship that didn't center on his research? "Do you think there's a connection between my lease and Marjorie?" She folded both hands around the warm cup.

"There's a good possibility." He edged his chair closer to the table. "The answers to so many questions could be connected to what we find. Are you ready for the answers?"

The intensity of his gaze was fixed on her as if he was assessing her strength and evaluating her courage. "I don't need to know everything about the past." She shifted in her seat and sipped her coffee with a hard swallow.

"What are you afraid of? I've met many people like you. They're cautious at first, almost resistant." He gave a shrug. "Once the leads started falling into place, little things, like the box, give life to unknown ancestors. They're not just dead people anymore. They had a life, and maybe a family. They were loved, hated, and possibly deceived. Emotions are timeless."

"You talk about forensic research and ancestry like they're the same."

"The two disciplines are not so different when it comes to how families react. In forensics, some people don't want to know the cause of death. They want the body buried and life to go on."

"That would be me," she murmured. "I rather not hear the details of the past."

"Too many wear rose-colored glasses when they start an ancestry search." He stared at the tartan tapestry on the wall. "I think we've already established that's not you."

"So why do they do it if they don't want to hear the bad with the good?" From the first day they'd met, she'd made it perfectly clear her ancestors' past contained things she preferred not to know.

"On the other hand, I've met people who have a feeling their ancestor is asking them to tell their story. They're not afraid of what I'll find and want every stone unturned." A slow smile curled his lip. He stood, walked to the wall, and put a hand on the old plaid. "When I started my research into the MacLennan clan, I thought your aunt Mary wanted me to learn everything I could for *your* benefit." He glanced over his shoulder.

"My benefit?" Sophia made her way toward the

plaid but stayed at a distance. She didn't want to encourage another haunting in the event another ancestor had something to say.

"It's your choice." He shrugged. "I'm beginning to think Mary had another reason. She could have wanted to uncover the truth about Marjorie." He glanced around the shop, returning his attention to the tartan. "Or maybe it's Marjorie, who wants her story told."

"Oh, please—a man who bases everything on science and fact is admitting some outside force is directing your research?" She raised a brow. "Do you believe in ghosts?" She liked his logic and believed there was truth in what he told her about Marjorie. How else could she explain the memories that surfaced when she touched objects belonging to her relatives? "You're the last person I would expect to hear that from."

"I don't rule out any possibilities and pick up information from many sources." He dismissed her comment with a sly smile. "Why are you so afraid of the truth?"

He blatantly addressed her fear. "Sometimes it's best to leave *sleeping dogs lie*."

"*Ach*, another of your father's proverbs."

"I believe its origins were French, not Scottish," she retorted.

"Touché." He gave her a mock salute. "Every family has ghosts in the closet. You should hear the stories my grandparents tell. The Campbell clan was not always popular. My family gets a good laugh over the old stories." He reached for her hands.

"You can't understand." She pulled away and wrapped her arms around her waist. "You have a family to share it with. I never had *anyone*." She just confessed her deepest secret. "My stepmother never said a kind word about my mother's family. She even told me all MacLennan descendants were terrible people. If something horrific happened and my ancestors left the farm, why is this important now?" She swallowed hard. "My mother and my aunt were kind people." She couldn't risk Ian discovering something awful and shattering her fond memories of her mother and aunt. She put their empty mugs on the tray and carried them to the bin under the counter.

"Marjorie was a woman ahead of her time." Ian followed and pointed out the window toward the van buried under shovels of snow.

"And if she was right?" Sophia followed his glance. A few letters on the van showed through the pile of snow.

"We can prove your stepmother was wrong, but you need to trust me. Work with me. I promise I'll only go as far as you want me to."

She did trust him. Her instincts for self-preservation had always been strong. She had already taken a risk when she expressed her fears to a stranger. The time had come to take another chance and open her heart.

Chapter 8

The offices of McNab, McNab, and Brown were in a charming, old building at the east end of Main Street. A horse-drawn sled parked out front would make it a perfect Currier and Ives scene. Sophia read the small brass plaque on the heavy wooden doors. The firm was founded in 1850—twenty years before Marjorie owned a brick-and-mortar bakery.

When McNab Senior presided over the reading of Aunt Mary's will, Sophia was seated in a small office. Today they were ushered into a conference room with portraits of generations of McNab partners circling the perimeter. A polished mahogany conference table filled the center of the room. An attractive blonde in her mid-thirties entered the room and stood under an impressive portrait of a distinguished young man. Her red designer suit was a sharp contrast to his perfectly pressed frock coat.

"Must be one of the original McNabs." Ian followed Sophia's gaze.

"Hi, I'm Megan McNab Brown." The young woman introduced herself. "The man in the painting is my two-times great-grandfather." She looked from Sophia to Ian. "My grandfather sends his regrets that he couldn't meet with you today. This snowstorm has caused havoc on the roads. He's not comfortable driving in this weather." She gave Ian a quick once-over. Her smile brightened, and her eyes twinkled.

Sophia bit back a smile. She wasn't quite sure how to introduce Ian. Was he a friend? Friends didn't make you feel like melted butter when they kissed you. "I hope you don't mind I brought Ian. He's a professor doing research on Aunt Mary's clan." She decided to keep their association on a professional level and avoid focusing on any kind of relationship—platonic or not.

"Not at all. Please be seated." Megan sat at the far end, in front of a laptop. "I've looked for the documents you're interested in." Her fingers moved quickly over the keyboard. "The original lease from 1870 was never scanned but should be in our archives. The paper on which old documents are written is often too fragile to put through a scanner. However, the latest lease is in the system." She pulled up a copy of the last renewal. "It states here this lease granted another fifty years to Sophia Forrest MacLennan."

"Sophia MacLennan was my maternal grandmother." Sophia folded her hands on the table. "My grandmother Sophia owned the shop before Aunt Mary. I've already done the math, and I don't have a lot of time left with the last extension." What happens at that point was something she hoped Megan could answer.

"I'm curious about something that might help explain the origins of the lease," Ian said. "I don't see a problem with Sophia's grandmother being the sole name on the renewed lease in the 1960s or 1970s. But…" He rubbed his palm along the scruff on his face. "There has to be an explanation of how Marjorie, a farmer's wife in the 1800s, came to own the shop. It's very unlikely a married woman of her time would have acquired property on her own."

"Do you mind if I take a look at your screen?" Sophia circled the sturdy wooden table, stopped behind Megan, and studied the words on the computer screen. Her math skills often helped her see patterns in dates.

"Do you see something?" Megan glanced over her shoulder.

"I'm thinking there's a pattern. They're common in math and exist in real life scenarios, too. Could there be a sequence of events—something in the original lease—that set it in motion?" she mused aloud.

Ian hurried around the table. "How did I not see this before?" He pointed toward the computer screen. "There is a commonality."

"I see it, too." Sophia looked closely. "The answer has nothing to do with numbers. It's all about gender. All the women who inherited the shop, by marriage or birth, had the surname MacLennan." She rubbed her forehead and glanced at Megan. "Did people do things like this back then?"

"Anything can be legally documented. The original lease should state that." Megan glanced at the computer.

"Very clever, lass." Ian put his hand around her waist and squeezed.

"I'm not so clever." Sophia shrugged. "I was looking for a complicated pattern. You saw the simple answer staring right at us. They're all female descendants of Marjorie."

"You don't give yourself enough credit." Ian pulled her closer.

Sophia relaxed against the dreamy intimacy of his

closeness. She hadn't felt this comfortable with anyone in a long time. Megan broke the spell with a question.

"Do you have many memories of your grandmother?" Megan flashed a warm smile. "Any stories she might have told you about her past could be helpful in locating the documents."

"Is there anything you can tell us?" Ian nodded. His hand slipped from her waist, and he parted a few inches.

"All I remember about Grandma Sophia was that she'd died the year I was born." Her knowledge of her family tree was limited to what Ian told her. She couldn't take the timeline back any farther. It hurt to go forward. A few years later, her mother was gone, as well. In recent months, the bad memories from the past were fading, and she liked it that way. She was happy in Highland Falls. "Why only female descendants?" She stared at Marjorie's name on the screen. If Ian was right, where did she fit in? She was a Porter, but her mother, Laura, was a MacLennan.

"Perhaps there were no male heirs." Megan stated the obvious. "When the lease was renewed your grandmother, and then her daughters, Mary and Laura, were the next MacLennan descendants entitled to the shop."

"*Ach.* I'm not sure that's true. I've done extensive research on the clan and discovered many of them were transported to the colonies after Culloden. My research in Scotland has led me here, but it's not conclusive. For some reason, moving forward from the 1800s, it's the females who dominate my findings." He cleared his throat. "The MacLennan name couldn't continue if there were no males. The shop and the women who ran it are just the tip of the MacLennans' story."

Ian was right. Grandparents, great-grandparents, and two-times great-grandparents all had to have at least one male heir to carry on the name. There would have been children, grandchildren, and great-grandchildren. The numerical possibilities were endless, and yet Sophia was alone in the world.

"The only way to know for sure is to locate the original documents." Megan reached for a pad and jotted down notes. "I'd like to find the bill of sale for the shop, as well. According to the will, you inherited the building without a mortgage. At what point was the mortgage paid off, or had someone set the conditions of payments?"

Megan was sharp. Sophia was glad she contacted the firm. "Do you believe something is stated in the original lease that allows for another renewal?" What if she was the loose connection? Unlike her mother, aunt, or grandmother, she didn't have the last name MacLennan. Was someone out there who could challenge her lineage? Of course, the land and the building were two different entities. No one could take the bakery. She inherited it outright.

"I'm sorry the last renewal document doesn't tell you anything you don't already know." Megan pointed to the line that read, *under the terms stated in the original lease dated 1870, I, Sophia Forrest MacLennan, am granted an additional fifty years.* "Hopefully, the original lease will provide us with the answer. We still don't know who owns the land or why Sophia is not paying rent."

"If the land is owned by a big cooperation with large holdings in the state, this little piece of non-income-producing property might be buried away." Ian glanced at the portraits. "Does your firm save après lawyer papers?"

"We do have files, but I'm not sure how far back they go. I'll have my associate check our archives," Megan said.

"What are après papers?" In a less-than-graceful move, Sophia sank into a chair. *Did she really want to know?*

"They're lawyer notes." Ian gestured toward Megan's pad. "Even today lawyers write side notes that are not officially part of a document. Before computers, they were often filed alongside official records."

All this legal talk gave Sophia a pounding headache. She rubbed her forehead.

"This can be overwhelming," Megan said. "I think we could all use a cup of tea."

"Tea would be nice," Ian answered for both of them. While they waited for the tea to arrive, he engaged Megan in a conversation about the founding partner in the painting.

Just like the first day Sophia met him, she watched as Megan fell under the influence of Ian's posh Scottish accent. The difference was that Megan knew the answers to his questions regarding family. Sophia half-listened to Ian ask one question after another. She couldn't figure out where he was going with all his questions. Megan's answers could be relevant to his research, but did not seem relevant to why they were here.

A young man in a designer suit entered with a tray. He set it on the table and poured an herbal infusion from a porcelain pot.

"This is a beautiful tea service. Ian's sister uses a similar tea set at afternoon tea." The teapot gave Sophia the perfect opportunity to change the discussion. At the chance of being rude, Sophia restrained from glancing under her cup to check the origin of the set.

"The set has been in my family for decades. It's always been used to serve our clients tea."

Sophia sipped her tea and studied the room décor and portraits. The furnishings and paintings were well maintained. She would have to ask Ian later what he thought of Megan's office.

"I'm a big fan of Sophia's lemon-fig shortbread." Megan passed around a plate. "My assistant picks up a dozen when he stops by the shop for his morning coffee."

"Let me know when he's coming, and I'll have a box ready." Sophia passed the cookies to Ian. "Do you like any other flavors?"

"My daughter loves the cinnamon sugar cookies, and my husband prefers the lemon shortbread."

"Judge Logan's favorite." Sophia had no claims on Ian and was relieved to hear the pretty lawyer was happily married.

"So, you know the judge?" Megan asked. "Are you aware of his research into old state laws and how they've changed?"

"He mentioned it briefly," Ian said. "Do you know how far back his research goes?"

"Exactly the time period you're interested in—1800 and forward. That's when the laws started to change. It might help your research."

"It was a time of reform, for sure." Ian rubbed the back of his neck. "I'd like to see his findings. They could be helpful, considering nineteenth-century lawmakers thoughts about the practice of women holding work-related property assets. Labor of wives belonged to their husbands and families and not to the individual woman."

Sophia understood where Ian was going with this because it bothered her, too. "So how did Marjorie own a brick-and-mortar business in her name?" She reached for the honey and stirred a teaspoon into her tea. The first revitalizing sip tasted sweet and minty.

"Could be several reasons—death being the most obvious. Divorce is possible, too." Megan glanced at the portraits on the wall. "It shouldn't be difficult to find proof of either of these circumstances. My predecessors maintained accurate records. The firm has protected them in an environmentally secure archive."

"Divorce in the 1800s?" The thought unsettled Sophia. An ancient curse to bring unhappiness to generations of MacLennan women was illogical and ridiculous, but it crossed her mind. She looked at Ian. Was their relationship doomed, as well?

****

"We have to find out what happened before we ask the whys." Ian reached across the table and filled the ladies' cups. He noticed the wrinkle in Sophia's brow and realized how badly she wanted to prove her stepmother wrong. "Let's not jump to any conclusions until we have all the facts," he said for Sophia's sake. "The acceptable standards for the time period suggest that an unusual circumstance allowed Marjorie to proceed with such an undertaking."

"I never imagined the answers to my elusive lease could be so deeply hidden in the past." Sophia sighed.

"Megan will deal with the lease, and I'll do the rest." Somehow, when he figured this all out, he had to find a gentle way to present his conclusions. He cared for Sophia and didn't want to see her hurt by the truth. She was a quick learner with little or no regard for academic protocols. What she lacked in well-defined actions, she made up with her enthusiasm. How far would he allow himself to go before he disregarded academic protocol?

Chapter 9

Winter was never Sophia's favorite season. In the past, it meant being stuck inside with Mother Malevolent. She often chose the brutality of the weather to her stepmother's vicious tirades. For lack of a better way to pass the hours, she would venture out with no particular destination in mind.

Life in Highland Falls was completely different. Baking routines and customer flow marked her days. Outside, the town thrived. The more snow, the better. With the holiday season approaching, not getting caught up in the Currier and Ives atmosphere was difficult. Just-baked, whimsical cookies would soon transform the window display from fall to winter. She placed a smiling Santa in a cherry red suit in the prime position and surrounded him with jolly, marshmallow-faced snowmen. When the last cookie joined the group, she stepped outside for a customer's view.

Tim and his grandmother, Granny Ulster, rushed toward her.

"What are you doing out here dressed like that." Granny pointed a finger at Sophia's bare arms.

"I came out to just check the new window display." Sophia exhaled a cold puff of air. "Why don't you come inside and join me for a warm beverage?"

"Maybe later. Granny's already late for the town's holiday decorating meeting," Tim said.

"You seem to have a knack for fancy decorating." Granny pointed a mitten at the window display. "Grab a jacket and join us."

"I can't. Alana is off today. I'm alone in the shop."

"Suit yourself." Granny slid an arm through her grandson's and tugged him toward the curb. "We have to hurry."

Sorry. Catch you later." Tim tossed his scarf over his shoulder.

He remained calm and attentive as he escorted Granny across the street.

Sophia hugged herself to ward off the cold and watched them disappear into City Hall. Granny Ulster could try anyone's patience. She took a final look at the window and rushed back indoors. Inside the ovens buzzed in harmony to the catchy Christmas music Alana insisted they play. She glanced around the shop. The tables were neat and clean. The feather duster sat idle in the corner. She had a few minutes before the next rush of customers. Might as well give the tartan a quick once-over.

The closer she got to the tartan, her skin tingled with the memory of the day Ian walked into her shop. A week passed since their meeting with Megan. Just the other day, he announced he was on to something. He preferred not to reveal his findings until he had conclusive evidence. She had an idea he might be looking into Marjorie's life. Before she could lose herself in recapping what they already knew, the bell over the door announced a customer.

A little girl in a pink ski jacket ran over to the display case.

"What would you like?" Sophia put away the

duster and stepped behind the counter. She glanced at the colorful display of snowmen in funky top hats.

The girl seriously studied the cookies. "I want that one. The snowman in the pink polka dot hat." She pressed her face against the glass.

"That's my favorite, too." Sophia held out the cookie. "This is a new design, and you look like my perfect taste-tester."

"What do you say, Amy?"

"Megan?" Sophia looked up, surprised to see her lawyer in the middle of the afternoon.

"We're on our way to the slopes for some late skiing. The fresh snowfall is hard to resist. I promised Amy a snack for the ride, but I have another reason for stopping by." Megan removed a sealed envelope from her backpack. "My assistant was diligent in searching for the documents you requested. We found the original lease deep in our file archives."

Sophia hesitated before taking the envelope. It wasn't very thick. She could see how something like this would be difficult to find, but somehow Megan and her staff had succeeded. "There's not much to it." Sophia held it gingerly between her fingers. "I would've thought something touching so many generations would be bigger."

Outside, the sun had melted snow off of her van. Bright-pink letters the color of the snowman's hat reflected through the window. She stared at the words, *Founded in 1870 by Marjorie MacLennan.* What would the lease tell her about her ancestor other than she really existed?

"I guess back in those days it didn't take so many words to explain something. The laws weren't so cumbersome," Megan said.

Sophia nodded. Apart from the modern conveniences that made baking easier, simpler, and more efficient, life in the nineteenth century had its appeal. "Do you have time for a warm beverage? I can put it in a take-away cup."

"Sounds good." Megan glanced at her watch. "We've got a few minutes before my husband picks us up. Why don't you check the envelope while we wait?"

"And what would you like?" Sophia asked Amy.

"Hot chocolate with whipped cream and marshmallows, please," Amy said.

When everyone was seated at the counter with cups of sipping chocolate, Sophia took a moment to glance over the lease. The old document, no more than two pages, was not what she expected. The lease was short, to the point, and handwritten in words that were nothing more than archaic legal gibberish. "Weren't there typewriters in the late 1800s?" She studied the swirling script.

"Offices started using typists at the turn of the century." Megan glanced over her shoulder.

At the bottom of the second page, Sophia ran a finger over her great-great-grandmother's signature. The tip of her finger felt warm. She pulled away, worried that further contact would ignite the paper.

"Are you okay?" Megan asked.

"Yes." Sophia gazed around the shop, stopping when she came to the tartan. According to Ian, the plaid was older than the words on the lease. An otherworldly sensation engulfed her. She turned away quickly and focused on the next signature. "Jonathan McNab, the founder of your firm witnessed the signatures."

"Yes, my two-times great-grandfather. He stayed with the firm until he died." Megan made a similar gesture to the one Sophia did over Marjorie's name. Unlike Sophia, she let her finger linger. "It's weird, isn't it? Seeing the actual written words from an old document has a surreal effect."

"They don't let you deny the truth." Sophia reached for the paper and pointed to another signature. The letters were not as clear. "Can you make out this name?"

"The name looks like Thomas O'Neil." Megan held up the copy to the light.

Sophia raised a brow.

"Is the name familiar?" Megan asked.

"I've seen it somewhere before." She had trouble keeping all the information she heard straight. How did Ian do it? Sophia thought hard. The air around her heated her cheeks. She remembered where she'd seen the name. "Thomas O'Neil's name was on an old receipt written by Marjorie."

"What kind of receipt?" Megan examined the signature.

Amy, oblivious to the impact of the papers, stirred the marshmallows in her cup. A long sip resulted in a creamy mustache on her upper lip.

Without missing a beat in their conversation, Megan handed her daughter a napkin.

Sophia felt a pang of envy for all the niceties she missed without a mother.

"The bill was for a large order of shortbread cookies to be delivered to a train station." The receipt reminded Sophia about payment for services. "By the way, how do you want to settle my bill?" Bringing the conversation back to the present cleared the flutter of unsettled thoughts from her head. She preferred the uncertainty of her future to the melted mess of the past.

"It's all been taken care of. Your aunt left a retainer account to cover any additional time the firm would spend assisting you," Megan explained. "Of course, once your year is up, whatever money remains will go to you."

"Aunt Mary must have been concerned that there might be costly problems." She had the lease so what further services could she need from the firm?

"It's not uncommon to run into obstacles in inheritance cases. Your aunt took the precaution of creating a substantial account," Megan said.

A tall, attractive man in ski clothes approached the window and waved.

"Daddy." Amy grabbed her jacket and raced to the door.

"I hate to rush out." Megan gathered their cups. "If I can be of any assistance to you or your charming friend, you know where to find me."

"Thanks for bringing the documentation."

Amy and Megan exited the shop.

Left with a swirl of emotions and questions, Sophia decided to spend the rest of the afternoon decorating the walls. Just before closing time, a late customer rushed in for a dozen cookies. Sophia looked at the trays still full and packed an extra half dozen.

The grateful customer left with a big smile.

Outside, the wind picked up. Snow wedged between the door and the jamb. A frigid breeze entered through the slightly ajar door. The wind whipped around the café, blowing napkins and loose papers to the floor. Sophia grabbed the lease before it fluttered to the floor and rushed to shut the door.

Fiona stood on the other side of the door, stomping snow off her boots.

"What are you doing in town at this hour?" Sophia looked past her but saw no sign of Ian.

"Ian and I were invited to the decorating committee meeting." Fiona stepped inside and removed her mittens. "I stayed in town to do some shopping." She followed her glance. "Ian's at the museum talking to Mr. Paisley."

"Why don't you have a cup of tea while you wait?" Sophia walked behind the counter, started the electric kettle, and removed a teapot and strainer from the shelf. Every couple of seconds, she glanced out the window.

"*Ach*. That brother of mine has a way of drawing everyone into his research." Fiona came up to the counter and reached for a broken cookie on the sample plate. "The other day he convinced Tim to accompany him to the Logans' paddock."

"What did he expect to find with all the snow?" Sophia refilled the plate with broken pieces of peppermint shortbread.

"Don't ask me. Highlanders can be fools sometimes. They never let the weather stand in their way." Fiona shrugged and popped the head of a snowman into her mouth.

Fiona often joked about her brother's most attractive qualities. Of course, she wouldn't see him the way Sophia did. "There's not much choice where you come from. I heard winters are brutal in Scotland." Sophia filled the strainer with loose leaves.

She replayed the day she braved the muddy field

with Ian, experiencing firsthand how neither wind nor rain deterred him. The image of his straight back and broad shoulders moving forward with long, determined strides remained vivid in her mind. Losing her train of thought, she reached for another box of tea. How could thinking about a man make her such a scatterbrain? She shook her head to clear her thoughts and placed the tea tin close to the edge of granite counter. The tin fell to its side and rolled onto the floor. "Oh, sugar." She kneeled behind the counter and brushed the mess into the dustpan.

"Everything okay?" Fiona glanced over the counter.

"No worries. Some tea leaves made a bit of a mess." She carried the mess to the trash with exaggerated care and lowered the pan over the bin. The door opened, and a few tea leaves flew off the dustpan. She jerked her head right.

Ian stood framed by the open door with a picture-perfect pose. Chubby snowflakes fell around him.

"Get in here and close the door," Fiona scolded, pretending to shiver.

"*Ye nivver dee'd o winter yit.*" Ian grinned and tapped the snow off his boots.

With her limited Gaelic, Sophia translated—no one dies of winter. The silly bantering between Fiona and her brother made her laugh and forget the tea leaves scattered across her shop. The laugh came out like a sad chuckle. How nice it must be to have someone to joke with the way they did.

Fiona responded with a playful tap across his chest.

"Hey, lass. Is that tea you're making?" Ian stared past Fiona and smiled at Sophia.

The intensity of his gaze disarmed her. A fiery heat ran down her arm. The sensation came not from the anticipation of seeing Ian, but from a whiff of hot steam from the kettle.

Ian rushed to her side and grabbed her arm above the elbow. He pulled her away from the burning vapor and held her in a one-arm embrace. With his free hand, he moved the pot a safe distance.

"Ouch. That looks bad." Fiona rushed forward.

"I'm fine. It's just a burn." Sophia shrugged. "This is one of many occupational hazards." She tried to ignore the sting, but it hurt a lot more than she wanted to admit.

"Do you have a first aid kit?" Ian ushered her to a chair and applied a cold cloth.

"I keep one under the counter next to the bakery boxes." Sophia couldn't recall ever being fussed over like this. All this attention for a burn the size of a maraschino cherry was embarrassing.

"It won't hurt for long." Ian read the ingredients on the tube of burn cream. "This cream has a numbing component."

He was always so practical and factual. Sophia smiled. Forgetting that as a forensic pathologist Ian had medical training was easy. She let him apply a simple dressing to the wound.

He placed a hand on her forearm above the bandaged area and gently squeezed down into the tense muscle.

"We could all use a good cup of tea" Fiona glanced at the dressing.

"I'll prepare a pot." Ignoring her racing heart, Sophia stood.

"We've got this," Ian insisted.

She didn't have the energy to argue. Today was a long day filled with chores and unexpected events. She walked toward the door and flipped the sign over to *Closed* before joining Fiona and Ian.

On the other side of the bistro-style table, Ian straddled the little chair. The soft, striped cushion yielded to his weight.

"I've got something to show you." She removed the envelope from her apron pocket. "Megan found the document we asked for."

"The lease?" Ian came around to where she was seated. He bent forward, resting his hands on the back of her chair.

"It's the original lease." Usually disturbed by people invading her private space, Sophia enjoyed Ian's closeness.

"Does the document answer your questions?" Fiona circled the table filling everyone's cup.

"It's a lot of old legal talk, but pretty straightforward." Sophia released an exasperated sigh. "The information is what we suspected when we visited the law office. The lease is granted by birth or marriage to MacLennan women. It states right here…" She positioned her index finger over the words. "The land is granted for the fee of one dollar a year for the first hundred years. The sum can be paid in full or over time. All additional renewals will be limited to fifty years with the same consideration. Megan found a receipt for a hundred dollars and another for fifty dollars when that lease was renewed." She glanced at Ian. "How did Marjorie pay the amount in full? Where would she have found the money?"

"It's possible she sold the farm." Ian took the lease and returned to the seat across the table. "How she got the money might remain a mystery, but we have proof she held the original lease."

"It seems like such a small fee to cover taxes and other expenses," Fiona said. "What about the building?

"The deed for the bakery was never in question. It was part of my inheritance." Sophia rolled her shoulders. "The question of who owns the land now is still unanswered. I have no idea if they'd negotiate a renewal or what it would cost." She did some rapid calculations. "With the high cost of land today, the renewal fee could increase astronomically."

"The property might be insignificant to the present owner." Ian stared blankly at the lease. "Or it could be buried so deep in the company's legal archives no one knows it exists. What did your lawyer suggest?"

"Megan said to continue the way I have been while her firm searches for the current owner." Sophia wasn't a pot-stirrer and agreed with her lawyer's suggestion. "She doesn't think I'll be contacted until the lease expires."

"You have nothing to gain or lose until then." Ian slid the lease across the table to Sophia.

"Did you look closely at the signatures at the bottom?" Surprised that he didn't comment on them, she pushed it back across the table.

"Thomas O'Neil. I'm not surprised," he said.

"Why not?"

"I was curious about Mr. O'Neil since his name appeared on the receipt for the cookie order. I stopped at the museum after the town meeting to review an article Mr. Paisley found in his newspaper files." Ian placed his phone on the table and opened his photo app.

Sophia looked at an old newspaper photo on the front page of the *Highland Falls Gazette*. Four men in dapper suits posed by a lovely lady in a fashionable dress. The group stood in front of what was now *Just Baked Cookies*. The structure of the building was similar, without the updates to the front window and roof. A bold font above the black-and-white picture read *Grand Opening*. The date was June 1870.

"Why isn't anyone smiling? Did they all have bad teeth?" Sophia found their facial expressions lacking.

"Today, people think no one smiled in old photographs because of their teeth. That's not true. Non-existent dental care was the norm. People weren't embarrassed to show their teeth. Cheerfulness, pleasure, or amusement in a photograph had a different connotation. Only the poor, the lewd, drunks, or entertainers looked happy in old photographs. If you wanted to be remembered as upper class and of good character, you would hold a serious expression." Ian's lips dropped to a frown. "A photographed image could possibly be the only likeness of you for eternity."

Was this the only likeness of her great-great-grandmother? Sophia wasn't sure she cared to see any others. More photos would only lead to more unanswered questions.

"That's an interesting topic, I never really thought about." Fiona reached for the phone. "How long did they have to stand there?"

"Good point," Ian said. "To capture a photograph could take from ten to thirty minutes. That was a long time to hold onto a grin."

Sophia agreed. Ian's facts were both exhausting

and thought-provoking.

"What's really important in this photo are the names printed underneath." Ian enlarged the font.

Sophia blinked once, then twice, until the letters came into focus. The first name was Thomas O'Neil. Three other men posed between him and the lady at the end. The list was an odd mix of prominent townsmen: the mayor, the doctor, and the blacksmith. The names didn't mean a thing until she read the name of the woman, Marjorie MacLennan.

She turned her head a fraction of an inch in the direction of her delivery van parked just outside. A soft gust of air gently caressed the back of her neck. It felt like someone had brushed by her. *I've got this, Marjorie.* She acknowledged the sensation with a subtle nod. In front of her was the tangible evidence. She had read the words on the truck so many times and was never overcome with nostalgia like she was now. "Marjorie really existed," she whispered.

"Did you ever doubt it?" Ian asked.

"I don't know." She shrugged. Maybe all this new information would shed a positive light on the MacLennan clan. She read the names again. "Why isn't her husband, Ross, in the photo? I don't see his name mentioned in the article." This waiting game was not her style. She was tempted to tell Ian to just get on with his work and leave her out of it, but he had stirred more than her curiosity. Like a kid who ate too many sugary cookies, her thoughts bounced all over the place. The unsolved story of Marjorie's life gave her a reason to see her handsome Scot every day.

Oh, Aunt Mary, what did you start?
****

"Old pictures are often hard to process mentally and visually." Ian promised Sophia the truth. "In today's world, we carry thousands of photos we can delete at will. It's hard to digest the historical significance of one faded old picture." He wanted her to understand the significance of the photo.

"Most people say a picture is worth a thousand words. My father always said Scots believe the opposite's true." Sophia tightened her hold on his phone.

"Simple words sometimes hold more power than a printed image." Ian nodded.

"What about missing names—like Ross MacLennan? Marjorie's husband isn't mentioned even once?" She leaned closer to the phone.

"No disputing he's absent from the event, but why?" Ian said. "Something must have happened to keep him away from such an important day. I'm checking the possibilities." The wrong words could result in an in-depth image being imprinted in her mind forever.

"Isn't it strange how Mr. O'Neil was so kind to Marjorie, a married woman? Why would he lease her land in her name for only a dollar a year?" She glanced at the bandage on her arm.

"Does the burn still hurt?" Ian assessed the dressing. "It's clean and dry with no sign of drainage. How's the wound feel?" He released her arm.

"Just a little sting." Sophia turned her focus to the teacup.

"I know a little about the man that might help explain his kindness." Ian cleared his throat.

"Go ahead, I'm listening." She sank into the seat

cushion.

"I want to hear how you explain this one, brother," Fiona said.

The bothered expression on Sophia's face disturbed him. "O'Neil was a childless widower and a philanthropist who obviously liked her shortbread." His answer was a bad attempt to lighten the situation.

"Mr. O'Neil enjoyed her shortbread two years before he helped her open this shop. The pen ladies' receipt was dated August 1868." Sophia looked around the cafe. "Don't philanthropists usually help widows and orphans?" She tilted her brow.

"I haven't found any evidence proving Marjorie was a widow." Ian was excited when Paisley gave him the article and expected Sophia to be, too. Maybe it was a mistake to show her the newspaper so soon.

"Then where was Ross?" Sophia leaned back and crossed her arms.

"I don't have all the answers, but I will," Ian said. "From the accounts of his life I read so far, Mr. O'Neil was a kind-hearted businessman. He might have had the foresight to see the potential and the need for a bakery in their town."

"There you go." Fiona laughed. "The granting of the land lease could be as simple as Marjorie having a benefactor who loved her shortbread." She filled everyone's cup with the remaining tea. "It makes sense to me to give the rights to the property to female descendants. In those days, it was beyond their sensibility to associate males with the cooking and baking. It could be a sweet story and nothing more."

"I doubt it," Sophia rushed her words. "I wish I could see it like a fairy tale. If anyone has a list of reasons not to believe in fairy tales, it's me." She turned to Ian. "I've told you my stepmother always described the MacLennan clan as less than reputable. What if Marjorie and Mr. O'Neil had something going on? What if that's the reason Ross isn't in the photo?" She reached for her cup and emptied it.

"That's a possibility, too." Fiona nodded.

"Don't play that game, lassies." Ian gave his sister a cross look. He got the impression she enjoyed his predicament.

"What game?" Sophia raised an open palm.

"*What if* questions invoke too much overthinking." His research didn't allow hypothetical questions. When it was challenged in the past, it was by reasonable academics that understood where it was headed. Sensible scholars relied on documented facts. "W*hat if* questions most often point to a disastrous dead end."

"I get it." Sophia released an exasperated sigh. "Like, what if I never came here? What if I stayed in the city? What if we don't pursue this?" She reached for a napkin and blotted a wet spot on the table. "Will Marjorie's legacy just fade into the history of the town? Would it be all my fault?"

"Those are illogical arguments grounded in unsubstantiated theories and personal feelings." Ian reached for her hands. "Without your help, I might still be trying to figure out who owned the crest. One lead fed into the next because of you. So far, every discovery has led down another path. The old pencil led to the pen club ladies, then to the cookie receipt for Mr. O'Neil. Your search for the lease has given my research a tremendous boost."

"I guess I don't see it that way. Every step forward

seems like a step back." Sophia pulled away her hands. "There are still so many holes. Maybe they don't want to be filled."

"Okay, let's take a break. I feel the burden of this information overload, and I don't have anything vested in it." Fiona stood, jostling the table. The cups and teapot did a soft shimmy. She reached for the empty pot. "I think it's time for some fresh tea." She slipped past Ian's chair and leaned in. "Be careful, brother. *As ye make your bed saw ye main lie on't.*"

Bed. He wanted to laugh. He was so preoccupied with research that he hadn't slept more than a couple of hours a night. He glanced at Sophia and his thoughts of being in bed were no longer on sleep or lying alone.

Sophia slid back her chair. "I'll make a fresh pot." She twisted her neck to the side and rolled her shoulders.

The soft sexy arch of the motion was meant to relieve her tension and not to drive him crazy. "Fiona can serve the tea." He reached for Sophia's arm just above the bandage. A strong desire to take her in his arms and soothe her worries overwhelmed him. He pulled back. His sister was right. The facts could be overpowering for an amateur, especially someone who was brought up to feel shame for the clan.

Sophia looked at him. Her tongue rolled over her bottom lip.

"I'm sorry," he said. "I was too harsh when you asked about Marjorie and Ross. He wanted to encourage her involvement—it was, after all, her family history. "Your insights have a personal connection, which is important too."

"So you do think Marjorie and Mr. O'Neil were

having an affair?" she asked.

"It's highly unlikely. If we find a society column, which alludes to a relationship, I wouldn't have too much stock in them. Most gossipy articles usually offer unconfirmed details. They're no more than someone's opinion of an uncertain situation." *Damn.* He didn't want her to think he was dismissing her contribution again. He should offer a positive comment on her observation. "Your curiosity about Ross is logical. Why don't you see what you can find?" If he had the leisure, it might be interesting to research a romantic notion between Marjorie and O'Neil—even if it led nowhere. Another venue would extend his visit here. His self-imposed deadline dictated his schedule and limited his freedom to sidestep his research.

She lifted her chin and met his gaze. "Maybe I will." She returned to her seat.

No matter how it came about, her interest pleased him. "An unfortunate event around the time Marjorie opened her shop could explain why Ross was missing." He offered his insight. "I haven't found anything significant that would have separated them for an extended period of time. If it's out there, I'll find it."

"Wouldn't you have come across a notification of his death by now?"

"I haven't ignored the possibility. I've touched base with a clerk in the state records office. If Ross is not dead, what course did his life take?"

"If he and Marjorie divorced, it's possible Ross married again. What if there's a whole other branch of MacLennan's?" Sophia's voice cracked. "Marjorie might not even be my great-great-grandmother. I might not have any right to extend the lease or own the shop."

"Don't jump to conclusions before you have the facts. The female descendants from another marriage would have no right to the legacy of Ross's first wife." Such a finding would be a minute point in his research but a monumental happening for Sophia. Ian tapped the screen of his phone. He needed to take a closer look and search for something he might have missed. The newspaper photo popped up. He enlarged Marjorie's face and saw something he didn't notice before. She might not be smiling, but she wasn't completely expressionless. She had an uneven tilt to her brow. It stung him. He knew that facial gesture.

"What are you looking at?" Sophia asked.

"Something I didn't see before." He turned the screen in her direction. "You inherited a quirky tell from Marjorie."

"All I see is a lot of serious people in their best clothes." She pushed away the phone.

"Look closely at Marjorie's face." He slid his chair closer to Sophia. Thinking she would notice the subtle quirk was foolish. She probably had no idea she had the same charming, telltale expression. "It's the little tilt of her brow. She's bothered by something."

"Yeah, most likely the time it's taking to shoot the photo." Sophia laughed.

"You do the same thing when you're uncertain or annoyed. It's a subtle trait, but I wondered from the day I met you who you inherited it from." Ian reached over and trailed a finger across her forehead.

"You noticed it the first time you saw me?" Her brow twitched upward.

She touched a side of him very few people experienced.

"And a few other *tidy* things." Resisting the temptation to move his hand along her cheek, he pulled away. He wasn't sure the timing was right for either of them to get too close.

Chapter 10

Sophia rolled over and glanced at the clock on the bedside table. Five a.m. flashed across the screen. She pulled the quilt over her head and sighed. The last time she looked at the clock it was three a.m. All night long, she twisted and turned, thinking about Marjorie's relationship with Mr. O'Neil.

"Going back to sleep is pointless." She tossed the blanket off the bed. Half awake, she slipped on a bathrobe and dragged herself downstairs. In the kitchen, she flipped on the light switch and set the oven's digital panels. The control lights flickered on and off, then on again. *Weird.* Was there an outage last night? She turned on her cell phone and checked for a message from the power company. Her photo app was still open to a copy of the newspaper article she copied from Ian's phone. She stared at the photo of Marjorie. Her ears started to buzz. "What are you trying to tell me?" An icy breeze brushed past her. She grabbed the edges of her robe and wrapped them closer to her body. Her busy schedule didn't allow for this kind of weirdness. She shut off her phone, walked over to the freezer, and removed a tray of frozen dough. Routine tasks helped shake the eerie feeling.

The ovens needed time to heat, and she needed a shower. She took the steps two at a time and slammed the door to her apartment. A loud hissing from the old hot water radiator greeted her. Listening to the sound of a running brook every time the heat went on took getting used to. Keeping the heat on all day was wasteful. The heat from the ovens would soon warm the apartment. She reached for a hammer and tapped the knob into the off position. The sound whittled to a wheeze, and she rushed off to shower. Even on a chilly morning, she didn't have the luxury to linger in a hot shower. She had cookies to bake.

On her way out the door, she grabbed a clean apron from the hook in the hallway closet. She paused for a moment and glanced at the old cardboard box on the shelf. The odds and ends in the box belonged to Aunt Mary. She hadn't thought about it since the day she put it on the shelf. Why bother today?

Downstairs in the kitchen, Alana was busy rolling the defrosted dough into flat sticky spheres. "Morning, chef."

"Yeah, good morning." Sophia pressed a palm to her forehead.

"Bad night?"

"I didn't get much sleep." She glanced around the kitchen. "The morning's been weird on top of it. Any problem with the power since you've been here?"

"Not that I noticed." Alana shrugged. "Anything I can do to help?"

"Maybe." The box would nag at her all day. "I found some of Aunt Mary's things. I could use some help carrying it downstairs."

"Let's go get it." Making room for the box, Alana cleared the back table.

The old, clumsy cardboard made it awkward to

carry. Somehow, they managed to get the carton down the stairs and onto the table. Sophia stared at the closed box.

"Don't tell me you changed your mind," Alana said. "Aren't you curious to see what's inside?"

"I'm not so sure now. One old box of relics should be enough for a lifetime."

"Your Hot Scot wouldn't agree." Alana opened the box "If you don't want to check it out, I will."

"Go for it." Sophia stepped back, but not so far away she couldn't see what was inside.

A cast iron gear peeked through the corrugated flaps. An old-fashioned, handheld eggbeater rested on top of old books and wooden kitchen tools.

Alana took the beater out of the box. "Wow, it works." Like a child unable to resist a new toy, she turned the handle. The gears creaked. "Can you imagine whipping egg whites to peaks with a tool like this?" She handed it to Sophia. "You try it."

"It's heavy." Sophia turned it over in her palm. "I see something on the side of the gear. It looks like some kind of engraving."

"It looks like the name of a company," Alana said.

"Not only a name, but a patent date, too." She read the inscription out loud. "Dover Eggbeater, Pat. May 31, 1870. "

"I guess that's how they did things back then," Alana said.

"That's the year Marjorie started the bakery." Sophia stared out the front window toward the bakery truck parked at the curb. "It's too much of an eerie coincidence." Surrounded by modern appliances and stainless steel counters and sinks, she felt a strange sense of wistfulness. Marjorie's laborious day of mixing and baking started hours before Sophia turned on her ovens. What did the kitchen look like back then? Did she use a butter churn, cast iron cookware, and dense wooden utensils? She dropped the beater back in the box and stepped away.

"Do you remember what Hot Scot said about the tartan the first day we met him?" Alana asked.

"Something about how seemingly meaningless things found in a closet or attic could have historic value." Sophia never cared about the tartan the way Ian did, but she was beginning to believe every old thing had a story to tell. She just wasn't sure she wanted to hear it.

"What are you going to do with all this? I'm not carrying it back upstairs." Alana put her hands on her hips. "Hot Scot might like a look through it."

"You're right. I should bring the box to Ian. He's meeting with Mr. Paisley later this morning. They can decide if any of these old things are valuable." Sophia pushed the box to the back corner of the table. She couldn't deny him the opportunity to find another lead. "Whatever's in box shouldn't mind waiting a few more hours. The ovens should be heated by now. We've got work to do."

Customers were in and out all morning. Sophia didn't think about the box again until things slowed down after the lunch rush.

"Why don't you take a break?" Alana cleaned the tables by the window. "Take the box to Ian at the museum. The two of us should be able to get it in the van."

Sophia drove the van the short distance to the

museum.

The young girl at the admission counter offered a dolly cart. She helped secure the box and roll it to the low, narrow door labeled Museum Curator.

Inside the tiny office, boxes and books were stacked side by side around the room. In the midst of all the clutter, Sophia discovered something warm and enchanting.

Ian was almost hidden behind the piles of books and old newspapers stacked on the desk. He held a magnifying glass in one hand and a small feather duster in the other. The scene was like something out of a movie—a smart, sexy movie starring a charming Scottish professor.

She held onto the image a long moment before clearing her throat.

"What have we got here?" Mr. Paisley stepped away from the bookshelf and glanced over the rim of his glasses.

Ian stood. "What a pleasant interruption. What are you lugging behind?" He rushed forward and wheeled the cart into the office.

"It's a box of old gadgets that belonged to my aunt."

Mr. Paisley cleared a space on a table hidden beneath piles of books.

"Let's take a look." Ian lifted the box onto the table.

"You have my permission to do whatever you want with the contents." She remembered what he told her when they found the box on the Logans' property. She didn't want the burden of deciding what to do with any of the items inside.

"You do the honors." Ian stepped aside for Mr. Paisley.

Sophia never expected such pomp and ceremony over the old box.

The curator reached for a pair of white cotton gloves. He closed his eyes and sighed before unfolding the flaps with a reverence reserved for a solemn act. "Our volunteer, Mrs. Worth, is going to love this." He removed the beater. "She collects old kitchen gadgets."

"This will be a party for her." Sophia turned to Ian. He was the reason she lugged the cumbersome box here. "Do you think we'll find something in here to explain what happened to Ross?"

"Let's go through it together," Ian said. "Mr. Paisley can have whatever we can't use."

"No rush." Mr. Paisley placed the old beater back in the box. "The office is yours for long as you need." He removed his gloves. "Ian told me you might be interested in reviewing society articles from old newspapers around 1870. Why don't I see what I can find?"

"That would be great." She smiled. Left alone with Ian in the confined space, she had no choice but to work close. Strangely enough, she didn't mind. The cluttered tables and dim lighting created a magical aura.

"You made Mr. Paisley very happy." Ian put an arm around her waist and squeezed gently. "Interesting old object. My mother had one similar to this." He glanced at the eggbeater.

"Mine, too." Earlier, she was overwhelmed by the coincidence of the patent date coinciding with the grand opening. In this room, surrounded by an odd mix of old things, a memory surfaced. She was standing on a stool at a tall kitchen counter. Behind her, her mother watched. Soft hands guided the motion of the beater. "She taught me how to beat an egg with one of these."

"Do you recall what you were going to make?" Ian asked.

"I don't remember much about that day. I wasn't more than four or five." Like most memories about her mother, this one was overshadowed by the years without her. "It's probably the only thing in the box I'm curious about."

"Did you check out the rest of the contents?"

"The majority of it looks like useless old junk." She glanced inside.

"How do you know if you haven't investigated?" Ian clasped his hands over the box. "Let's take a look." He reached in and pulled out a small blue book. "What about this?"

"*Lizzy Leslie, A Lady's Recipe-Book.*" She read the title out loud. "I'm not a fan of old cookbooks—too much detail and hard-to-find ingredients." Something compelled her to open the book to the title page. The copyright was 1847. The date was impressive but not so shattering as the handwritten note under the title.

"Find something?" Ian asked.

"There's an inscription." *To my sister, Laura. Great find at a yard sale. Happy Birthday. Your loving sister, Mary.* She put the book to her face and inhaled. Was she only imagining the sweet yet sensual smell of some ancient recipe?

"An antiquarian bookseller told me he could date a book by its scent." Ian inhaled. "It's the lignin, an organic substance that keeps plants rigid and woody. When made into paper and stored for years, the chemical breaks down and smells quite delicious."

"Vanilla?" She sniffed again. The notes overpowered the scent of musty book. "It smells almost good enough to eat."

He placed his hand over hers and brought the book to his face. "A hint of vanilla and grassy roots." His eyes glimmered with a faraway look.

"Do you miss Scotland?" In spite of the chill from the old drafty window, his fingers felt warm where he touched her hand. She imagined a wild likeness of him walking in the footsteps of his ancient Highlander ancestors.

"Except for Fiona, my family is still there." He stepped back. "*Ach*, lass, but this is home now. Fiona and I have our work and friends."

Family was a topic Sophia preferred to avoid. "I'll save this for Alana. She loves cookbooks. She's thinking of writing one." She closed the cover and placed the book to the side.

"Did you notice how some of the pages are dog-eared?" He flipped to a marked page. "Someone must have found an interesting recipe."

"You read it." Masking her interest, she crossed her arms over her chest. The truth was, she did wonder who tabbed the page and why.

"Beat with the proper stroke and place wooden rods in a shallow, flat-bottomed earthen pan." He read each word with emphasis.

Mesmerized by his posh Scottish accent and the eloquent description of a simple task, she listened. "The author's words create such a vivid picture." She imagined Marjorie with a wooden stick whipping just-laid eggs in a heavy cast iron Dutch oven.

"People used to speak that way back then. Should I continue?"

She nodded.

"The coldness of a tin pan retards the lightness of the eggs. For the same reason, do not use a metal eggbeater." He glanced at the old wooden beater. "I suspect that's not true today?"

"Baking is a science as well as an art," she said. "Maybe what the author wrote was true with the crude metal tools they used in the 1800s. Today chefs and bakers use top-grade stainless steel. What else does it say?"

"Put the eggbeater to the bottom of the pan. Continue till the surface is mirror-smooth. The beaten egg will be as thick as boiled custard." He studied the page. "Does it make any sense?"

The words flooded her mind with a memory. "My mother must have marked the page. Until today, I didn't remember where I learned the technique. Whether she was mixing by hand or using an electric beater, all her eggs were beaten to the same rich, golden texture."

"That's a grand recollection from your childhood. Want to tell me about it?"

"That's all I remember. It's just a silly thing that came back when you read the recipe."

"Should I go on?" Ian placed the book on the table.

"I've hit my quota of memories for the morning." She couldn't deny him the opportunity to find something useful for his research. "Let's see what else is here." She blindly reached inside.

"Do the memories disturb you?" He reached for her hand and guided it away from the box.

"Who said I'm afraid of remembering?" Considering her inner turmoil, she maintained her composure. She never kept it a secret that she wasn't fond of old things. Today, the perfume of the old books, the serene environment, and Ian's touch brought comfort.

"I see it in the way you're afraid to hear or see something that reminds you of your past." He clutched her hand with both of his. "Your memories are wonderful. When you identified the crest by its motto, you helped save precious time with my research."

The heat of his skin cascaded along the length of her arm. "I'm happy I could help." She paused, looked at his hand, and pulled away. "But I don't choose to live in the past." Was she lying to herself? In the past couple of weeks, so much of her life before Mother Malevolent came into focus. The secret bond of events and sayings she shared with her father were exposed. Afraid of her stepmother's evil tongue destroying those memories, she'd buried them next to the ones about her mother. Not until she met Ian had she shared any of those memories.

"That day in your shop when I showed you the damage on the tartan, you did your best to hide your feelings." He leaned back against the desk and crossed his arms.

She appreciated his retreat and the small distance between them. "How do you know? I never said anything."

"I saw it in your face and how you pulled away from the plaid. What did you remember?"

"A secret my father told me." She didn't see any reason to elaborate. Her father told her never to talk about the wedding photo he carried in his wallet. At a young age, she understood the repercussions if her stepmother found out. Telling Ian wouldn't have the same backlash, but she wasn't ready to share the secret. She twisted her sweater cuff between her thumb and forefinger.

"Moments like that are common." He uncrossed his arms and reached for her hand.

She sighed and released the sweater. "I can't take control of these memories. They surface at odd moments. Under the right circumstances, like today, those recollections take no time to appear." She steepled her fingers close to her face. "Thoughts about my mother are not something I create in my mind. They linger there, just below the surface. Before I moved to Highland Falls, I never let them out." From the day they met, he encouraged her memories. He listened eagerly—without judgment.

"Too many memories at once can be overwhelming. We can finish this on another day." He started putting things back in the box.

"Wait." She placed a hand on his forearm. "Let's go through the rest."

"Are you sure?" he asked slowly.

She took a few seconds to reconsider. "Let's do it. She reached into the box. "A thick, heavy book rests on the bottom." She tugged, but the book didn't yield.

"I'll get it." Ian held up the book to the light. "It looks like a well-reconditioned family Bible. See the deeply recessed decorations on the cover?" He turned the book in her direction. "I'd guess it's over a hundred years old."

"Is it a MacLennan Bible?" Sophia ran her fingers

over the letters, *BIBLE*. She was anxious to see what was written inside but not anxious enough to open it.

"We'll find out soon enough." Ian opened the book and scanned the first page. "It's here—the MacLennan family history." He pointed to names and dates written in an assortment of handwritings.

With her hands locked behind her back, she looked at the first faded page. Ink smudges dotted the corners. She gasped, but no air filled her lungs. The stuffy room closed in. Sitting in front of her could be everything they wanted to know—births, deaths, and marriages—maybe even divorces.

"We don't have to read this now." Ian placed an arm around her shoulders. "The information is not going away. We'll take it back to your shop and have a look later."

His thoughtful consideration touched her. He put her feelings before his need to gather the facts. She relaxed against the safe contours of his body. Her head rested against his chest, just below his heart. The strong, even rhythm soothed her. Her anxiety slipped away. Her breathing slowly returned to normal.

Sophia and Ian meandered back to her shop. She didn't object when Ian took the Bible, the eggbeater, and Lizzy Leslie's cookbook. They left a note for Mr. Paisley to give the remaining contents to Mrs. Worth. After hours spent in a room filled with memories and sweet-smelling books, the cold air felt refreshing. By the time they reached Main Street, Ian managed to calm her apprehension with a ridiculous story about a man who registered for the draft after his family Bible verified his correct age.

"Other documents stated he was too old for the

draft. A state attorney used the Bible to confirm the man's right age." He finished the story just as they arrived at the bakeshop.

What unexpected facts would they find in the MacLennan Bible? Sophia opened the door and stepped inside.

"Welcome back. Find anything in that old box?" Alana put a tray of dirty cups behind the counter.

Sophia shrugged a shoulder. "Some books, like this old cookbook." She placed the book next to the tray. "I'm not a fan. Why don't you keep it?"

"I can't take this." Alana wiped her hands on her apron and opened the book. "The book belonged to your mother."

"You know I'm not a fan of cookbooks." Sophia shrugged. "Mary would want you to have it." Her assistant was one of the few people who knew what Sophia's childhood was like. Sophia couldn't think of a more worthy person to give the book. Alana and her two older sisters were orphans brought up by a loving grandmother. Alana dreamed of writing a cookbook honoring the recipes served in the family pub for the last one hundred years.

"I'll treasure it." Alana hugged the book to her chest.

"Can you stay until closing?" Sophia asked. "Ian and I have something we need to go over."

"No problem. Get out of here." Alana shooed them away with the skirt of her apron.

Midway up the stairs, Ian stopped.

"Is something wrong?" Sophia glanced over her shoulder.

"We should approach the Bible on a full stomach. I

can order a pizza." He reached for his phone.

"I've got a better idea. Follow me." Inside her apartment, she directed him to the kitchen. "It won't take long to put together a meal of toasted cheese sandwiches and salad."

"What can I do to help?" Ian leaned against the counter with his arms crossed.

"Salad bowls are on the top shelf." She pointed to the cabinet behind him. "Cut salad and dressing are in the fridge."

"Yes, ma'am." He gave her a mock salute and opened the refrigerator.

"If we didn't have work to do, I'd heat up a delicious shepherd's pie and a side of mushy peas Alana brought over from her family pub."

"No problem. Cheese toast is fine. I'm anxious to see the Bible."

"Can you hand me the cheese and butter?" She maneuvered her way around him toward the stove. Ten minutes later, supper was ready.

Ian carried the plates to the living room and placed them on the coffee table.

She sat on the couch.

"Everything looks delicious." He joined her on the sofa.

She reached for a sandwich and shifted uncomfortably to the end of the sofa. The last time he was here, they just touched the surface of Marjorie's story. Not far from their reach, the Bible rested on the coffee table. Every so often either she or Ian would casually glance at it, like it held some mystical power.

"Your talent is not limited to baking cookies. You make a pretty good cheese sandwich." Ian took a bite of the sandwich.

"You toss a pretty decent salad." She carried the plates into the small kitchen and placed them in the sink.

"I'll dry." Ian reached for the dishtowel on the counter.

"I can finish the dishes later." She turned to face him. Her sudden change of position, in the cramped corner, sent her elbow into his chest.

He didn't flinch.

"Oh, no. Are you okay?" She placed an open hand against his chest.

"I'm fine." He smiled without moving away or dropping his arm from the counter.

With her hand still on his chest, she inhaled, afraid if she released her breath the minuscule space between them would disappear. Her body felt warmer than the inside of an oven.

Ian reached behind her with his other hand.

She let out her breath and swallowed. Was it possible to be any closer?

"Lass, the sink is going to overflow." He shifted to the side and shut off the running faucet. "You've too much on your mind at the moment."

His sweet sexy smile simmered to the surface. A tingling traveled up her arm, raising her skin in tiny goose bumps. "My shirt's damp. I'm going to change." She slipped under his arm. "Meet you in the living room."

"Bring paper and a pencil with a good eraser," he shouted after her.

When she returned, Ian had poured himself a glass of whisky from the bottle on the kitchen shelf. The

Bible was open on his lap. She was glad he started without her. "Find anything?" Sophia considered sitting next to him, but after their close encounter at the sink, she reconsidered. She sat on the floor with her back against the sofa—a safe and more conducive distance away.

"Looks like the documentation goes back over two hundred years." Ian turned the pages carefully.

"What exactly do you hope to find?" She drummed her fingers on the coffee table.

"Important facts are often documented in family Bibles. All we need for now is to prove Marjorie and Ross were married." Ian slipped off the sofa and sat on the floor next to her. "Write the dates, occasions, and names as I tell them. I'll put the data into my computer later."

Shutting out all the fine attributes of Ian's strong, masculine body, Sophia stared at the list of MacLennan events—would they offer more clues to her ancestors? Mixed emotions clouded her thoughts. How much did she want to find out? Did she really want to discover more than she already knew about Marjorie's life?

"Events are listed as far back as the 1700s. Mary was correct in suggesting I use the MacLennan clan for my research. They had a strong presence in this part of the state for centuries. It eliminates searching various locations and allows me some control over the independent variables."

"Okay." *Yeah, right. I got that. Please don't disappear into professor-mode.* She flipped the pencil between her fingers and waited patiently for something to write on the paper. Much like baking, you couldn't rush a research project.

"It's here, the proof of their marriage." Ian's finger traced the listing. "In 1840, Ross Robert MacLennan married Marjorie Anne Cleary."

"Is this proof enough?" Sophia scribbled the names, the date, and the event. "Wouldn't an official record be more validating?" Then she remembered the story about the man who got drafted on the documentation in the family Bible.

"I doubt they would've falsely documented a marriage in a holy book. If anything were incorrect, it would be the dates. Events weren't always added in true time." He ran a finger over the page. "Births are here. They had three sons—Alex, Simon, and Kirk. All the boys were given the middle name Robert just like their father."

"Is that odd?" Sophia paused with her pencil on the paper.

"Honoring an ancestor was a common family tradition. I've come across the name Robert MacLennan before. However, the time period was earlier than I'm interested in."

"My mother's middle name was Roberta, Laura Roberta MacLennan Porter," she said.

"When my research is done, I'll go back through my notes and look for a Robert MacLennan."

"It's not necessary." She dismissed the suggestion. More dead relatives would only turn up more unanswered questions. The answers to those questions might not be something she wanted to hear. "Did they have any daughters?" Sophia wondered which one of the sons was her great-grandfather.

"Doesn't look that way. If a daughter died, her name and birthday would be documented. What have you written so far?" He glanced at the notes.

"The names of the sons and their birthdays," Sophia said.

"The last son, Kirk, was born in 1860. For the sake of accuracy, it would be wise to start our search a year or two prior to the birth of the last child." Ian stretched to the right and turned on the table lamp. "We'll gradually widen the search back, and forward, in time. Ross had to be in the picture when the lads were born. That way we can estimate whatever happened to Ross Robert MacLennan happened sometime between 1855 and 1870."

"That's fifteen years of newspaper articles and public records." It made sense that 1870, the year Marjorie opened the shop and Ross was absent from the photo, was the cut-off date.

She glanced at her watch and realized hours had passed. Was this how Ian spent his days, lost in some university library, completely oblivious to time or place?

"The data seems to end with the birth of their last son, Kirk." He turned the page. "It's blank."

"Shouldn't there be records of the boys' marriages and family deaths?"

"It's odd that the last recorded death was Ross's father, Manus Robert MacLennan." Ian turned to the previous page and ran a thumb back up the list.

The way he bounced back and forth in time, gathering information, made her dizzy.

"What do you think happened after Kirk's birth that caused Ross and Marjorie to stop recording?" Sophia scribbled Manus' name and date of death, April 1825, on the top of her paper. If the dates were correct, and Ross was born in 1820, he was only five when his father died. "What was life like back then for a child without a father, especially such a young boy?" Sophia sighed. Marjorie was not the only one with a story to tell. Ross also had a story.

"Laws didn't exist to protect children," Ian said. "If his siblings were old enough, they could have gone out on their own to help support the family. A younger child, like Ross, was most likely sent to a relative willing to care for him." Ian leaned back against the sofa.

"The events of my childhood are not so different than those of my two-times great-grandfather, Ross Robert MacLennan. We both lost a parent at a young age." She didn't grow up with two loving parents, but her father provided for her. "I always had a roof over my head, I received a good education, and I never wanted for anything. Ross might not have been so fortunate?" Curious to find out more about Ross, she took the Bible from his hand. "It says here that Manus MacLennan married Siobhan Kerry. Sounds like Ross's mother was an Irish girl."

"There's the Irish on your mother's side, which you spoke about the day we met." His forefinger rested on Siobhan's name.

"I was a little rude to you that morning, wasn't I?"

"*Ach*, lass. No worries. I was a stranger with a lot of questions. My questions had no meaning to you back then." He pushed a loose strand of hair off her cheek. "Your bit of Irish heritage is documented right here."

"My stepmother never missed a chance to make sure I knew I wasn't of pure Scottish blood—like it makes a difference. After all, everyone's a bit of this and that. Isn't that what this whole ancestry craze is about?"

"'*Tis.*" Ian nodded.

"It's all so exhausting," Sophia said. "How can you constantly play this waiting game?"

"The desire to learn more is a slow, steady burn that consumes you. You've got the fever now, lass." Ian put an arm around her shoulders and pulled her close. "It's not a game."

"Are you familiar with the puzzle book where you search a crowd for the boy in a striped shirt?" She inhaled Ian's heavy masculine scent and rested her head.

Ian shook his head. "I don't recall such a book."

"It's a picture book." Sophia laughed at the silly turn the conversation had taken. "Once you spot him, it's like he's been right in front of you all along."

"You're really getting the knack for this kind of work." Ian placed a soft kiss on the top of her head.

The kiss was as challenging as it was rewarding. Like the day outside the museum, it left her wanting more.

"Don't worry, lass. When all this comes together, that's exactly where we're going to find your two-times great-grandfather—in plain sight."

"Your mind is better organized than mine." Her thoughts fluctuated between pride for what they accomplished in a short span of time and caution for what else was out there. She never doubted Ian's ability. She was unwilling to face the truth once he found the answers. She walked over to the window. Mesmerized by the strings of twinkling lights across Main Street, she blocked out the risk of learning all these new facts. Once they discovered what happened to Ross, did she want to chance the possibility Mother Malevolent was correct? Was a shameful secret hidden in her ancestors' past? Ian would tell her it was a silly, meaningless notion.

"I'd like to take the Bible with me." He placed his hands on her shoulders and massaged deep into her tired muscles.

"I never imagined you were the religious type." She turned and looked up.

"I'm far from it." He laughed. "I'm not interested in the words of the gospel. Something helpful could be hidden between the pages."

"Like a pressed flower or memento?" She raised a brow.

"Exactly. A flower indigenous to this area could be further proof they resided here. I'm thinking along the lines of the time of year it would have bloomed. I could save valuable time by narrowing the dates to a specific season over a few years."

"A page-by-page search could take days." She walked past him toward the coffee table and grasped the Bible by the binding. "Why not just give it a shake and see what falls out?"

"Don't do that." Ian rushed forward and grabbed the book. "Although it's been professionally reconstructed, I wouldn't trust the integrity of the binding."

"If you want to go through the mumbo jumbo of each page, it's all yours." With her blessing, she released it into his confident charge.

"I'll let you know if I find anything." Ian took his jacket off the chair.

"You should get some rest." She yawned and walked him to the door.

At the door, he stopped and gazed in her direction.

A strange, faintly eager looked flashed in his eyes. For an awkward moment, neither of them spoke. She met his glance and saw a lazily seductive eagerness. Did he agree the night was over too soon?

He leaned forward and placed his hand under her chin.

Without any coaxing, she lifted her face. Their open lips met. She tasted the remnants of the peaty Scotch. Moaning softly, she rested her head on his chest and leaned into the hard contours of his body.

"It's late. I should go." Ian stepped back and held her at arm's length.

He broke the spell. All this was so new. Doubtful, she'd say the right words, she didn't argue.

****

Ian never planned for the evening to end this way. He placed a finger on her lips. "Good night, lass," he whispered, refusing to let words come between what just happened. The door shut behind him, leaving him with an emptiness he couldn't explain. Research *was* a solitary task. He often worked alone in out-of-the-way places. So why was the sudden emptiness in his gut so weird? The logical explanation was simple. However, the sassy pastry chef who simplified his research with an analogy to some lad in a striped shirt was far more complicated.

Outside, the cold air refreshed him. He looked at the window over her shop. Sophia was framed in the twinkling reflection of holiday lights. Was she smiling? He couldn't tell. He waved.

She waved back and disappeared.

When he arrived in Highland Falls, meeting Mary's niece was at the top of his list, but falling in love with her was the furthest thing from his mind.

Chapter 11

Ian drove to the B and B in a fog of uncharted emotions. His research was progressing, as was his relationship with Sophia.

Fiona was in the kitchen, preparing batter for tomorrow's breakfast. "Are you hungry?" she asked over her shoulder.

"Depends, I had a bite earlier." He glanced at the pan on the stove. "What are you cooking?"

"I'm experimenting with vegan oatcakes for a guest. You're just in time to be my guinea pig. Alana suggested I try this recipe from an old pub menu. I'm replacing the dairy products. I need to make sure I've got the texture and consistency right."

"Smells good. I'll give it a try." Preoccupied with the events of the afternoon, Ian heard half of what his sister said. He tossed his jacket onto the chair and took a seat at the cluttered table. He rested the Bible within reach.

Fiona placed a plate with a stack of round flat cakes in front of him.

"Looks like a Scottish bannock," Ian said.

"I adapted the recipe for my guest." Fiona stood across the table with the spatula still in her hand. "How do they taste?"

"I taste the oats." He chewed slowly. "And a hint of coconut." He tasted better oatcakes, but never ate one made with a vegan recipe. "Something's missing." Lying to his sister would serve no purpose. She'd spot it a mile away.

"Like a ton of fat. I had to replace the animal fat with coconut oil." She pressed her lips together. "What can I do to improve the taste?" She handed him a jar of homemade jam. "See if this makes it better."

Ian added a heavy smear. "*Aye*, it does. Actually, it's quite tasty this way." He swiped the last piece of oatcake around the plate and covered it with sweet thick blackberry preserve.

Fiona started another bowl of batter. This time, she added a tablespoon of maple syrup before putting it into the griddle. "Taste this." She piled another short stack on Ian's plate. "Where have you been all day?" She glanced at the Bible. "At church?"

Of all the Campbell siblings, Ian was the least likely to attend mass. In a structured pattern, he worked his way through the food on the plate. An exact smear of jam covered every bite before he brought the fork to his mouth. He chewed slowly, making it impolite to answer his sister with a mouth full of food. When he was done with the first forkful, he repeated the process. The sticky syrup added just the right amount of liquid and sweetness.

"You're going to run out of food eventually and will have to tell me where you've been all day." Her hands rested casually on her hips.

"In town." He knew a simple two-word answer would not satisfy her curiosity. "I spent the afternoon with Sophia."

"It's way past afternoon." She glanced at the wall clock.

"She found a box of Mary's things and thought I'd be interested."

"And...?" She held out an open palm. "Where'd the Bible come from?"

His research never interested her before now. Now that her friend was involved things changed. "Mary's box." He avoided the emotional side of the day and stayed with the main events. "It's a MacLennan family Bible."

"Reminds me of the one Granny has." She shared a half-repentant grin.

Ian nodded. Neither of them had visited family in Scotland in awhile.

"How far back does it go?" Fiona picked up the book. She opened it to the first page. "Births, deaths, and marriages..."

"Far enough, but it ends suddenly. Nothing is recorded after 1860."

"I'm sure you'll figure it out." She handed him the Bible. "I'm going to clean up and call it a night. I suggest you do the same."

"Want some help?" he asked.

"I got it." She dismissed him with a wave of her hand. "See you in the morning."

Ian was relieved. No doubt, the conversation would have touched on the more delicate events of the evening. Upstairs in his room, Ian sat in the overstuffed chair by the window. He wouldn't be able to sleep without at least one run through the Bible. Thinking about Sophia's quirky suggestion to shake the book made him smile. Kissing her was divine pleasure.

He reached for his laptop and started a search for a silly boy in a crowd. What did she say the lad was wearing—polka dots? No, he wore stripes, red-and-white stripes. He typed stripes hiding on a beach. He played around with the words, but it wasn't the boy in the striped shirt he was thinking about—it was Ross MacLennan. He looked at the Bible. *Are you hiding in there somewhere in plain sight?* He shut the computer and picked up the Bible.

The Bible was an amazing find. He opened it midway. It would make no difference if he searched forward or backward. His only option was a page-by-page inspection. If the tedious task were successful, the long process would be worthwhile. A letter or note placed randomly between the pages, no matter how simple, could reveal a lot. His other option was to search for a passage with meaning to Ross and Marjorie, but that would take even more time. Unfortunately, his knowledge of biblical writings was limited.

How much time had passed? He took his gaze off of the pages long enough to glance at the bright light of the alarm clock next to his bed. *Two a.m.* He yawned and placed the book on his lap. Too tired to continue, he leaned back and closed his eyes.

When he woke, the sun was shining. The book had slipped off his lap onto the floor. He reached down to retrieve it. A faded slip of paper lay off to the side. Could this be the answer they were looking for? He pulled back his hand.

The paper, with its worn edges, could be decades, if not centuries old. He stepped around the paper, picked up the Bible, and placed it on the chair. A pair of white gloves rested on the desk. Until he knew the condition of the note, he would proceed with caution.

He slipped on a glove and placed the paper on top of the book.

The noise of activity in the kitchen echoed in the stairwell. The day was starting for Fiona and her guests. New discoveries needed a clear head and a lot of caffeine. He left the artifacts and went downstairs for a strong cup of Fiona's coffee.

Thirty minutes later, he was ready for the task. A colleague who translated old documents always said three things were needed for this kind of work. The first was patience. Ian had lots of that. The other two essentials—fantasy and a bit of luck—Ian didn't consider imperative.

Filled with caffeine, he was prepared to spend the morning deciphering words written over a century ago. Someone had folded the paper into quarters. Except for a deep crease along the fold, the paper held up to the test of time. The note, written with a nib pen, was dated April 1869—one year before Marjorie opened her shop. He read slowly, word-by-word.

Dearest Marjorie,

He turned to the front of the Bible and compared the handwritings. The writing matched the other documented family events. Was Ross the official recorder?

Do not be worried. I will endure this, but you must move on.

The courts will grant you a divorce for the supposed crime they believe I committed.

"What was your crime?" By today's standards, it could have been nothing more than a misdemeanor that resulted in his incarceration.

Ross explained how it would be best for her and

161

the boys to disassociate from him.

Did Marjorie listen? So far, he hadn't found any records documenting a divorce. He couldn't make a judgment call on the uncertain outcome of Ross's life without understanding the laws of the time period. He picked up his phone and dialed Judge Logan's number.

"Logan residence." On the other end, a man with a heavy Brooklyn accent answered.

"John? Didn't expect you back so soon." Ian quickly dismissed his thoughts of their first encounter and John's attention to Sophia. He couldn't remember a time when he'd felt so protective of another human being.

"Taking advantage of all the snow," John said. "Want to join me in a cross country run?"

"Maybe another time," Ian politely declined. "Is your grandfather home?"

"Come on out to the farm. He'll be back soon. I'll leave a message to expect you."

Okay, maybe the guy wasn't so bad. Ian hung up and called Sophia. Any information about Ross' incarceration might be easier for her to digest coming from the judge.

****

Sophia smiled at the line of jolly snowmen on the counter. She placed the last dot of red frosting on the last snowman and reached into her apron pocket for her phone. The phone rang before she had a chance to snap a photo. Ian's name appeared on the screen. She placed the phone between her chin and shoulder and cleaned her hands on the nearest towel. "Good morning." She was surprised to hear from Ian so soon. "Did you sleep last night?"

"Not much. I'm on my way to see Judge Logan," he said. "Can you meet me there?"

She heard a subtle hint of excitement in his voice. "Did you shake something out of the Bible?"

"A letter slipped out." He laughed. "You'll see when you get here. I need to check the laws of the time period with the judge before I say anything."

"Sounds important." She glanced at the clock. "Alana should be here any minute." A half hour later, Sophia was on her way to meet Ian. A box of the judge's favorite cookies rested on the passenger seat. The lemon buttery scent of the just-baked shortbread filled the car. The scent did little to calm her over-active thoughts.

A letter from Ross to Marjorie would be different than a letter from Marjorie to Ross. She wished Ian had given her a hint of what to expect. He told her not to play *what if* games. She should wait for proof before jumping to conclusions. That might work for him, but scenarios ran rampart in her mind. A simple *Dear John* letter to Ross might lead to proof of a divorce. Was Marjorie the kind of woman willing to face the difficulties and scandal of a divorce? Extenuating circumstances leading to such a decision could not be ruled out. If the letter came from Ross, it might explain a conflict that kept him away from his family, leaving Marjorie with no alternative other than to accept Mr. O'Neil's kindness.

Ian's lessons echoed in her mind. *Look at only one possibility at a time. A lead was never useless. Any new lead allows you to rule out a probability.*

Yeah, right. Sophia hung onto her theory that O'Neil and Marjorie had an affair. Although not ideal, this explanation was the least complicated and easier to grasp. In spite of last night's snowfall, Sophia arrived at the Logans' in less time than it would usually take. She stepped from her car and navigated the slippery incline of the driveway. At the door, she rang the bell and waited. No one answered.

She walked around the south side of the house toward the atrium. Everything was quiet, except for the barking dogs. Where was everyone? She circled back along the north wall and spotted a window with a light. She leaned close and saw Ian and the judge sitting in front of the computer. She tapped on the window, but no one moved. Back at the front door, she tried the door handle. It opened, and she let herself in.

The setters sat guard in the entrance hallway. They barked when she entered.

"Hi, boys," she spoke softly to each dog. "How's your day going?"

"I thought all that commotion was due to either you or my grandson, John." The judge came to the door. He signaled for her and the dogs to follow.

"John's back?" she asked.

"He had a few days off and wanted to take advantage of all the snow."

"Is he here now?" She smiled. John was the unsuspecting Cupid who brought her and Ian together when he suggested they visit his grandparents.

"No, he's out doing some cross-country skiing. Lily's at a pen club meeting." He ushered her into the den. "I'm afraid, for now, you'll have to tolerate a couple of bookish academics."

"And what are you two super scholars studying at the moment?" Sophia returned his warm smile.

"Ian and I were just going over early prison records."

"Prison records?" Sophia lost the euphoric mood. Her mouth went dry. Was it too late to turn around and leave?

"I'm sorry. I thought Ian told you about the letter." The judge lifted a brow.

The word prison sent her back a step. "He told me he discovered a letter." She shook her head. "But I have no idea who wrote it or what they wrote." Reluctantly, she followed the judge into the office.

"I found something," Ian said from behind the computer screen. "I hit a link in your database that took me to prison reforms in the nineteenth century."

"Prison reform…" She froze and stared.

Ian glanced over the computer monitor. "I didn't realize you were here." He pushed back his chair, hurried across the room, and reached for her hands. "I'm so sorry, lass."

An apologetic cloud settled over his face. "You said you found something in the Bible," she said. "Does it have to do with Ross and prison?"

"It's a letter from Ross to Marjorie," he said. "Do you want to hear what happened?"

His serious expression gave her pause. "Go ahead. This letter is the reason I'm here." She glanced at his hands. His thumb caressed the back of her hand in gentle circles. Her mind reeled with the possibilities of what was in the letter.

"Ross instructed Marjorie to divorce him because of his incarceration."

"Ross went to prison? What did he do?" She searched her mind for a reason a supposedly good man would go to prison. Or maybe Mother Malevolent was right—Ross wasn't a good man. "Was it forgery, was he a thief…" She bit her lip. "Was he a murderer?" The word stuck in her throat. In spite of the roaring fire in the fireplace, she shivered.

"I doubt it was murder." Ian pulled her against his chest.

The strong rhythm of his heartbeat and heat from his body soothed her. A long moment of stillness stopped the world—present or past didn't exist.

"Definitely not murder." The judge broke the moment.

"Do you want to see the letter?" Ian led her to the chair at the computer desk. "It's pretty straightforward."

"Ross's name would have come up in a previous search if he committed a heinous crime." The judge offered her a glass of Scotch. "Back then sentences were passed for misdemeanors. Today the same crime would be punished by the imposition of a fine."

"I never drink this early." She shook her head. "I need a clear head to absorb everything Ian's saying."

"Then we'll move on." Ian reached for the glass of Scotch. "Can't let a good whisky go to waste."

She watched the movement of his Adam's apple as he drank it in one big swallow. Was it an attempt to get the bitter taste of what he just told her out of his mouth?

Without missing a beat, he leaned forward to point out something on the computer.

"I found this piece written by the judge." He nodded at the judge. "The paper discusses the result of prison reform in the late 1800s."

Confident and intelligent, Ian's words drew her

back to the reason she was here. She came this far and wouldn't run away now. She was here to see the letter and learn what happened to Ross.

"I remember writing that particular piece. Archaic laws and poor management of the prisons made it necessary to change the way the system was handled," the judge said. "How does this fit into your research?"

"Yes, how will this help us find Ross?" The word prison echoed in her head.

"To answer your question..." Ian looked at the judge. "You know my grant is to study the Scots who resided in this area. Ross's life was less than ideal, but it proves he was integrated into every social aspect." He squeezed Sophia's shoulder. "Unfortunately, not everyone lived happily ever after."

If anyone didn't believe in fairy tales, it was Sophia. Unlike Ian, she experienced firsthand the harsh realities of separation from the people she loved. The journeys that brought them to the bakeshop were worlds apart. How had Marjorie moved forward in a time when the men around her defined a women's life?

"Perhaps the crime was not as serious as it seems." Judge Logan tossed a log onto the fire. "My article explains how due to overcrowding, many inmates charged with lesser crimes were granted parole after serving part of their term. If that was Ross's case, then it would suggest his crime was insignificant."

"Just like that—they released men convicted of crimes?" Sophia asked.

"The prisons were in a bad state with little money allotted by the government." Judge Logan referenced his article. "One solution was to release inmates who committed lesser crimes. After one or two years into their sentence, the magistrates believed their thievish instincts had cooled, and they were released into society. In spite of an attempt to live within the norms of what judges and lawyers considered society's morality, many locals found it hard to forget a neighbor had spent time in prison."

"There must be records." She didn't doubt what the judge said was true. She just wasn't ready to accept this without proof. "Could you find concrete documentation showing Ross was released early?"

"The cruel and disinterested wardens and guards spent little time keeping records. Most records were incomplete." The judge poured another glass of whisky.

"Can I see the letter?" After hearing all this, she briefly considered asking for a glass of whisky. Remembering her last experience with the pungent drink, she decided against it.

"I prepared a neat binder with notes and documents." Ian opened the folder to the page with the letter. "I've scanned the original and put it in a safe place."

"This letter's dated 1869. That's a year after Marjorie delivered cookies to Mr. O'Neil on the train." The air around her felt cold. "And a year before she opened her shop. Was Ross already in prison?"

"It's possible, but we don't know for sure," Ian said with a note of caution. "We now have a lead to Ross's story."

"Do you think they were divorced?" She hugged her arms around her waist.

"Divorce was not easy in the 1800s." The judge opened a folder on the computer and pulled another article. "Laws varied from state to state. By not granting divorces, the judges believed they were protecting moral values. However, in Marjorie's case, she was the wronged party. A divorce might be granted on the grounds of abandonment. Divorce was often allowed under the condition that neither party remarry."

"Marjorie could have felt the stigma of divorce would have compounded her already degrading situation." Sophia had to think like a nineteenth-century woman—someone at the mercy of the men in her life. What was she supposed to do when her man was gone? "Maybe Marjorie never followed Ross's instructions. More and more evidence points to her not divorcing Ross."

"You make a valid point. If we can't find a recorded divorce, we'll have to find another way to search for Ross after he left prison." Ian scribbled in the margin of his notes.

"So where's the boy in the striped shirt hiding?" Sophia asked out loud.

"Perfect analogy. I love a good puzzle." The judge laughed.

"You're familiar with the books?" Sophia asked.

"I've never met the chap personally, but I'm pretty good at picking him out of a crowd." His brows flickered. "I've got a slew of grandchildren to impress."

Ian didn't join the conversation. He was busy skimming through his notes.

"Did you find something?" Sophia placed her hands on his shoulders. His muscles tensed.

"You were on the right path when you questioned why there was no mention of Ross in the article." Ian showed her the pages of the old newspaper in his folder. "We were so caught up in the article and the picture that we didn't read anything further." He turned the pages. "Let's see what the gossip column reporter has to say about O'Neil escorting Marjorie to the town's annual celebration."

Over his shoulder, she read the column on page six. "Is she insinuating they had more than a business relationship? She failed to mention Ross' absence."

"Society columnists were always a gossipy bunch. The shop opening was a big event, but scandalous gossip sells papers. Any whisper of an impropriety would be newsworthy to a gossip columnist." Ian pointed to the frequent mention of Marjorie's name in print. "You're correct. There's no mention Marjorie was recently widowed or divorced."

"Poor Marjorie." Sophia pressed her fingers against her temples.

Ian turned to face her. "I asked Mr. Paisley to do a more thorough search of local newspapers, obituaries, and social events. Marjorie was a prominent figure. A divorce or a death in her family would be newsworthy."

"If they were still married, why didn't Ross return to his family when he was released?" She folded her arms across her chest.

"Without proof, I'm not going to jump to conclusions." Ian shrugged and handed the copy of the newspaper to the judge. "What do you think?"

"Ross might have seen the article about the opening and assumed Marjorie followed his instructions to get a divorce." The judge glanced at Sophia. "A year passes, and he suddenly finds himself released with no rights to his previous property or family."

"Did they have newspapers in prison back then?" Sophia looked away. A feeling of sadness engulfed her.

"Not likely, but cruel prison guards with information about life on the outside were not above tormenting a prisoner with news like this."

Sophia's heart ached not only for Marjorie, but her great-great-grandfather, too. "I don't believe Marjorie got a divorce." She sighed and sank into the chair next to Ian. "She loved him enough to wait until he got his act together."

"I'm beginning to believe you're right. They never got divorced." Ian combed his fingers through his hair. "I can't jump to conclusions without documented proof."

Ian was hardly likely to speculate. She studied his face. He was too hard to read in professor mode. Did he believe he was pacifying her when he agreed? She preferred the Ian she was with last night—down-to-earth sexy.

"We could check surrounding counties," Judge Logan offered.

"How far do you want me to go?" Ian asked Sophia.

"Let's see where the judge's suggestion takes you." Her decisions were easier when they first started. She didn't care to know about her ancestors. She learned a long time ago life wasn't all rainbows and unicorns. Marjorie had her fair share of life's ups and downs, too. Sophia had little choice and accepted the burden to tell Marjorie's story. Once again, Ian was right. Without conclusive evidence, Ross deserved a pass for his incarceration until they had more information. The bakeshop and the old gadgets brought her great-great-grandmother to life. Now, the Bible and the letter did the same for Ross. She couldn't stop now without knowing what happened.

Ian carried the Bible and his notes to his car.

Sophia helped the judge bring the dirty glasses to the kitchen.

"Your aunt was smart to give Ian a heads-up about her clan. The leads he followed are a treasure chest of material and sources."

"A researcher's dream." Sophia smiled in spite of her uncertainty of how all this would turn out. Whatever the consequences, she owed it to her great-great-grandparents to find actual proof of the circumstances that caused them to separate. Their story brought her and Ian together and could separate them, too.

Chapter 12

Ian followed his reluctant assistant out the front door toward her car. "You've been a tremendous help. Can I take you to dinner as a reward for your inquisitive and inspiring questions?" He placed his arms on the hood of her car, locking her in place.

"I'd love to, but Alana has already covered for me this afternoon. It's our late night. I couldn't ask her to stay."

Sophia's interest in his work brought a new perspective to his research. After her initial shock of finding out about Ross's time in prison, she accepted the situation and asked for more information. Her empathy for Ross and Marjorie made him pause and think about her ancestors' internal motives. He didn't want to be the bearer of bad news. Forensics trained him not to get involved and to always separate fact from personal feelings and romantic notions. For years, he taught his students to concentrate on facts and use a broad base when questioning the circumstances of a victim's history. Exploring a personality was more complicated than fact-finding. Discarding his knowledge and experience, he wondered how Ross and Marjorie endured their separation. *Keep to your research. You've got a deadline.*

"We've done a lot for one day." Sophia's fingers rested on the handle of the roadster, but she made no effort to open the door.

Her inviting smile warmed him to the core. Snow clouds turned the sky gray, and flurries started to fall. Was he imagining or was she waiting for a kiss? The thought raced through his mind at high speed. If he were wrong, he'd find out soon enough. He leaned in to test his theory.

She shifted toward him.

Her soft moan excited him. He'd made the right move. He was always good at reading people, but she was different. Sophia wasn't just anyone. He wanted to know her intimately.

A cold wind blew a whirlwind of snow around them. He wrapped his arms inside the puffs of her jacket. She snaked her hands inside his open coat, curling her fingers into the wool of his sweater. The folds of his outer garment flapped at her sides. He pulled her closer. Their bodies touched with her face resting on his chest. For a long moment, neither of them moved.

****

Secure and warm in the folds of Ian's jacket, Sophia felt a rush of heat and a vibration against her hip. "Your phone's beeping." She nodded toward his pocket.

Ian stood rooted to the spot. He wrapped an arm around her back and moved his free hand to her face. He caressed her cheek.

"Don't you think you should answer?" Through the layers of quilted down, she felt his touch. Her heart responded with a rapid beat.

His mouth swallowed the rest of her question.

The wind picked up. It blew across her skin like a

cool caress. Powerless to resist, she snuggled closer. Somewhere in her mind, she knew they should stop. They couldn't stand on the Logans' driveway much longer and kiss in the midst of a snowstorm. The persistent beep of a text message took control of the situation.

"Damn." Ian released her and pulled his phone from the pocket of his jacket.

"Something important?"

"It's a text from Tim." Ian read the message out loud.

—Working on my grandmother's boiler. Found a box of interesting stuff in her basement.—

"Is it always like this?" She made no effort to hide her disappointment. "Do you ever get a break?"

"Interruptions at times like this are always an inconvenience." He released a sigh that was almost a growl. "When I'm deep into my research...they can't be ignored." He slipped his phone into his pocket. "Three boxes in a short time. You know the old Scottish proverb, *treas uair fortanach*," Ian brushed his lips against hers and stepped back.

"Third time lucky—I know it well. It's one of my father's favorites." The mood was broken. She leaned against the car door. "I'm not surprised Tim found a box of odd things in his granny's basement. I don't think she ever throws away anything. You should check it out."

"You know Tim's grandmother?" he asked.

"Everyone in town does. Jenny Ulster showed up to check me out five minutes after I arrived in town." She shook her head. "Granny Ulster knows everything that has happened or is happening in this town."

"Is that a problem?" He tossed his car keys and caught them in his palm.

"I don't know how she'll feel about you going through her stuff. You might want to bring her a little gift to soften her up."

"Don't you think my Scottish charm is enough?"

His eyes sparkled with a playful twinkle. "Not for Granny Ulster." She didn't doubt in his line of work he ran into resistant old women like Tim's ninety-year-old grandmother.

"Any suggestions?"

"She loves sweets and a good whisky." A bit of forewarning might make his case easier.

"Maybe I should drive back with you." He paused. "I could help you bake a fresh batch of those delicious whisky shortbread."

"If you start with a bottle of good Scotch, you'd stand a better chance of getting her to talk." The thought of snuggling up with Ian while they waited for the cookies to bake was tempting. She dismissed it with a giggle. He had bigger cookies to bake. "If things work out, I promise I'll bake her a batch of cookies." She placed a hand over her heart.

"There's always the chance I won't succeed." He squeezed her hand. "I'm going to hold you to your promise either way."

"You two might just get along fine. Something in your bag of charm might get through."

"I've faced similar challenges before." He opened the car door and smiled. "One sassy little baker comes to mind."

"I'll admit I wasn't an easy sell about all this ancestry stuff." She ran a gloved finger along his jaw and slid into the driver's seat.

"And now?" He rested a hand on the open door.

"I'm still not sure about the ancestry, but I'm a sucker for a man who looks good in a kilt." She slipped off her gloves and started the car.

"And what about the charm you suggested I use on Tim's Granny?"

"Maybe a bit of that, too," she teased.

"I'll stop by later and tell you what Tim's found." He reached for her hand and kissed her palm. "That's a promise." He shut the car door.

A soft shiver ran along her arm.

****

Sophia was glad to be back in her shop. Despite the rapid-falling snow, a nice après ski crowd had stashed their gear and found their way to the bakery. She refused Alana's offer to stay and help serve the late crowd.

Customers shared small tables with strangers. They sipped hot beverages and chatted about their day on the slopes. Their conversations were a refreshing break from her afternoon of research and fact discovery.

A family of four came into the shop just before closing. They ordered cups of thick, warm sipping chocolate. The youngest in the party looked like she was going to fall asleep in her cup. Before her head hit the table, the girl's father picked her up and carried her to the car. The mother stayed and paid the bill.

Sophia followed them to the door and watched the family drive away. Her father had carried her like that. Sophia often fell asleep on the couch, waiting for him to come home from a late surgery. Her stepmother would turn out the lights and leave her there.

Regardless of the time he came home, he'd carry her upstairs, tuck her in, and kiss her forehead. "*Ordhche mhath a bhobain,*" she whispered. "Good night, my heart." She was about to turn the lock and call it a night when Ian appeared.

"You look surprised to see me." He stepped inside, placed his hands on her cheeks, and gave her a quick kiss.

"Your hands are freezing. Don't you have gloves?" The hands on her cheeks were cold, but his lips were warm. "It's late, and the roads must be a mess." She glanced at the wall clock. The little handle was on the ten.

"I followed a snow plow into town." He tossed his jacket over a chair and rubbed together his hands. "You know what they say about a true Scot?" He winked.

"You never wear anything under your kilt?" She laughed

"That's for another time." He struggled to keep a straight face. "I was referring to my promise to see you later."

"I've never doubted you were a man of his word." She turned the door sign to *Closed* and dimmed the lights. "There's still some coffee in the pot, or I could turn on the kettle for tea."

"A cup of coffee sounds perfect."

"How was Granny Ulster?" She walked behind the counter and poured two steamy cups of coffee.

"You were right. She's a bit of a *crabbit.*" He winced.

"That bad?" Sophia was not at all surprised by his wry smile.

"When you've lived as long as she has, you don't

have to apologize for your bad temper."

"I take it she didn't let you go through the box."
She tried not to laugh at his experience. Ian's iron-
willed determination was a suitable match for the
headstrong old lady, but he was too much of a
gentleman to pursue something Granny wasn't willing
to share.

"We didn't exactly discuss the box Tim found. I
caught him on his way out. We had a brief chat. Except
for a book with an interesting publication date, the box
was filled with mostly junk. He said the risk of being
caught snooping would be worth it if it would help our
research."

An uneasy feeling gripped her stomach when Ian
said our research. She still wasn't sure she wanted to be
so involved, but he kept turning up facts that piqued her
curiosity. "What was the date?"

"Eighteen ninety-nine," he said.

"That's way past the time Marjorie and Ross were
separated." Sophia did not see any reason to consult a
book published almost thirty years later. "We don't
know if they were even alive by then."

"Let me explain, and you'll see where I'm going
with this." Ian held up a palm. "Tim thought the title
and the author's name were a curious combination." He
hesitated. "Her name is Audrey Robert. Her book is
titled *The Unusual Events of a Scot's Life, as told to me
by my father, Ross Robert*."

"So what? Neither of those names came up in your
research." She placed the cups on a tray next to creamer
and sugar bowls and stepped around to the front of the
counter.

"I haven't gotten that far, but think about it." He

caught her hand.

"Are you saying there's a possibility Ross *Robert* is Ross *MacLennan*?" She followed his thought process. "It could all be a coincidence. I'm sure Robert was a common name."

"It's a long shot," he murmured and released her. "Robert is a name with meaning to the MacLennan clan. The middle names of Marjorie and Ross's sons were all Robert. You mentioned your mother's middle name was Roberta."

"Why would Ross change his name?" She pulled a tall stool close to the counter.

"To protect his family," Ian said.

"Did Tim have a chance to read any of the chapters?"

"He said she'd be aware if a page was turned."

"You should know her bark is worse than her bite." Sophia preferred to talk about Tim's contentious grandmother rather than this possible twist of events. She climbed on the stool, reached for a mug, and passed one to Ian.

Ian remained standing.

"Cream or sugar?" she asked.

"I'll take it black." He shook his head and reached for the mug. "Tim's granny is traditionally the matriarch of the family. Out of respect and love, no one will cross her. It's best to tread lightly in cases like this."

"I never thought of the Scots as a matriarchal society." Sophia slipped off the stool and walked over to the plaid on the wall. Her father told her a few tales of kings, lairds, and clan chiefs. None of the chiefs was ever a woman.

"What are you thinking, lass? Do you remember something?" Ian set his mug on the counter and followed.

"A silly tale about a boy bitten by a snake just popped into my head." The memory was a strange one to surface now, but the wall hanging never asked permission before intruding on her thoughts. "Maybe it's because I was thinking of my father before you came in."

"It's a tale about Ireland." He gave her shoulder a squeeze. "Tell me what he told you."

"You know the story?" She smiled.

"Aye. Tell me your father's version."

"It starts with the grandson of an ancient king who was bitten by a snake." She leaned back against the softness of his wool sweater.

"Tell me more." He wrapped his hands around her waist.

"The man who cured the boy told him he would travel to an island to the west where his descendants would settle." She heard the energy of her dad's voice in her head. "That's it or at least all I remember."

"You've only told me the beginning of the story. Want to hear the rest?" he whispered against her hair.

"Go ahead. I'm listening." She closed her eyes and allowed Ian to her draw into a mythical tale of ancient times. Outside the snow fell, and the wind blew. A strange aura filled the quiet space in the dimly lit shop. Sophia didn't want to move.

"The boy's descendants defeated the mystical *Tuath de Dinan* of what was then Ireland. The surviving group migrated to what is now France. After a period of time, a group returned to Ireland and asked for land."

Ian wove the story in images so vivid anyone listening would believe they were experiencing the event. The eerie way he focused on the ancient names imitated the inflections in her father's voice. She took a deep breath and waited for him to go on.

"The Irish king took pity. Years of wars left Ireland with too many widows. The king was wise, like kings can sometimes be. He had a rather brilliant plan." His voice faded to silence.

"You know what happened next, don't you?" Sophia opened her eyes. Shadows from the streetlight danced across his face. "What was his plan?" Like a kid around a campfire staring into the flames, she waited for a dramatic end.

"You're going to find his solution very interesting." He spun her around and smiled.

Tiny goose bumps covered her skin where his hands rested. She shook it off as nothing more than the anticipation of hearing the rest of his version of the story.

"The king let them settle in Scotland and gave them the Irish widows to marry."

"Okay, seems like a logical plan." Sophia shook off his hands.

"I'm not done." He stepped back and guided her to a chair. Before he continued, he placed his jacket over her shoulders. With slow, carefully calculated words, he told her how the story ended. "They had one important condition. Future rulers would descend through the wives' descendants."

"The story ends similar to Mr. O'Neil and Marjorie's." She hugged his jacket close. "His deed granted Marjorie's female descendants ownership of the shop?" Caught off guard by the conclusion of his story, she blew out a long, slow breath. The plaid had done it again. It evoked a memory that circled round to Marjorie and O'Neil's story.

"Mr. O'Neil could very likely be a descendant of those settlers. Their ancestors include the prehistoric Irish king, Niall of the Nine Hostages, who all O'Neils are descended from."

If someone else told the story, she would say it was a fabrication for her benefit. "You're saying Marjorie's Mr. O'Neil was following in his ancestor's footsteps when he granted her descendants the shop?" She shook off the haunting effect. The story was just a silly fairy tale Ian stored in his vast intellect for the right moment.

"The historical facts are there."

A sharp academic glare replaced his dreamlike gleam. She'd enjoyed the story until it turned into a mirror of reality she would rather not hear. The similarities to her current situation weren't Ian's fault. Storytime was over. "Tell me about your visit to Tim's grandmother." She stood. "Did she drink your Scotch?"

"*Aye*, she did." His mouth twitched with amusement. "Brought her a fourteen-year-old bottle of good Caribbean Cask whisky." He leaned across the table and smiled. "Didn't soften her one bit."

She caught a whiff of his sixty-proof breaths and resisted the urge to taste it.

"It's been a long day. Best we get a good night's sleep. You have an early start to your day." He glanced at the exit leading to her apartment. "I'll call in the morning."

"Will you try again to get Tim's grandmother to show you the book?" She handed him his jacket and walked him to the door.

"It's not necessary. It would be easier if she decided to share what she knows, but I've got a good enough lead." He slipped his arms into the sleeves of the jacket and placed a kiss on her forehead. "Tomorrow I'll call my research assistant. I'll give her the necessary information to start a search for any publications written by Audrey Robert. Good night," he whispered.

A tingling sensation lingered on her forehead. Tonight, as on previous nights, she found herself with a void in her chest and unanswered questions about her great-great-grandmother. She turned the lock in the door and shut the lights. In the work area, she checked that the ovens were off. She reached for the old beater on the counter, picked it up, and weighed it in her palm. The metal was heavy but was the beginning of better gadgets in the future.

Marjorie lived in a time ripe for change. Many reformers fighting for women's rights managed to make subtle changes in the laws. Women fought for things Marjorie was granted because of a generous benefactor. She was allowed to receive wages and sign business agreements.

Mr. O'Neil was Marjorie's wise king. Were the lease and his kindness due exclusively to personal feelings, or did he have the foresight to understand that one day the laws concerning women could change?

Sophia had no wise man to share her dilemma. How far did she want to go with Ian's research? Would the end result make her feel better or worse about her family? Even her relationship with Ian was questionable. Soon his research would end. Late-night visits, drives out to the Logans', and quick kisses under stormy skies would come to an end. Her quota for difficult decisions was filled. She could sure use a fairy godfather.

Chapter 13

Cold weather was good for more than just the skiing business. Sophia looked around and smiled. Every table in the shop was taken. Customers lingered over warm cups of fragrant herbal tea, hot cocoa, and fresh brewed coffee.

For the past few days, every conversation in the shop revolved around the weather. The townspeople never tired of the topic. The conversation finally took an interesting turn when Mr. Durand brought up the Snow Queen parade.

Sophia joined Alana behind the counter. "What's all this talk about a snow queen?" she asked with an exhausted sigh.

"The queen is a big deal here. Her float will be the main event in tomorrow's Christmas Eve parade. The early settlers believed she watched over them from a mountain hideaway. I love the story." Alana sighed. "When I was a little girl, I pictured a tall, willowy woman floating over the mountains."

"She did more than watch over them." Tim edged in and took a broken cookie from the plate on the counter. "The Snow Queen taught the early settlers necessary survival skills. In return for sharing her knowledge, they kept her mountain hiding place a secret."

"If you believe in that kind of stuff." Sophia

poured Tim a cup of freshly brewed coffee. "I believe in making your own destiny."

"That, too." Tim took a sip. "Hmm, good blend. Is it new?"

"It is. The ad promised its extraordinary flavor would leave you with that first-cup-of-coffee feeling all day long." Sophia preferred to start her day with a cup of tea. Today, Tim's invigorating expression convinced her to try coffee. She took a sip, wrapped her hands around the mug, and thought about tomorrow's celebration. "The parade honoring the queen will pass right by the shop," she said. "What if we do a window display in her honor?" She didn't have to believe to take advantage of the situation.

"What a great idea." Alana clapped her hands. "We'll make everything out of shortbread, shortbread trees, shortbread creatures, and a shortbread snow queen."

"We'll cover the cookies in a sparkling white frosting and add a dusting of powdered sugar." Sophia picked up a dirty napkin and slam-dunked it in the trash. "We'll roast vanilla beans so the shop has a warm, inviting atmosphere inside, too."

"I love it." Alana hugged Sophia.

"We don't have enough time for anything too elaborate." Sophia was not used to physical gestures of affection. She slipped from the embrace and took another sip of coffee. "If we want a decent display set up in time for the parade, we'll have to work late." She stopped short. "Hmm, what can we use to cut the queen's shape?"

"How 'bout I carve a set of wooden cookie cutters in her likeness?" Tim reached for another cookie

187

sample.

"Are you sure you have the time?" Sophia handed Tim a perfectly formed snowflake cookie from the display case.

"Consider it done. It won't take long. The image is instilled in my mind since I was a kid." Tim went out to the alley.

A curious group of locals followed.

Sophia filled a pot with hot coffee and brought it outside. She lingered for a while, listening to the stories.

"She was snow white and lived in a cave in the valley," Mr. Durand from the hardware store said.

"Where'd you hear that nonsense?" The man next to him shook his head. "She was green and lived under a hidden canopy of trees deep in the forest."

The cold finally took its toll. Unnoticed, Sophia went back inside to start her cookies. In the late afternoon, she needed a break from rolling and cutting. She reached for her jacket and stepped outside. A funnel of cold air whistled as it swirled between the walls. She stood in the doorway with the closed door to her back and surveyed the group. The townspeople stood shoulder to shoulder between the buildings. Either their close proximity to each other or the heat from their argumentative natures allowed them to ignore the frigid cold wind. She noticed Ian tucked into the doorway of the opposite building.

"Hey, Doc." Tim gestured for Ian to move closer. "You know all about the past. What do you think really happened?" He reached for a piece of sandpaper.

Sophia remained in her doorway and listened to Ian's interpretation.

"There are many twists and turns given to tales over the years." Ian abandoned his cozy corner. "I appreciate hearing all your tales." He looked around. "There's some truth to each one."

Signs of agreement shifted and murmurs of disapproval resounded as the crowd dispersed.

"Did you enjoy the story?" Sophia tucked her hands inside her jacket. She wanted to hear more of what Ian had to say.

"Folklore is interesting in its own right, but it's the facts that I concentrate on." He joined her in the doorway. "Even you were inspired by the tale. News about your plan for the front window display is the talk of the town."

"What do you guys think?" Tim blew the last bit of dust off the finished cookie cutter.

"Your work is amazingly detailed." Ian ran a thumb over the narrow grooves. "I take it these will imprint the folds of her gown."

"It's perfect." Sophia took the cutter from Ian.

"I'll get this all cleaned up." Tim looked at his feet.

The snow was covered with a fine layer of wood shavings.

"No problem," Sophia assured him. A little bit of wood shavings outside her shop was a small price to pay for this beautiful carving. No one ever gave her such a precious gift. She would cherish her new gadget, even if her window design failed. "I better get started. I've got more cookies to cut and frost."

"Looks like you could use another set of hands." With a sweeping bow, Ian gestured for her to pass. "I'm at your service, lass."

"We'll need dozens of cookies, not only for the

window display, but to sell, too." Sophia giggled at his gallant gesture. So used to going through life's challenges on her own, she was willing to work 'til dawn if necessary. Life in Highland Falls was so different from her past experiences. Her stepmother never offered assistance or celebrated her successes. Living in Highland Falls had restored Sophia's faith in people.

"Hard work and long hours are right up my alley." Ian smiled.

"Are you sure you have time for this? I don't want to interfere with your search for a copy of Granny's book." She gazed at Ian's brilliant blue eyes. *Am I ready for this?*

"No worries. My assistant back at the university is diligent in her quest to locate Audrey Robert's book."

"I'm really sorry, guys." Tim shook his head. "I wish I could have approached the subject with my grandmother."

"You did what you could. We'll find another copy. In the meantime, this lass and I have some work to do." Ian took the cookie cutter from Sophia and ran a finger over the edges. "If it's precision and accuracy you need, I'm your man."

She looked from Ian to Tim. A warm feeling filled her chest. "I'm not turning down anyone's help." She experienced firsthand Ian's ability to maneuver his way around Fiona's kitchen. She had no doubt he would conquer the tedious task with methodical rigor. *Thank you,* she nodded a wordless acknowledgement to the power of the Snow Queen. With the cutting and baking covered, she'd concentrate on finding the perfect consistency for the frosting.

"It shouldn't take more than an hour to go over my latest findings with Mr. Paisley," Ian said. "I want to put him in contact with my research assistant before she takes off for the holiday. To avoid repetition, I'll go over the resources she's already checked."

"Take your time. We won't be able to get the window dressed during business hours." She rubbed her finger over the smooth edges of the Snow Queen. "The dough's ready to go. The cookies won't take long to bake."

"See *ye efter*, lass."

His slow, easy smile made her heart flutter. "Yeah, later." She leaned back against the cold brick and watched Ian disappear around the corner.

"Sometimes that guy is too serious." Tim laughed. "Precision and accuracy. What about creativity and imagination?" He wiped his tools with a soft cloth.

"Tell me about it." Every relationship needed a thinker for situations where common sense should not rule the heart. Like most academics, Ian had a quiet confidence, but she knew firsthand he was not *only* about academics and research. She saw the romantic twinkle in his eyes after he heard the Snow Queen's tale. Imagination alone would not get this project done, nor would just precision. They would need a good mixture of both.

"Let me know if you need anything else." Tim slipped the knife into a pocket of the pouch.

"Your tools are well cared for." Sophia studied the craftsmanship of Tim's whittling knives and the detailed stitching of the well-worn leather bag.

"My grandfather, Granny's husband, left them to me." He secured the case with a string. "Granny made the case." He ran a finger over the wrinkled leather. "Grandpa Sam handcrafted the handles for each tool."

"Every item has stood the test of time." Sophia felt a wistful chill. Before inheriting the shop, she had only her memories of her father's proverbs and the wedding photo. Thanks to Aunt Mary, she now had the MacLennan tartan, the clan crest, and a wonderful bakeshop.

"Speaking of my grandmother, is it okay if she watches the parade tomorrow afternoon from your shop instead of the grandstand? She's never missed one since she rode on the first float."

"I'd be honored to have her."

"Great. I've got some last-minute work to do on the floats so I'll drop her off early in the morning." Tim gathered his tools and left the alley.

He was an easy guy to like—like a cousin or younger brother she never had. Her list of reasons to stay in Highland Falls was growing longer every day.

Ian returned to the bakery before closing. After setting up the background for the window display, Sophia sent off Alana under the condition that she'd call if she fell behind. She didn't foresee that happening.

"Just point me in the right direction." Ian removed his jacket, rolled up his sleeves, and washed his hands.

She watched him lather, rinse, and rinse again with surgical precision. When he rotated his arm under a stream of water, she noticed a simple, bicolor tattoo inked on his left forearm. "*Albe Cu Bratc.*" She read the words written over the blue-and-white flag of Scotland. She handed him a paper towel. Her finger traced the outline of the flag and rested on the words, *Forever*

Scotland.

His muscle flexed, giving life to the flag.

"I never imagined you were the type to get inked," she said. "I guess it's true when people say a Scot is a Scot even onto a hundred generations."

"Aye, lass. The town of Highland Falls is proof of that." He dried his arm and tossed the towel in the trash.

"When did you get it?" Sophia never doubted he was a true Scotsman. He was highland born and raised, educated at the University of Edinburgh, and wore a kilt with style and confidence.

"One evening, when I was at university, a group of mates and I had a dram too many. This was the result." He flexed his forearm.

"I like it. It's subtle and says a lot about who you are." She was never attracted to this form of art, but Ian wore it well. "Any others that I can't see?" she dared to ask.

"Why don't I save the answer for later?" He winked. "We've too much work to do for you to find out right now."

"I was just wondering if…" she stammered. "Yes. Let's get started." She looked into his steady, seductive gaze. A rush of heat warmed her cheeks.

"No worries, lass. I'm a Scot who wears a kilt. I've been asked more personal questions." He winked. "And cared less for the women asking them."

Heat rose in her cheeks again. Her skin must be as bright as a maraschino cherry. She looked away. "I'm going to step outside for a minute. I want to get a sense of what people passing by will see." She dried her hands on her apron and stepped outside.

The cold air revived her and cooled her heated

swirl of emotions.

She stared into her shop and watched Ian. She was impacted by much more than the way he looked at her or the feeling she had when she touched his tattoo. A bone deep comfort surged through her when he was around.

"How's it look?" Ian came outside and rested a hand on her shoulder. "I think some twinkling lights would work well." His thumbs slipped under the neck strap of her apron. In lazy circles, he rubbed the sides of her neck.

"I like that idea." She stepped away. "I've got a box of lights somewhere. I'll look for them when the cookies are all done."

"There are still a few dozen more cookies to cut." Ian followed her inside and returned to the pastry counter.

Every few minutes, she glanced up from her frosting and looked in Ian's direction. He was making amazing progress.

"All ready to bake." Ian pointed to a tray of cookies ready to be slipped into the warm oven. He cut the remaining dough into two dozen, whimsical shapes. His placement of each cookie cutter maximized every inch of the dough.

"Wow, they look great." She placed the empty pastry bag on the counter. Achiness and stiffness from squeezing and piping infused her fingers. She clenched, unclenched, and wiggled her fingers to relieve the cramps in her joints. She looked across the counter and sighed. Still more cookies remained to decorate. She reached for a second tub of frosting.

"Don't you ever take a bloody break?" Ian gently

took hold of her wrist.

"Not until the work is done." She attempted to pull away and hide her hands in the pockets of her apron.

Ian slid his hands to her palms and cradled them. "What will you do if your fingers get so stiff you can't place the cookies in the window?" He ushered her toward the sink and placed her hands under hot running water.

At first, the temperature stunned her. Each quiver of the heated water massaged her stiff joints. The combination of heat and massage felt too good to pull away.

Ian placed her hands on a towel and patted them dry. With his thumbs, he stroked the inside of each wrist. His fingers moved across her skin with a firm pressure. Before moving to her palm, he signaled in advance, massaging the top of her hand between the bones. All his concentration was on her hands. "Our palms contain some of the most powerful muscles in our bodies. I'll have to apply a little more pressure to make it effective," he warned without looking at her.

His skill eased the tension in not just her hands—her entire body melted like butter. She was completely at his mercy. The convection oven hummed in sync to the movement of his fingers. Outside, a rhythmical rattle of tires crunching over packed snow mixed with the harmony of distant carolers. Lulled by the sounds of the season and Ian's soft caresses, she leaned back against the sink, closed her eyes, and let him work his magic. Strong fingers lingered at each connection. He traced the lines of her hands like he was committing each ligament and joint to memory.

A loud *bing* from the oven timer broke the spell.

Sophia jumped.

"You've done enough today." He slipped a restrictive arm around her waist. "I'll get it."

His expression was not judgmental but concerned. They were working nonstop since he arrived. "That's the last batch. You plate the broken cookies; I'll turn on the kettle."

The teapot whistled.

She poured two cups and placed them on the café table where she spent many nights after the shop closed discussing Ian's latest discovery. This evening was different. She liked working in the kitchen with him. He was efficient, clever, and, most of all, attentive to her needs. Over the last three months, he drove her crazy, stirred hidden passions, and ignited her deepest emotions. Was this what it was like when you connected with someone emotionally and romantically?

****

"You're a whirlwind of energy." Ian bit into a cookie and chewed slowly. A hint of lemon offset the buttery sweetness. "You need to rest and stop thinking." He watched her pour the tea. He could get into this kind of baking. Everything was detailed without any room for inaccuracy. "What's next?"

"When the icing sets, we'll place the frosted white cookies against the backdrop." She sat and folded her hands in her lap. "And voilà, we're done."

"You're sure that's it?" he asked.

They drank their tea in silence.

"What are you thinking?" Should he broach the subject of Granny's book? Not saying what was on his mind would be out of character. Honesty and candor were always his motto.

"How do you know I'm thinking about something?" She cocked a brow.

"By the way, you tilt your brow." He took a sip of tea and waited in a metaphoric sense for the cookie to crumble.

"Is there something you want to talk about?" Sophia retorted.

"Ladies first." He wasn't in the habit of playing games when something needed saying. His colleagues would never beat around the bush. They'd ask questions and resolve the problem. However, Sophia's game had a seductive quality. The mysterious quality of the unknown enticed him.

"Well, here it is." She folded her hands around her cup and leaned forward. "You said you were looking for another copy of Granny's book. I believe something's revealed in the book Granny prefers to keep secret."

"I already suspected as much. Granny made that pretty obvious the night I shared my whisky." He crossed his arms and leaned back. "What do you have in mind?"

"She's going to view the parade right here." Sophia tapped the table firmly with the tip of her index finger. The cups clinked against their saucers. "I'm going to find a way to ask her about Ross. I don't intend to bring up the book. If anyone around here knows MacLennan history, it's Granny."

"What if she won't talk?" Ian reached for a napkin and wiped a spill off the table.

"That's my point." Sophia threw her arms in the air. "If she refuses to talk, it's better if the truth isn't revealed." She sighed. "I'm sure she has her reasons."

He shrugged and reserved his thoughts. The decision to continue with this part of his research had to be made by Sophia. His colleagues would debate the rationale of such an option. What he had with Sophia was on an entirely different level. Communication in a relationship wasn't about convincing your partner your impression was right. Understanding their side of the story was what it was about.

"You don't agree?" She leaned back. "Do you think Ross had another family?"

"Maybe," he said. Never leaving a stone unturned had brought him to Highland Falls, the MacLennan Clan, and Sophia. He had more than he needed, but that's not to say more couldn't be discovered. "I've no problem with your decision," he conceded and drained his cup of cold tea.

"Well..." She cocked a brow. "Let's get this window decorated."

He saw the uncertainty in her expression. Maybe she was right about Granny's secret. Was the truth important enough to his research to disrupt the status quo in this quiet little town? He'd keep searching until he found the answer.

Chapter 14

A loud noise woke Sophia from a restless sleep. Her first impulse was to pull the covers over her head. "What's going on?" Reluctantly, she eased out of bed and glanced out the window. Float trucks rumbled down Main Street toward the other side of town. She was about to turn away when the Snow Queen's float rolled past her shop. Sparkling glitter and shifting shades of white mimicked the store window. Like magic, the queen's float turned the corner and disappeared. Event workers would stop in early for hot drinks.

No more lingering. She reached for her bathrobe, slipped on her slippers, and dragged herself downstairs. She rushed around the cold kitchen, preheating ovens and preparing coffee pots. In the café, the tables were set with festive tablecloths decorated with snowmen and snowflakes. Confident everything was ready for the big day, she went upstairs.

A quick shower didn't wash away the tired feeling. In the living room, she stared at the inviting, overstuffed sofa. Today was going to be busy. A short power nap before the first customer arrived might help. She grabbed a blanket off the chair and cuddled into the sofa. She closed her eyes and dismissed any thoughts of Ian's trip to Edinburgh. In a disturbing dream, she walked through the Highlands beside a faceless man in a kilt.

A loud noise from below woke her from the dream. *No one has dreams with sound effects?* The loud banging wasn't part of her dream. She reached for her chef's jacket, adjusted the Santa pin, and rushed downstairs.

"Didn't think you'd want to keep your customers waiting." Granny Ulster brushed aside Sophia and walked into the shop. She pulled off her heavy woolen mittens and rubbed together her hands. "They could freeze to death out there."

Sophia wasn't sure if Granny's tight expression was from the cold or a sign of her displeasure that she waited for Sophia to unlock the door. "I'm sorry. Tim mentioned he was going to drop you off before the parade." She glanced at her watch. "I didn't expect you so early." She looked past Granny. "Where's Tim?"

"He had to make last-minute adjustments on the floats." Granny removed her jacket, exposing an ugly Christmas sweater.

Jingling bells and bright ribbons overwhelmed Sophia's senses. She took a breath and a step back. The smell of mothballs over-powered the buttery scent of the shortbread in the display case. "Interesting sweater." She wrinkled her nose.

"I've had it for years." Granny removed a spec of lint from the sleeve.

"It's very nice." Sophia forced a polite smile.

The bell over the door rang not a moment too soon.

"The window is amazing." Alana walked in and hugged Sophia. "I love the details. The white on white, sugar sprinkling, and Tim's cookie cutter sitting in the center bring everything together. Inside and out everything is perfect." She glanced over Sophia's shoulder. "Oh. We have a customer. Merry Christmas, Mrs. Ulster."

"She's going to view the parade from our shop," Sophia said.

"How's your charming grandmother?" Granny acknowledged Alana with a nod. "I haven't seen her in a while."

Sophia noticed a hint of distaste beneath Granny's courteous nod. She never heard her assistant talk badly about Tim's grandmother. However, town talk suggested the women had a falling out.

"She's visiting with relatives in Albany for the holidays," Alana said. "I'll tell her you asked."

"Send her my best." Granny studied Alana. "You look like her when she was young."

"So I've been told," Alana said.

Granny shrugged. "Enough chatting for now. You two better get to work." She sat with a jingle and dismissed them with a wave. "The town wakes up early on Christmas Eve day."

Sophia linked an arm with Alana's and retreated behind the partition. The oven-warmed air and the smell of fresh-brewed coffee were a welcome relief from the sight and smell of Granny's sweater.

"The parade isn't for hours." Alana reached for an apron with a snowman on the front. "I hope she doesn't scare away our customers with her ugly sweater." She rolled her eyes and waved a hand in front of her nose. "Did I smell moth balls?"

"Don't worry. The cold air from the opening and closing of the door will get rid of the odor." Sophia put on her apron and toque. "I've got this covered."

Dealing with this kind of drama was a piece of cake in contrast to the daily strife of living under the same roof as Mother Malevolent. *Not here. Not now.* She wouldn't let those memories ruin her day. *Today will be a great day—lots of Christmas floats, lots of sales, and lots of men in kilts.*

"I'll help get her settled." Alana arranged some whisky shortbread on a green holiday plate. "Tim told me she likes her tea very hot with a pot of milk on the side."

Sophia reached for two small pots. She poured hot water over the loose leaves in the first pot and steamed milk into the second. She downed a quick cup of coffee while she waited for the tea to brew.

Alana helped carry the tea and cookies to Granny's table.

Outside, the town was waking up. Locals noticed Granny sitting by the window and waved.

"Is the milk warm enough?" Sophia made sure Granny was settled before the customers started coming.

"No need to stand over me and watch me drink." Granny Ulster dismissed them with a wave and a jingle.

Sophia turned on her heels and positioned herself behind the counter. In no time, the shop filled with locals participating in the parade. She filled takeaway cups with hot beverages and boxed dozens of Snow Queen cookies. The sound of the cash register was a welcome ring.

"I'll take four coffees to go." Mr. Durand from the hardware store engaged the lady behind him in conversation. "Did you notice the window full of snowflake cookies?"

"Wonderful work, Sophia. It's magical how it appeared overnight." The lady smiled.

"Thank you. We're thrilled with how it all came together." Sophia gave Alana a high five. Even in daylight, the all-white forest scene twinkled against the lights Ian set in the background. The overnight appearance added to the magical aura. "Ian and I worked into the *wee* hours of the night. It feels good to have our hard work noticed." She glanced across the shop. The line was out the door. At the corner table, Granny held court and watched the comings and goings on Main Street. Unlike the cosmetically injected lady at Fiona's tea, Granny wore her wrinkles well. They deepened when someone she didn't care for greeted her and enhanced the smile around her eyes when she was pleased. *Nothing gets past this woman.*

By mid-morning, the crowds decreased.

Alana took advantage of the break in the morning rush. She refilled the napkin dispensers and cleaned tables.

Sophia used the time to approach Granny. She offered the old woman a fresh pot of hot water and extra teabags.

"I hear you have an adequate knowledge of Gaelic." Granny gestured toward the plaid on the wall.

"Just little bits here and there. Things I remember from my father." Sophia suspected Granny was about to reveal her reason for coming to the shop so early.

"Do you remember coming here with him after your mother passed?"

"I was very young. Aunt Mary and Uncle Charles were very kind." She looked away from the wall. "I was always afraid my father would leave me with Aunt

Mary."

"Your father would never pass off his responsibilities. Has anyone ever told you how your stepmother finagled her way into his life?" Granny didn't wait for an answer. She nodded toward an empty chair. "Take a seat."

With trepidation, Sophia sat. No one could accuse Granny of beating around the bush.

"He never should have hired such a misery of a woman to care for you. I never understood how such an intelligent man like your father fell into her web. Next thing I knew, they were married. I prayed for you." She frowned. "Are you still in touch with her?"

Sophia shook her head. She'd organized Edna's finances and did whatever she could to leave her in a comfortable situation, which was more than she could say about her life with that evil woman. She didn't feel the least bit guilty they lost contact.

"You didn't like her. I can see it in your eyes and hear it in your silence." Her gnarled crooked fingers patted Sophia's hand. "Don't blame you. She was a sour-faced crone, even when she was a young girl. How she trapped your father into marrying her is still a puzzle to everyone here."

Sophia forgot Mother Malevolent grew up in the Highland Falls area. "I was only five when my mother died. I guess my father thought she would be a suitable wife." She never blamed her father for marrying such a miserable woman.

"Nonsense. The woman trapped him. She made him feel guilty for what she believed was his wrongdoing to her sister." Granny raised a brow. "Don't you lie and tell me Edna was a good mother."

204

"She tried her best." Sophia sighed and relaxed her shoulders. Talking about her stepmother always made her tense. She spent her younger years always trying to please. She never asked for anything and tried to be strong all of the time. After many agonizing years, she realized she was not responsible for the evil woman's actions.

"Edna didn't have a best." The wrinkles around Granny's eyes softened. "Do you know her sister's story?"

"I didn't know my stepmother had a sister." Not sure she cared to hear any of this, Sophia stood.

"Sit," Granny ordered. "You'll want to hear what I have to say."

Sophia really wanted to discuss her two-times great-grandfather, not her stepmother. Ross and the book would have to wait until Granny got this off her chest. She sat on the chair across the table.

"After completing his medical degree in Edinburgh, your father came to New York to visit relatives." The old woman stirred her tea. "Edna's family wanted a marriage between your father and her sister, but he fell in love with a much nicer girl."

"My mother?" Sophia sighed and placed a hand over her heart.

"What a dear Laura was. She and your father were a perfect couple, always happy and smiling." Granny formed a lopsided steeple with her fingers. "The sniveling sister never married. She was a foolish girl. Your father never gave her any sign he was interested. Edna's family always blamed him for her early passing. They said she died of a broken heart." She looked over her shoulder and spit a puff of air. "Hogwash."

"My stepmother never said a nice word about my mother's family." Refusing to let the memories of Edna's words affect her, she stiffened her spine. She was too young to differentiate between the time she was the nanny and then her stepmother. "How long after she came to Brooklyn were they married?" It didn't matter now.

"My memory is vague, but it wasn't long after she came to help out. Maybe your father married her because he needed more than a nanny and wanted you to have a mother." She reached out and ran a hand along Sophia's cheek. "Who knew your father would be killed in an accident and leave you alone to deal with her? She was always a helpless fool. Did she give you a hard time when you left?"

"I don't think she'd ever admit she was sad to see me go. I realized I stayed too long in the same house after Dad died."

"Edna Frost was never a warm person."

"Mother Malevolent," Sophia murmured under her breath. She always whispered the name in her head. She'd never said Edna's name out loud until this moment. It felt good.

"A very appropriate name, I'm sure." Granny turned her attention to the door. "The mayor's secretary has arrived for her morning order."

Sophia pushed back her chair. "The order's ready. I'll go get it." She watched Judy push her way to the front of the line. No one fussed. The town's holiday spirit and kindness had taken some getting used to.

"Stay. I enjoy your company." Granny placed her hand on Sophia's elbow. "Let Alana wait on her."

Within minutes, Judy stood next to the table.

"Merry Christmas, Jenny. I noticed you've been sitting here a while. What tales have you been telling, dear Sophia?"

"Nothing that concerns you," Granny said.

"I have some news for Sophia," Judy said. "A man came to City Hall the other day, asking about the local business real estate. Did he stop in here?"

Sophia looked over the rim of her teacup and fought the urge to laugh at Judy's sweater. The sweater was as hideous as Granny's. "Why would he come to my shop?"

"Well…there *is* the issue with the land lease." Judy looked around.

"And how would a stranger have that information?" Granny asked.

Sophia waited for a chance to inject her thoughts on the matter. She wouldn't let anyone dampen her Christmas spirit.

"It's my job to welcome visitors to the town and answer their questions." Judy hiked her nose and jutted her chin.

"You'd best not discuss Sophia's business with strangers." Granny furrowed her brows. "Since when did you become our welcoming committee?"

"I *am* the mayor's secretary." Judy grabbed her box of lemon cookies, turned in a huff, and exited the shop.

"Do you think someone is interested in the lease?" Sophia didn't like being talked about.

"Don't listen to that foolish woman." Granny stood and approached the tartan. "I hear your handsome professor is almost done researching the MacLennan clan." She glanced at Sophia from under her heavy eyelids. "What has your boyfriend learned so far?"

"Nothing you don't already know." Sophia wasn't sure if Granny would take her comment as a compliment.

"I know most everything there is to know about the people in this town." She pointed a bent finger to her head. "All the stories passed down by my family are stored in here." She smiled. "How deep is that handsome Scot into your family's history?"

Sophia ignored the heat rising on her face. This was her chance. A quick glance at Granny with her gaze transfixed on the plaid urged her to act now. She might not get the opportunity again. "We know a great deal about my great-great-grandmother, Marjorie. That's where we hit a wall. With Judge Logan's assistance, Ian discovered Ross went to prison." She studied the lines on Granny's face.

The old lady didn't twitch a wrinkle.

"Ian couldn't find any trace of him after his release."

"Maybe he didn't want anyone to find him." Granny turned toward her. "Let's see how good your Gaelic is. *Is ná clois a gcloisir? Is má fusfraítear, Abair ná.*"

"Don't hear what you hear. And if you're asked, say you don't know," Sophia translated. What was Granny not telling her?

"Well done." Granny walked back to the table, lifted her cup, and sipped her tea.

She thought Granny's silence would be enough to justify her not wanting to know any more. A secret kept for so long was better untold, or so, she believed until Granny's evasive answers gave her second thoughts. Surprisingly, it piqued her curiosity. Ross's incarceration was certainly reason enough to give credibility to her stepmother's mean-spirited remarks, but something still bothered her. She sensed so much more existed. Where would it end? Would learning what Audrey Robert wrote in Granny's book prove Mother Malevolent right or wrong?

Chapter 15

Even on Christmas Eve, Ian's critical thinking skills for evaluating and analyzing data never rested. He couldn't put off Mr. Paisley's request to stop by and see him. Must be something important—no one in this town missed the parade.

Pre-parade chaos filled the narrow cross streets leading to the museum. Twirlers, elves, and town dignitaries hustled back and forth between the floats.

Mr. Paisley stood outside the museum. "Amazing, isn't it?" He adjusted his glasses and gestured toward the street. "All this chaos will eventually become an organized event."

Ian nodded. The robust sound of an off-key tuba drowned out his reply.

"Let's step inside. I have something to show you." Mr. Paisley covered his right ear. "It won't take long." He led the way to his office.

Ian watched the museum curator shuffle through a mess of papers.

"Here it is." He held out an open book. "You don't have to read any further than this page," he said. "Ross Robert and Ross Robert MacLennan were the same man."

"We've suspected as much. Can I take the book and read the details later?" Ian ran a hand through his hair.

"It's all yours." Mr. Paisley pointed to another book on the cluttered desk. "I have a copy. Will you share it with Sophia?"

"Not today. I don't want to ruin her holiday if I can help it." Ian shook his head. "If she asks, then I'll have to tell her."

"Don't agonize over it. You'll make the right decision when the time comes."

They stepped out into the cold air. In the short time they were inside the museum, the parade led by a gaggle of twirlers rolled off toward Main Street. The high school band played a cheery holiday tune on key.

Mr. Paisley disappeared in the cheering crowd.

"Hey, Doc. What are you doing here?" Tim approached with a screwdriver in his hand. "I thought you'd have a prime seat in Sophia's shop. It's the best view in town."

"Had some last-minute business with Mr. Paisley," Ian said. "What about you?"

"Just made a few adjustments to the mayor's float." Tim tucked the screwdriver into his tool belt.

"I'm glad I ran into you. Got a minute to walk with me to my car? I've got a small token of my appreciation for all your help." Ian tucked Audrey Robert's book securely under his arm. He welcomed the unexpected encounter with Tim. He had more time to consider how to approach the inevitable discussion with Sophia.

"I'm headed that way, too." Tim stepped off the curb.

"Watch it." Ian reached for Tim's arm, avoiding collision with a float full of elves that came to a sudden halt.

"Hey, what are you doing?" Tim shouted at the

driver.

"No worries. I got this, man." The driver waved. "Just testing the brakes."

They wove their way through the crowd and arrived at the parking lot without further mishap. Ian popped the trunk of his car and revealed a boot full of gifts and a large wreath. The wreath's sharp, peppery fragrance brought back memories of playing with his sister in the Caledonian forest. Not being with family was hard this time of year.

"That's a lot of gifts." Tim let out a slow whistle.

"They're for Fiona and her staff. They've been a big help." Without any ceremony, he reached in and handed Tim a brown paper bag from the hardware store. "Sorry. I didn't have time to wrap this one."

"Thanks, Doc." Tim beamed at his new power drill. "I've got something for you, too." He reached into his jacket pocket and pulled out a small box. "The bow was my mom's idea. She does the wrapping in my family. Go ahead and open it."

"Wow…it's amazing." Ian untied the bow and struggled to find the right words. "Thank you." He inspected the intricate details of the hand-carved stamp of the Campbell clan crest. His practical, but impersonal, gift paled in comparison to the beautiful, handcrafted present.

"My pleasure, Doc. I wanted to give you something personal and easy to pack. We don't want you to forget us when you're off to Scotland." Tim looked down and shuffled his feet. "I suggest you take the back streets to the bakery. Main Street will be difficult to navigate."

"Good suggestion." Ian grasped Tim's hand in a

firm shake. "Thanks again." He crossed the street.

Inside the bakery, warm scents of vanilla and peppermint welcomed him. Organized chaos reflected the excitement outside. He noticed Sophia behind the counter. He could see by her smile and laugh that her day was going well. He would hate to be the one to change her holiday mood. "Good morning, ladies." Ian joined Granny and the City Hall clerk at their table.

"What's he saying?" the clerk asked.

"He said hello." Granny leaned closer and screamed into the woman's ear, before turning to face Ian. "Where have you been, young man?"

"I had some last-minute business with Mr. Paisley." Ian hid his smile. Age had its privileges. The first day he met her, he realized she made a habit of asking a question that she already had the answer to.

"Oh." Granny raised a drooping eyelid.

The loud sounds of the marching bands drowned out any opportunity for idle conversation.

The arrival of Santa's sled announced the end of the parade. Silver and gold streamers and delicate snowflakes surrounded the jolly man in the red suit. The clerk and other customers left to join Santa in front of City Hall. The noise level dropped considerably, except for an occasional horn blast from a passing driver.

"Where are you off to, young man?" Granny asked.

"Sophia and I are spending Christmas Eve with my sister." He assumed the question was a roundabout way of asking if Sophia was part of his holiday plan.

"Good." Granny smiled. "I would imagine Sophia didn't have many merry Christmases growing up. She probably spent too many holidays alone with her miserable stepmother."

"We're determined to see she has the memorable evening she'd missed all those years." Ian stood. "Will you tell her I'm going to pull the car around?"

Granny nodded.

Ian navigated through the post-parade traffic. He parked behind Sophia's delivery truck and rolled down the window for a better view of the display. The scene was really magnificent.

Sophia approached the car. "Don't bother getting out. I've got this." She tossed a holiday scarf over her shoulder and opened the back door. She stacked several neatly tied bakery boxes on the back seat, threw her winter jacket over them, and placed a pink-and-purple-plaid overnight bag on the floor.

In the rearview mirror, Ian saw Judy rushing toward them. Too late, he placed a hand on the horn to warn Sophia.

Judy stood by the car with arms full of gifts. She rearranged the packages, handed Sophia a small box, and glanced in the window. "Enjoy your holiday, Professor Campbell."

"You, too." Ian nodded and reached across the passenger seat to open the door. "We've got to get going. I promised to help Fiona prepare a hot punch."

Sophia slid into the passenger seat. "Judy surprised me with a gift." She glanced at the side view mirror. "The whole town is going to think we're sneaking away for the holiday."

"Well, that's sort of true." He winked and pulled the car into the flow of traffic.

"I made a point of telling her we'll be at the B and B with a house full of guests." She leaned back against the headrest and closed her eyes.

"*Dinna fash*, lass." He didn't want her to worry about what one gossipy lady might have to say. "If we skipped out on my sister, she'd really have something to talk about." He was tempted to turn the car in the opposite direction and drive to a romantic inn a few towns over, but plans were made to accommodate Sophia. His suggestion to share his room with Sophia was quickly dismissed by Fiona. She reminded him Sophia was invited as her guest, not his.

"Tempting, but not today." Sophia opened one eye halfway and smiled. "I wouldn't do that to Fiona."

"Aye. Maybe some other time." He closed his hands around the steering wheel and drove out of town. By the time they reached the highway, Sophia looked relaxed.

"How was your visit with Mr. Paisley?"

"It went well." Avoiding the real reason for his last-minute visit to the museum, Ian kept his answers benign. "We discussed the possibility of the museum working closely with the state university when they begin digging on the Logans' property."

"That's an interesting development. Couldn't the information wait until next week?" She raised a brow. "Is that all you discussed? Are you avoiding something you're afraid might ruin my holiday?"

He pulled the car off to the side of the road. The tires bumped and crunched over plowed snow. He shifted the gear into Park and reached for her hands. He wouldn't lie. "With help from my assistant, Mr. Paisley located another copy of the book at the university library."

"The same book Granny Ulster won't let anyone

see?" She stared out the window.

"Word for word as told by Ross Robert's daughter, Audrey," he said.

"What is it you're trying so hard to not tell me?" She turned toward him.

He reached out to place a hand on her shoulder.

She inched back.

Her features were deceptively composed. It began with the wrinkle in her brow and spread into the inquisitive depth of her dark eyes. An uncomfortable silence followed.

"Ross never had a daughter with Marjorie." She shook her head vigorously. "How can you be so certain she's writing about the same man?"

"Events in the book are aligned with the facts we've uncovered about Marjorie and Ross. The author wrote about incidents she claims her father told her. Those events parallel Ross MacLennan's life as we know it."

"You believe those references are enough to conclude Ross was the father of the girl who wrote the book?" She clenched her fists in her lap.

"What's bothering you, lass?" He didn't want to upset her, but he promised the truth if she asked.

"We don't even know for sure if Marjorie divorced Ross. Now you're saying he changed his name and had a child with someone other than Marjorie…"—her voice cracked—"Why is Granny Ulster so protective of this information?"

"The Ulster clan might play an important role in this part of the story."

"I suspected as much." Sophia held up her gloved palms. "Let's start with an old lady who knows everything happening in this town. This particular woman just happens to have a mysterious book she won't let anyone see." She sank deeper into her seat. "Granny is obviously protecting a family secret. Is her family history as notorious as the MacLennan clan's?" She raised a brow. "What do you think now that you've seen it?"

"I haven't read through the entire book." In the past, Ian dealt with irrational families of homicide victims. Keeping them focused was difficult. By sticking to the facts, he'd get them back on track. *Sophia* was different. His involvement was on a personal level. "I don't disagree with what you're saying. The Ulster clan is somehow connected to Ross. Give me time to read through it." Although irrelevant to his research, he would explore the connection for Sophia's benefit. Many people jumped from one subject to another to avoid listening. Sophia was no exception.

"It doesn't matter what Mother Malevolent said." She put her hands over her ears in a childish matter. "I don't want to hear anymore—not today or ever."

"You don't have to make the decision at this moment." He reached for her hand. "I'll do everything I can to learn more if you change your mind." *Everything I can to help you prove your stepmother wrong.* He worried the facts could prove otherwise. He kept the thought to himself.

Someone tapped on the window.

Next to him, Sophia jumped.

"Hi, Doc." Sheriff Maxwell signaled to roll down the window. "Do you need assistance?"

"Everything's fine." Ian stepped from the car. "The car felt like it was dragging a branch."

The sheriff followed Ian around the car. "I don't see anything." He stopped at the passenger side. "Hey, Sophia. You taking a staycation at Fiona's?"

"Just an overnight." A half smile tilted her lips.

"I've heard she charges a pretty steep rate to spend a night there." The sheriff laughed. "You paying for it in cookies? I meant to stop by and pick some up for the family." He gestured toward the bakery boxes on the backseat.

"We appreciate how busy you've been with all the holiday tourists." Ian scrubbed a hand over his hair. "What's the family favorite?"

"It's hard to say." The sheriff rubbed his chin.

Ian shifted impatiently.

"The wife loves the gooey cherry chocolate. Jim Junior likes his shortbread plain. Rosie will eat anything sweet and buttery."

Ian opened the back door and handed the sheriff a box marked *variety*. "Here's a box for your family. Wish them a Merry Christmas."

"Thanks! Let's make sure the rest of those cookies get to Fiona's in one piece. Follow me. I'm heading in the same direction." The sheriff returned to his patrol car and turned on the siren.

Ian climbed into the driver's seat and waited for the sheriff's car to take the lead.

"Is he going to escort us to Fiona's?" Sophia rolled her eyes.

"I'm afraid so." Ian started the car.

"At least, the red light is festive." She shrugged.

He couldn't tell if she found the situation annoying or amusing. The reflection of the red light flashed around the inside of the vehicle. He watched it flicker across her face.

"What?" she asked.

"The light makes your eyes sparkle like a peppermint candy." He swirled a finger in the air.

"You look deliciously festive, too—like a candy cane." She stared at his face and laughed.

The siren created quite a commotion when they arrived at the B and B.

"How are you going to explain this?" Sophia asked.

"I have no idea." Ian shut off the engine and stepped from the car. The police escort and flashing lights momentarily relieved the tension between them, but he still had to deal with Fiona.

"What's with the police escort?" Fiona slapped Ian across the chest with the back of her hand. "Were you speeding?"

"Evening, Miss Fiona. I didn't mean to cause such a ruckus." The sheriff exited the patrol car. "Just a little car trouble. I wanted to make sure they got your cookie order here safe and sound. I'm afraid you might be short a few."

"We gave a dozen to the sheriff for his trouble." Sophia bit her lip.

Ian noticed the tilt at the corner of her lip, and her attempt to hide her smile. If he hadn't just told Fiona a white lie, he, too, might find the predicament amusing.

"No worries." Fiona glanced from Sophia to the sheriff. "Car trouble?"

"Yes, ma'am. There's nothing to worry about. Your brother thought he caught a branch. All good now." Sheriff Maxwell tipped the brim of his hat. "You and your guests have a happy holiday." He climbed into his vehicle and drove away.

"A branch?" Fiona raised a brow. "You must be getting soft, brother." She removed the cookie boxes from the car. "What happened to the reckless lad who learned to drive in our *da's* old truck? You dragged more than a branch off the winding roads of the Highlands and never stopped."

Ian didn't have time to come up with an acceptable response. He released a sigh and watched the guests walk back to the inn. No one wanted bad news to ruin a holiday.

Fiona tossed her braid and followed her guests inside.

"I never pictured you as the reckless type." Sophia grunted a soft chuckle and reached for her suitcase. "Are you going to stand out in the cold all night?" She glanced over her shoulder.

"I'll be right behind you." Ian stood over the open trunk and slowly gathered his gifts. He'd let everyone warm up and absorb the holiday feeling before he joined in.

Sophia might have left the upsetting conversation on the road, but Fiona wasn't buying any of this. She wouldn't be happy if she knew why he really stopped.

The entire situation was unnecessary and ridiculous. He had no one to blame but himself. Fiona warned him not get Sophia involved in his research. He never intended to upset anyone, especially today. The sooner he tied up the loose ends on his research and left for Scotland, the better for everyone.

Chapter 16

Delicious holiday smells overpowered Sophia senses the moment she stepped inside the B and B. Tonight was about being with friends. She pushed all thoughts of her conversation with Ian from her mind. "Hmm, spiced cider." She walked over to the stove and inhaled deeply. "Cinnamon, anise, cloves, and something else…"

"Cardamom." Ian stood beside her. He stirred the pot and scooped two pieces of ginger onto a wooden spoon. "It's a family favorite. We'll add some rum before it's served."

Sophia gave him a weak smile. She had no favorite family recipes to share. Her stepmother wasn't much of a cook. No matter the occasion, Sophia prepared simple dishes she could heat quickly.

"Keep stirring." Ian handed her the spoon. "Don't taste before it's done. I'm going to wash and change before dinner."

"Is everyone dressing for dinner?" Sophia watched him disappear up the kitchen staircase.

"Not at all." Fiona adjusted her apron. "Some of my guests belong to a cross-country ski club and are comfortable in joggers and jeans."

"Hope I'm not over-dressed." Sophia gave the liquid a final stir and placed the spoon in the sink. With her hands free, she smoothed an imaginary wrinkle from her skirt. She chose her outfit carefully—a winter-white wool skirt and a muted-red sweater with just a hint of sparkle.

"You look more than fine, lass," Ian shouted from the top of the stairs.

"Now he's a fashion expert, too?" Fiona winked at Sophia. "You look very nice."

"Can I help?" Sophia reached for an apron.

"Would you mind taking these out to the guests?" Fiona handed her the tray of Scotch eggs in exchange for the apron. "Then I want you to relax and enjoy the evening. Ian will be down soon enough. You've both been working hard." She smiled. "I made him promise no research talk."

"Let's see how long he can hold that promise," Sophia said. Torn between her uncertainty regarding Granny's book and her spiked curiosity, she promised not to let it ruin her evening. Christmas should be about fun, food, and family—not ghosts from her past. She carried the tray into the dining room. Tonight, she'd make up for all the holidays she never spent with a real family.

Holiday glitter and twinkling lights on the fresh-cut tree gave the room a magical sparkle. A soft Christmas soundtrack played in the background. Fiona's guests consisted of a redheaded family of four, a young couple in matching holiday sweaters, and the group of skiers. They gathered around the punch bowl and enjoyed a rosy-red cup of holiday cheer.

A nice-looking man smiled from across the room. "Can I take that?" He glided toward her with the loose-arm swing of a cross-country skier and reached for the plate.

"I've got it, lad." Ian stepped off the bottom step and stood beside Sophia.

The lilt of his accent and his confident presence attracted everyone's attention the moment he entered the room. The men grabbed the eggs while the women stood there staring at her beautiful Scot in a kilt.

"I thought you only dressed like this for weddings, bar mitzvahs, and the occasional christening." Sophia leaned toward Ian. Tonight, he wore a more casual red-and-blue-plaid kilt. The chunky, navy sweater complemented his loch blue eyes. He had every detail covered.

"*Ach*, lass. You remember what I said the night of the Kirkin?"

"And a few other things." She smiled. She glanced at the brown leather sporran hanging by a loose chain from his belt buckle. "Is the crest engraved in the leather?" The detail impressed her. Each letter was cut with laser precision. *OMG.* She glanced away from the pouch.

"You can get a closer look later." Ian grinned.

A young woman with a head of tight blonde curls sashayed closer. "Fiona forgot to mention men in kilts when she advertised a Scottish Christmas." She reached for an egg and nibbled around the edges "The egg is delicious. What's it wrapped in?" She smiled seductively at Ian.

Sophia refrained from rolling her eyes.

"It's a hard-boiled egg wrapped in a sausage patty." One egg remained on the tray. Ian reached for it and took a bite. "Pork sausage is traditional. Tonight, my sister settled on a healthier option." He chewed slowly. "I believe she used turkey patties."

Nothing was sexy about the eggs or turkey meat. Curly-Head tightened her grip and flashed an I'll-be-all-yours smile.

The artfully, artless way Ian gave the egg center stage made Sophia wonder who was seducing whom. His good looks and charm were as much a part of him as the facts rolling past his lips. He spoke eye-to-eye to each person.

"There are many stories about the origin of the Scottish egg. The truth is the egg is not Scottish." He held up his half-eaten egg. "The Scotch egg was invented in the eighteenth century by a famous London department store. Originally, the meat was covered in fish paste." He worked his way toward the fireplace.

Sophia surveyed the room. Every detail exemplified her idea of a true family Christmas. Bright, plaid stockings hung from the fireplace mantel—one for each guest. She felt like she'd stepped into a children's picture book full of holiday colors, a roaring fire, and an exuberant storyteller. A comment from one of the skiers brought her attention back to the group. She watched him mesmerize the guests with animated hands and a lively energy.

"Must be getting a bit toasty under that kilt."

"*Aye*, lad. It can get a bit drafty, too." Before anyone could ask any personal questions about his kilt, Ian waved a hand toward the sporran hanging from his belt.

"You've got no pockets, mister. Can you put your cell phone in there?" One of the little redheads tugged on the kilt and pointed to the pouch.

"*Aye*, lass. There's room for some chocolate, too." He winked and signaled for her to dig in. "A kilt has no pockets. That's why I wear a sporran. Sporran is Gaelic for purse. Reach inside and see what you find."

The little girl reached in and pulled out a candy bar.

Across the room, Sophia noticed Curly-Head sitting at the edge of her seat. She nudged Fiona. "Should we help your brother before someone's ringlets get stuck someplace they shouldn't?"

"He's got it. He's in his element." Fiona led her to the spiced punch bowl.

The bowl shimmered under a string of white lights. Everything was magical. She watched Ian play the room. Although, the group was nothing like the tea ladies, they were just as dazzled by his charm.

"I bet you could fit a *wee* bottle of Scotch in there." The father of the redhead pointed toward the sporran.

"I'll have to give it a try." Ian led him to the bar and poured everyone a dram. His little friend followed at his side. "*Ach, caieag bheag*, this is not for you." He reached for her hand and guided her toward a smaller punch bowl. He filled a cup half way and handed it to the little girl.

The combination of how he looked in a kilt and his sweet concern made Sophia's heart race and her knees weak. "*Caieag bheag.* My little girl," she whispered. The words aroused a strange feeling—not just a memory, but also a sense her father was here with her. He would like Ian. She filled a cup and raised it in a silent salute to her father's memory.

Like bees on honey, the aromas of Fiona's labor drew the guests to the table. Platters of succulent roast chicken, meat-and-onion pies, and fresh-baked biscuits sat family-style in the center of the table.

In a well-calculated move, Ian positioned his seat between the two little redheads.

"Are you sure you're okay sitting between them?" their mother asked.

"No worries. Fiona and I come from a big family. We have lots of nieces and nephews to contend with at holiday dinners." With precision, Ian diced a slice of chicken into bite-sized pieces for the youngest girl.

Across the table, Sophia watched the girls interact with Ian. With their reddish hair, the girls could easily be mistaken for his daughters. How many of her ancestors had red hair? Under the pretext of knowing his understanding of genetics, she'd ask him later. If Ross were a redhead, would his mysterious daughter have his hair color or the color of some unknown woman who suddenly appeared on Sophia's family tree? Lost in the genetic probability of her and Ian producing a redheaded child, she didn't realize Curly-Head had passed a dish. An intentional elbow in her rib drew Sophia's attention back to the dinner table.

"Potatoes?" Curly-Head shoved the bowl at her.

The bowl slipped to its side.

Sophia was quick, but not quick enough to prevent a spoonful of mashed potatoes from landing on her white skirt.

"Can I help?" Ian reached for a napkin.

"I'm fine. It's nothing a little stain remover won't take care of." She laughed it off. Too many of her holidays were ruined by some trivial incident. She didn't want to be responsible for doing that to the girls or any of Fiona's guests. The incident was her fault. Her mind wandered to silly things she shouldn't be thinking about—especially not Ian and babies. She pierced a piece of chicken with her fork.

Several courses later, Fiona gathered her guests in the main room for desserts.

After the last cookie was eaten and the last cup of hot cocoa emptied, Sophia watched the guests go off to their rooms. The skiers would need a good night's sleep if they wanted to enjoy an early start.

"Don't worry, *caieag bheag.*" Ian assured the sleepy little redheads. "We'll leave a plate of Sophia's sparkling shortbread cookies for Santa."

Although exhausted by holiday overload and an over-indulgence of dessert, Sophia didn't want the night to end. She and Ian relaxed in the big chairs by the fireplace after everyone retired for the night.

"Don't move. I've got something for you." Ian walked over to the tree and pulled a haphazardly wrapped shipping tube from behind the nativity scene. With calculated steps, he approached Sophia and handed her the gift.

"What is it?" Sophia balanced the odd-shaped gift with both hands.

"You're not supposed to ask."

"I'm afraid my experience with receiving presents is limited to practical things like socks, gloves, and scarves." She carried the tube to the table.

"Go ahead and open it." He crossed his arms and leaned back against the table.

Curiosity and eagerness to look inside roused her from her food coma. She ripped the crinkled paper, pulled off the end cap, and peeked inside. It smelled of old paper and briny, black ink. The oddity of the gift and its imperfect wrapping made her smile.

"It won't bite," he said.

His excited anticipation was contagious. Sophia removed a rolled parchment from the tube. The delicate paper looked and felt like an old document. "It's my family tree." She shuffled two steps back from the table. "It's amazing." No one ever gave her such a personal gift. One year, Mother Grinch surprised her with a worn cookbook she bought at a thrift shop. The present didn't come close to this intimate gift. "Did you draw this by hand?" She ran a hand across the words.

"I used a standard template and traced the dates all the way to Scotland in the 1700s."

"Robert James MacLennan." She pointed toward the name at the top of the page. "He's the Robert the family honored for centuries." She skimmed the next few generations. "I see some familiar names, Ross Robert MacLennan and his three sons." With an index finger, she traced the connecting lines of children, grandchildren, and great-grandchildren. The paper crinkled under her finger.

"Do you remember the story I told about a skilled group of Highlanders and their closely guarded guild techniques?"

"The glove makers." No matter how dull or boring, she never forgot anything he told her.

"I didn't come upon the story by chance. My research of your clan started in Scotland over a year ago. That's when I first discovered the group of glove makers who were granted land by Sir William Johnson. Your ancestor, Robert James MacLennan, was a guild member who migrated to this county around 1760."

"You mentioned the glove makers that day in the paddock. You never said they were led by a MacLennan."

"I recently came across the details when I reviewed my notes." He shrugged. "Unlike discovering the box, the information about the glove makers didn't seem to interest you."

"Was I that obvious?" She felt bad he noticed how easily she was bored with historical details. Her attitude changed once she got to know him. The more involved she got in his research, the more she realized he never brought up a fact without good reason. Under Ian's tender but vigilant gaze, she followed the branches of her family tree. The box and the chart were tangible evidence of her heritage.

She stopped her finger on the line connecting Marjorie to Ross by marriage. All the sons were married, too. According to the terms of Mr. O'Neil's lease, their wives inherited the bakeshop and the land lease. Now it all fell into her hands. "This is a wonderful gift." She thought about buying him a gift, but she couldn't find anything suitable. Nothing she thought of would have come close in emotional value as this family tree. She traced her fingers back to Ross's name. The chart held no sign he was divorced and married again.

"I purposely left it blank. If you want to know more, just tell me." Ian placed a hand on her shoulder.

"I don't need to know anything else." She promised herself she wouldn't go there tonight. She breathed a heavy sigh and rejected the possibility that Ross MacLennan and this Robert guy might be the same man. "Will you use Ross's history in your research?"

"What he did after prison bears mentioning." Ian shrugged. "However, his personal life is irrelevant to my research topic."

"If you believe what this woman wrote in her book is true, how can you ignore the fact Ross had another family?" Sophia bit her lower lip. The book was written proof he had a child, legitimate or not, with someone other than Marjorie. Did Marjorie know? "For the sake of Marjorie's memory, I'm taking it one step further than Granny Ulster's theory. *Is má fusfraítear, Abair ná.* Don't say what you know, should include don't say what you don't know."

"If you're comfortable with not knowing, I'm okay, too. I have enough to finalize my research. I know you're a direct descendant of James. Your parents didn't reside in this part of New York state for long, but their ancestors left their mark on this town. Your shop is evidence of that."

"If the woman who wrote the book was really Ross's daughter, her descendants could be in Highland Falls?" She thought of all the people she came across with good Scottish names. Working with Ian taught her anything was possible. Any of them could have descended from a marriage between Ross's daughter by another woman and a McBain, a Simon, or even an Ulster. An Ulster. Was that Granny's secret?

"It's possible and would make a nice sidebar." He squeezed her hand. "I'll only continue if you want me to."

"No. I don't want to know." The possibility of the unwelcome ramifications reinforced her answer. "Don't tell me if you've already traced that branch of Ross's family tree. A prison term, a divorce, and a child out of wedlock were enough fuel to scorch Mother Malevolent's nasty tongue." She threw her hands in the air. "What else could I possibly want to know?"

"You don't have to decide now. I never intended to upset you. Let's forget about the book and your ancestors for now." He took the parchment from her hand and rolled it.

"Your gift was lovely. I don't want you to think otherwise." She stood on tiptoes and kissed his cheek. "Thanks."

"No worries, lass." He touched his cheek and stepped back. "Hey, I promised Fiona I'd fill the stockings before I went to bed. Want to help?"

"I'd love to." She walked around the room, blowing out the candles. Sadness crept over her as the flames changed to smoke. She inhaled the remains of the holiday scents, cinnamon, cloves, and her favorite Snickerdoodle. This wonderful night was almost over.

"Each stocking gets an orange, a chocolate, and a bar of soap made with herbs from Fiona's garden. The two stockings on the end are for the little girls. They get hair ribbons and clips." Ian handed her blue-and-yellow-plaid bows.

"The ribbons are a lovely contrast to the girls' red hair." Sophia rolled the silky bands in her hand. "What's the probability of a brunette and a ginger having a child with red hair?" She glanced from the ribbon to the reddish bristle on Ian's face.

"It would depend on whether or not the dark-haired parent inherited red hair genes from her ancestors. I'm certain there were plenty of redheads in your family tree." He ran a hand over the scruff on his chin. "Any particular redhead you have in mind to father those children?"

A humorous lift appeared at the corners of his

mouth. She should have known he would find this amusing. "The little girls had me wondering about the odds. I was just making a scientific observation." Sophia's cheeks heated, and a warm flush crept along her arms. Ian might attribute her flushed skin to the heat from the fireplace, but she knew differently. He was irresistible, full of surprises, and a little dangerous.

"Only two percent of the population has red hair, with eighty percent of them having a gene variant. Red hair can originate from changes on the modified gene. If one of these changes is present on both chromosomes, then the respective individual is likely to have red hair."

"Can you explain in English?" She laughed.

He took the ribbon from her hand, wrapped an arm around her waist, and pulled her close. "The gene for red hair is recessive. If your partner carries the gene for ginger hair, there's a one in two chance your child will have ginger hair." His free hand brushed a stray strand of hair off her face. "Black hair is dominant. It might take a few tries to produce a redhead."

His gaze, suggestive and sexy, made it difficult to fight what was happening. "So all I need is a recessive gene passed down and a partner with…"

"Red hair." He danced her backward and stopped under the mistletoe hanging by the stairs.

His lips touched hers with tantalizing precision and passion, shattering her composure. She melted into the contours of his body.

With a subtle tilt of his head, he nodded toward the stairs.

Her lips were still warm and moist from his kiss. The suggestion was more persuasive than she wanted to admit. Her disciplined emotions reminded her that willing and wanting were not the same. She wanted him like she never wanted anyone before. His arrogant intellect, stolen kisses, and comforting embraces wrenched forth her suppressed feelings. He was a handsome Highlander she'd only imagined in her dreams. He was strong in body and spirit and sometimes a bit overbearing. She was attracted to these traits from the first time he walked into her shop. Her life was about finding and losing things—more on the losing end. The intimacy of his suggestion made it hard to let him go. She rested her head against his chest and listened, for a brief moment, to the inviting beat of his heart. "Not tonight," she whispered and slipped from his embrace.

Chapter17

Sophia sat behind the counter going over yesterday's receipts. The days following the New Year brought an expected slowdown in business. Across the street at City Hall Park, workers removed strings of holiday lights. A spark of disappointment surged through her. She sighed and looked around the shop. Change wasn't always bad. Adapting to a new life worked for her. Along Main Street, trendy concept shops were scheduled to open in time for the spring tourists. A variety of new businesses would be good for the town.

"How was the soft opening of the rolled ice cream shop?" Alana refilled the takeaway cups next to the coffee pot. "I read an article in a trade magazine about its growing popularity."

"I liked the concept. The customer gets to decide what they want to add," Sophia said. "Some choices were a little odd. The lady in front of me chose black licorice rolled into vanilla ice cream. The combination made a great photo to post on social media." She made a sour face. "Anise, fennel, and tarragon in ice cream didn't sound right."

"Ugh. I agree." Alana scrunched her face.

"You should come with me next time."

"I'll think about it. Ice cream is not my thing in cold weather," Alana said. "What ingredient did you add?"

"Tea and crumpets. They rolled chunks of an Earl Grey shortbread into cream and froze it on a cold tray."

"Sounds much better than licorice. Do they bake their own cookies?" Alana asked.

"For now, they're baking small batches to experiment with. I offered to take over some samples this morning."

"Great idea. I'll wrap each flavor separately so the stronger tastes won't overtake the subtle ones." Alana reached for a bag. "What did Hot Scot think of the experience?"

"I suggested he taste a new flavor, but no, not Mr. Purist. He stuck with traditional chocolate chip."

"He might have thought differently if they sold a whisky candy." Alana giggled.

"You could be on to something. An adult-only ice cream is a good idea. I'll tell the owner, Matt."

"Speaking of Hot Scot, he should have been here by now to pick up Fiona's cookies." Alana glanced out the window.

"It's still early." Sophia reached for her duster and walked toward the wall with the plaid. She had time for a quick dusting before delivering the cookie sampler. She ran a hand over the imperfection Ian showed her the day they'd met. A chill slivered up her arm. "Ignorance can oftentimes be bliss while those looking for trouble will often find it," she murmured.

"Did you say something?" Alana asked.

She glanced over her shoulder toward the counter where Alana placed the last cookie in the bag. "Just thinking out loud." She put down the duster and joined Alana. "I'll drop these off at the ice cream shop while it's still quiet. If Ian shows, don't let him leave."

"Wouldn't think of it. I don't know how you're going to manage without your daily dose of Hot Scot." Alana put the back of a hand to her forehead and faked a swoon. "Any idea when he's leaving?"

"He's submitted his research. His defense is at the end of the month," Sophia said. "I think he's disappointed I didn't share his passion when he finalized his research."

"I don't mean to pry." Alana gave her a hug, almost crushing the bags of cookies between them.

"He's leaving soon. I don't know the exact date. When we're together, we don't talk about it." Sophia untied her apron, tossed it over the back of a chair, and grabbed her jacket.

"No need to rush back." Alana gestured to the empty shop.

Sophia had no intention of lingering. She and Ian didn't have much time left to spend together, and she cherished every moment.

****

Most of the stores on Main Street weren't open yet. A chilly mountain breeze scattered a newspaper someone left on the bench in front of the bakeshop. Sophia gathered the papers, tossed them into the trash, and crossed the street. She saw a light on in the front of the ice cream shop but didn't see anyone. She walked along the alley to the back and knocked.

"C'mon in." Matt opened the door. "You're just in time. I'm experimenting with a variety of sweet and salty combinations. I'd appreciate your opinion."

"Maybe next time."

"Whenever you get a chance," Matt said. "Thanks

for the cookies. Gotta run. I left cream on the cold tray."

"We both have work to do. I'll come by later in the week." Anxious to see Ian, Sophia rushed down the alley.

"Back already?" Alana pointed toward the corner table. "Megan and Ian are waiting."

"Did they come in together?"

Alana nodded.

Sophia glanced toward the corner table. Ian wore a blue plaid shirt that made the color of his eyes stand out. This morning, his usual sparkle was missing. His features rarely showed disapproval. A foreboding chill surrounded her. "Everything okay?" She approached with trepidation.

Ian stood, hooked a chair with his foot, and gently eased her onto the seat. He stood behind her with his hands resting on her shoulders.

"Is someone going to tell me what's going on?" She glanced from Ian to Megan.

"There's been a recent development regarding the land lease." Megan folded her hands on the table.

"I'm listening." Sophia stared over her shoulder at Ian. His silence said volumes. "This isn't going to be good, is it?"

"There's no reason in over beating this." Megan opened her laptop. "The owner of the lease surfaced. He's challenging your right to renew. Since you're not a direct offspring of your Aunt Mary, any future lease renewal was ruled invalid by the court."

"That's insane. How is it even possible?" Sophia's heart raced. She moved to the edge of the chair. "I'm more MacLennan than any of the women who married into the family. I've got a direct bloodline through my mother." She struggled to keep the anger from her voice. Megan wasn't to blame. The fault lies with the ruling judge who made the decision without knowledge of the people involved.

"Is there any legal action we can take to fight this ruling?" Ian asked.

"What about my mother? She was a MacLennan," Sophia protested. She had the same feeling of emptiness in the pit of her stomach, like she did the day Ian told her Ross spent time in prison.

"I'm sorry. The court didn't consider your mother significant in this case. She was a MacLennan by marriage, but she never owned the shop. We searched for a pay slip, a silent partner, or any evidence of a financial connection to the bakeshop." Megan muttered something about the unfairness of the court's interpretation.

"Who knew about the lease?" Sophia remembered how difficult it was for the law firm to produce the original document.

"No one until recently. A current descendant of Mr. O'Neil has spiraled into financial trouble." Megan turned the computer screen toward Sophia.

Sophia stared at a headshot of an average-looking man about her age. "What did he do to get in such a bind?"

"Mostly bad investments." Megan hit a link. "He's in desperate need of a tax loophole. His attorneys searched through every nook and cranny to see what they could dig up."

"And the land lease was what they found?" Things were going too well. She shouldn't be surprised someone snuck up and sucker-punched her again. It was the story of her life.

"They're desperate. They're going after any forgotten inheritances and family heirlooms." Megan's motionless expression grew serious. "The property this shop is on is prime real estate with a high price tag. The present Mr. O'Neil can donate the land to the town and receive a huge tax deduction to help him out of his situation. The town, in turn, can auction it behind closed doors to the highest bidder."

"Didn't you tell me the original Mr. O'Neil was a childless widower? Who's this ancestor?" Sophia glanced at Ian.

"The O'Neil family was prosperous for many decades." Ian straddled the chair next to her. "Property holdings and businesses were passed down to nieces and nephews, as well as offspring. Some still sit on the boards of the family businesses." He turned away. "I didn't feel the need to search any further than the mid 1900s. If I had, I would have discovered the current ancestor and his financial problems." He stared out the window.

"You researched the O'Neil family after the point of Marjorie's connection?" She had no right to question his motives. Nothing about this unexpected development was his fault. She was to blame for thinking her life would run smoothly now that the shop was a success.

"O'Neil's connection to the Scots in this area interested me." With a heavy sigh, he turned and faced her.

"Do you know how the present O'Neil got around this loophole?" If she learned something from her time helping Ian in his research, it was to collect your facts before reacting.

"Their legal team was able to get a judge to interpret by birth or marriage as meaning the next generation of the current owner, not beyond. Mary had no daughters or daughters-in-law," Megan said. "We wouldn't be having this conversation if your mother ran the shop."

"What are her options?" Ian clutched Sophia's hand.

"My team is looking for a loophole in Sophia's defense. The only way to fight such a ruling is with a long, drawn-out, and expensive defense." Megan shook her head.

"Didn't you say Aunt Mary left a retainer?" Sophia worked too hard to give up easily.

"She did. You don't want to waste it on a nasty court battle that you might not win."

"No. I have another plan." Sophia placed her palms on the table. "Ian proved my family's past, good or bad, is tied to this area. The best way to honor my female ancestors and their fairy-godfather benefactor is by making this shop a huge success." Now was the time to fight for Marjorie and Aunt Mary. If Mary knew what was happening, she'd be turning in her coffin. "Can I bid on the property?" she asked.

"I don't see why not." Megan nodded. "I should warn you, some major international developers are interested in Highland Falls."

"If they win, I'll be at their mercy." She pressed two fingers to each temple to ward off a sudden ache. "New owners can raise my rent and put me in the position where I'll have to sell the shop. Worse yet, if they refuse to renew the lease under terms of such agreements, the building can also revert to the new landowners. I could lose everything." By her calculations, she had only weeks left on the lease. "When does this ruling go into effect?"

"Immediately," Megan said. "O'Neil's legal team was effective in processing the paperwork necessary to donate the land."

"Your staff did a great job digging up this information," Sophia said.

"I wish I could give them all the credit." Megan gestured toward City Hall. "Small-town gossip can be more efficient than hours of archive searches."

"Judy? Did all this information come from the mayor's secretary?" Who else knew everything that happened? Sophia swallowed past the lump in her throat. Had Judy leaked this information to help her? She and the mayor were fond of her cookies and might not want to see her lose the shop. Her reasoning was a poor excuse, but it was valid in a town where everybody knew other people's business and protected their neighbors.

"And others," Megan said.

Sophia stood slowly and glanced around the shop. "This all teeters between tragic and ridiculous." She was no longer a lonely child at the mercy of Mother Malevolent. She wouldn't let her stepmother's demons take charge. Aunt Mary's foresight provided her with a strong emotional arsenal and an unexpected gift—Ian. Her life changed the moment he walked into her shop. She wasn't going back.

"Are you prepared to fight this battle?" Ian asked.

"This is about more than the bakery; it's about the

honor of my ancestors." She quoted the words on the MacLennan crest. "I don't think I'll be alone." Megan made it clear the town was behind her. She dug deep into a mysterious place that helped her survive living with Mother Malevolent. In the past, caring was an illusion she learned never to trust. She allowed herself to try it again. The townspeople were all on her side— Mr. Durand at the hardware store, Mr. Paisley at the museum, and even nosy Judy at the mayor's office.

"The bidding will get steeper," Ian said.

"So far, the shop has turned a nice profit." She did a quick calculation in her head. "I received a decent inheritance from my father." She glanced at Megan. "And the balance of the retainer account at the law firm reverts back to me at the end of my first year." She gave him the details supporting her decision, without mentioning the exact amount. They knew so little about each other's personal affairs. She knew Ian, the Hot Scot, the forensic expert, and the genealogist. He was full of facts and details, honest, and sometimes elusive. He knew everything about her past and accepted her reluctance to learn more. Did he truly understand how important this decision was? Maybe she misread the direction of their relationship, and she was not part of his future.

"*Aye.* You're in a good position to accept any financial challenge." He cocked his head to the side. "Are you ready to go the course?"

"I've worked hard to make the shop successful. I'm not letting some outsider walk in and force me out." She focused on the situation. Going back to her life with Mother Malevolent was not an option. She'd tighten her apron strings to make this work. She could do anything with Ian by her side. But would he be?

"My office is behind you, if you need any assistance." Megan closed her laptop.

"I'll call you soon." Sophia pressed her lips together and forced a smile. She didn't have time to wallow in self-pity. A few customers were waiting at the counter.

Alana gestured with a wave that she had it covered.

Reluctantly, Sophia took the seat across from Ian.

"I know today hasn't gone well." Ian stood and joined Alana. "I have something I hope will cheer you up."

Sophia watched him whisper in Alana's ear. What were they up to? Despite the mystery, she was grateful for the distraction and avoided his gaze.

From behind the counter, Alana picked up a package in a plain brown paper. "This is why Ian was late today. He ran into the postmaster." She carried the box to the table.

"The pink rose petals from Bulgaria?" Sophia glanced at the box with an overseas postmark. She sniffed the box. The delicate scent of roses lifted her mood. "How did you get it?"

"I passed Mrs. Grant on the street." Ian stood with his arms crossed and watched her examine the parcel. "She said you were expecting a delicate delivery, and the mail truck was already out. I offered to bring it here. She didn't have a problem with my signing. It's a small-town courtesy you won't find in a big city."

"Thanks. Alana and I have been waiting for this package." The package, as a light as a feather, was a welcome surprise. She planned to use the contents for spring designs and tastes.

"I'm happy to put a smile on your face after the not-so-good news." He squeezed her shoulder.

Avoiding his forced cheerfulness, she looked up and turned to Alana. "Can you cover the shop while Ian helps me open the box?" She hated to deprive her assistant of the thrill of opening the package, but she needed to talk to Ian alone. This was as good a time as any to talk about his departure. Her day was already marked by disaster—why not go for all the bad news at once? "We'll work in the back."

"No problem, boss."

Ian picked up the package and followed.

"Put it here." Sophia cleared a counter.

"Do you want me to do the honors, or do you want to open it?" He pulled a Swiss Army knife from his pocket.

"I'll do it," Sophia said.

"Be careful. The blade is sharp." Ian slowly placed the closed knife in her open palm.

"Don't worry. I use sharp objects all the time."

"Sending all the way to Bulgaria seems like quite a process to get rose petals." He crossed his arms and leaned against the opposite counter. "Wouldn't it be simpler to buy rose water or rose extract from your supplier?"

"Too much extract can make your cookies taste like soap." She wrinkled her nose. "These petals can be crushed and measured to the exact amount." The knife was cold and heavy in her hand. She secured the bottom of the box with her right hand and pushed the blade through the packing tape with her left hand.

"I'd imagine soapy cookies are never good for business." He smiled.

"You're so right." She glanced at his heart-stopping smile for a long second. "Ouch." She dropped the knife and put her index finger between her lips to stop the bleeding.

"I told you to be careful." Ian cupped her hand and assessed the damage. "You've done a good job. It's fairly deep and needs a couple of stitches."

"Nonsense." She pulled away her hand, walked to the sink, and let the cool water wash away the blood. "I've sliced a finger before." The water continued to flow red. All this blood from a little cut?

"Apply pressure." Ian handed her a clean towel. "I'll be right back." He removed his car keys from the pocket of his jeans.

"Where are you going?" She was hesitant to tell him she hated needles more than the average person. "There's no need to get your car. I'm not going to the ER."

"I'm not forcing you to do anything you don't have a mind to. I've got a medical bag in my car." He winked. "I'm pretty handy with a needle and thread."

"Oh no. I don't need stitches," she said to his back. "This isn't how I planned to spend my afternoon." Her day just turned from bad to worse. First there was the news from Megan. If that wasn't enough, when she found the perfect moment to bring up the subject she and Ian were avoiding—this happened.

After applying pressure for several minutes, she unwrapped her finger to see if the bleeding stopped. "Yuck. This doesn't look good." A line of blood spread beyond the narrow, but deep, laceration. She felt lightheaded, and lowered her head between her knees. When she looked up, Ian stood in front of her with a black doctor's bag.

"Are you okay?" He reached for her wrist and placed two fingers on her pulse. "Strong and steady." He nodded. "It's not uncommon to have a vasovagal response at the sight of your own blood. You'll feel better once I close the wound."

"Exactly. The blood made me a little queasy. I'm fine now, really." She swallowed and forced a smile. The last thing she wanted to hear was a long explanation about how her body reacted. She looked around the work area. "Where are you performing this procedure?"

"Upstairs." Ian pointed to the door to her apartment. "I can create a sterile area on your kitchen table."

"Are stitches really necessary?" Before following Ian upstairs, she tapped on the glass partition, waved her bandaged finger in the air, and signaled to Alana she was going upstairs.

"Oh my goodness." Alana stared at the bloodstained bandage. "I saw Ian rush out to his car and return with a doctor's bag, but I had no idea…"

"He's stitching me up." Sophia winced.

"Just stare at his handsome face. You'll be fine." Alana looked at the wound and faked a shiver. "I had my share of cuts and burns, and I suffered as an old sourpuss ER doc was sewing me up. Enjoy it." She went out front to wait on a new customer.

Sophia crept up the stairs.

Ian was in the kitchen, setting up his instruments. Before donning gloves, he removed a sterile cloth from his bag of tricks. He placed everything he needed on the kitchen table and filled a paper cup with warm water and a reddish-brown antiseptic. "Let your finger soak in here."

"Have you done this often?" Her voice cracked with anxious anticipation. She swirled her finger in the solution, creating a spiral in the colors of chocolate and cherries.

"Many times when I was teaching forensic medicine." He dried her finger with clean gauze.

"I don't doubt your skill, but the bodies you worked with were dead. They couldn't feel anything." She ignored the sting and concentrated on his face like Alana suggested.

"Forensic humor?" He laughed. "I can apply a numbing cream, if you'd like. It'll take about twenty minutes to work."

"I've got nothing but time. Go for it." This was the best thing she'd heard all day. Twenty minutes with nothing to do but sit here and talk to Ian. Wasn't that what she wanted?

Ian applied a thin ribbon of clear sticky gel and covered it with clean gauze. "Can I make you a cup of tea while we wait, lass?"

The topical anesthetic stung. "I think I should go into this with an empty stomach." She swallowed a wave of nausea brought on by her anxiety.

"Don't worry. I promise you won't feel a thing," Ian said.

The numbing medicine started to work its magic. Engaging Ian in conversation about his trip to Scotland would help to distract her. But, Sophia couldn't make her mouth work. She was afraid of the truth. What if he said he didn't know when he'd return or something worse? Before coming to Highland Falls, her mind was cluttered with lists and strategies. In her head, she'd carried a suitcase of tentative plans to get away from her stepmother. Random events occurred that made her feel guilty about leaving. When Aunt Mary's bequest offered the opportunity to take action, she didn't second-guess the consequences of such an impulsive decision. Just a short while ago, she reacted to Megan's news with decisive action. *Put on your big girl apron and do it again. Ask him about his trip.* "Is everything ready for your presentation?" She fiddled with a gauze pad.

"It's been a long, slow process." He reached for a pointy nosed tweezers. "A dissertation starts with having the will to write it. I have a thousand pages of information." He assessed the edges of her wound with the tweezers.

"That's some term paper." She thought of the long evenings they spent together in her apartment or the bakeshop.

"My notes were very detailed. I eliminated what wasn't relevant and put the remainder in chronological order."

"Just like that?" She snapped the fingers on her good hand.

"It took two years of determination and sleepless nights." He applied gentle pressure to the wound and wiped away the blood. "Do you feel anything?"

"No." She avoided looking at the wound. "What's your next step?"

"After the sutures are done?" He pushed the first stitch through the skin

"I'm not referring to the stitches, and you know it," she retorted. "Are you purposely avoiding a conversation about your trip to Edinburgh?" She felt a slight pressure as he placed the second and final stitch.

"*Aye*, lass." He tied the last stitch in a delicate knot and wiped off the antiseptic. "We've both been avoiding the subject." He wrapped a small bandage around her finger. "I've given it some thought. The solution is simple."

"How simple?" She took the first deep breath since her mishap. Just like that, he was about to offer a practical conclusion to something she agonized about since that night at Fiona's when she'd turned down his offer to spend the night.

"Come with me to Scotland." He extended a hand.

She placed a hand in his and eased away from the chair into the circle of his arms. Excited by the offer, she waited until her hammering heart found its rhythm. "If our circumstances were different, I would ask you to stay." She broke away. "But, I won't. You worked too hard to pass up this chance to present." She studied the hard angles of his cheekbones, challenging blue eyes, and the curve of his lips. She would have liked nothing more than to hike the hills and mountains with this harshly handsome Highlander. For a fleeting moment, the idea had merit. Standing in Aunt Mary's kitchen reminded her everything here was at stake.

"Since when did you become so logical?" he asked.

"I had a good teacher." For months, she anticipated this day. Knowing he wanted her with him should be enough to believe he was coming back. But it wasn't. She never had the opportunity to tell the people she loved not to leave. Her father, her mother, and even Mary were here one day and gone the next. "Any idea how long you'll be gone?" She tossed the used gauze into the trashcan.

"It's impossible to predict. I've got some other matters to tend to while I'm there."

His smile said everything would be fine, but his words were contradictory. She reached for a cloth and spray to clean the table and stopped short. "Don't you have a round-trip ticket?"

"I only bought a one way. My return is open."

"It's always the last line that gets you." *My return is open.* The words cut through her like a sharp knife through frozen dough. She clutched the edge of the table.

"What's wrong?" he asked. "Is the anesthetic wearing off?"

"I'll be fine once I adjust to having my finger wrapped like a Christmas present." She waved the cumbersome dressing in the air.

"It's only for today—in case there's any blood oozing." He took the cleaning cloth from her. "I'll clean up."

"Ugh. It's a bit of an inconvenience. Alana will have to unpack the rose petals." Purposely distancing herself from their conversation, she thought of all the things she had to do. "And tomorrow?"

"A small bandage and glove will protect the wound. You can still roll dough and bake, if you follow my instructions." He cleaned the table with an antiseptic wipe and shut the light. "I'll pack my instruments and meet you downstairs."

Sophia entered the shop and waved her bandaged hand. "Alana, can you unpack the rose petals, please? I won't be much use today."

"Doctor's orders." Ian stood behind her with his

doctor's bag. "She has to rest today. Tomorrow, she can do light work."

"Got it, boss." Alana glanced from Sophia to Ian.

Sophia pointed to Ian. "And you have a delivery to make. Fiona's cookie order is packed and ready to go." She reached for the package on the counter and shoved it at him. "It's best you get them there in time for her afternoon tea."

"Are you sure you're okay?" He rubbed the back of his neck.

"Everything's under control," she lied and watched him walk away. His genuine concern pierced her heart. A dash of sadness tilted her smile, and a heaping spoonful of desire coursed through her. Christmas at Fiona's flashed through her mind. Today was the second time she let logic dictate her actions. If driven only by desire and emotions, she would never have refused either of his tempting offers. She looked around for something simple to do and reached for her duster. The plaid on the wall was no longer an inconvenience. She found comfort in the tedious task. If a little blood leaked through her bandage onto the fabric, it wouldn't do it any harm. The tartan had seen much worse than a cut finger. Her thoughts wandered to her great-great-grandmother and Ross. What was it like when they'd parted? Marjorie must have expected Ross to return some day, but he didn't. Was her life destined to take the same course as her ancestors?

****

On the drive back to Fiona's, Ian thought about the things he said. He should have phrased his answers better and been more specific about when he would return. He had focused on the closure of the wound and failed to see a clue as to why her attitude was so dismissive. Bloody hell. *She thinks I'm not coming back.* He smacked his hands on the steering wheel. Of course I'm coming back. In most cases, he was a quick learner. Fiona would agree his lessons in relationships fell short when it came to practical application.

He found her in the kitchen, preparing for afternoon tea. Tea wasn't what he needed. He reached into the cupboard for a bottle of whisky and poured a dram into a china teacup. The notes of wood and leather said a lot about the quality of the drink. "This whisky is precisely what the doctor ordered." He took a sip and nodded.

"Would you like a shortbread with that?" Fiona motioned for him to take a seat and pushed the plate in front of him. She sat across the table and waited.

There was no way around this. Fiona, with her usual instinct for knowing when something was bothering him, would sit there staring until he folded. He started with Megan's news about Sophia's lease.

"What are you going to do? Will you just walk away and leave Sophia to deal with the situation on her own?" Fiona shook her head.

"Sophia's more than capable to handle any business dealings." He lifted the delicate cup to his lips and downed the remaining Scotch in one sip. "She's the one with an accounting degree."

"I don't doubt she can maneuver her way through this financial mess," Fiona agreed. "You're ahead of schedule. Have you thought of delaying your dissertation until Sophia can travel with you?"

"The idea crossed my mind. Timing is important if I want to attend the conference that follows. I'll have an opportunity to network with archeology, genealogy, and forensic departments of several universities. These connections are vital to my plan to settle in Highland Falls."

"What's to keep you in Scotland after you meet all these people?" She shook her head and stood.

"I have other matters to attend to when my academic obligations are done."

"Other than visiting family?" She reached for a teapot with one hand and a plate of cookies with the other. "Hold that thought. I'll be right back."

Ian walked over to the sink and rinsed his cup. Maybe his sister was right. He should come back sooner than he planned, but he already put things in motion.

"Cora's dealing with the guests." Fiona returned with an empty teapot and placed it in the sink. "I'll put on the kettle, and we can talk."

"It has to do with Granny Ulster's book. Did you read the copy I gave you?" Ian straddled a chair and studied his sister's face.

"I did the night you gave it to me." Fiona set clean cups on the table. "There's a lot of stuff in there that can upset a lot of people. You have to respect Sophia's request."

"I told her about the book. She wants nothing to do with it." He did his best to live up to his promise to stop if what he discovered was upsetting. But he could not understand not wanting to know what the book could reveal.

"So, case closed?" She filled their cups.

"For now." He learned never to try and anticipate how Sophia would react in the future.

"Okay, then." She threw up her hands and sighed. "What else is on your itinerary other than a visit to *Ma* and *Da*?"

"I called Sophia's grandfather, Finn MacLennan. I explained my research and my interest in seeing his brooch." He waved off the milk she offered. "I was surprised by how well I was received."

"Did you happen mention how fond you are of his granddaughter?" She placed her hands on her hips.

"I might have mentioned we saw a lot of each other." He crossed his arms and leaned back. "Finn MacLennan returned to Scotland a few years after his daughter, Sophia's mother, died. Considering what I know about Sophia's upbringing from that point forward…"

"Her wicked stepmother might not have acknowledged his letters or calls." Fiona finished his thought.

"It would be a terrible thing for the man to leave this world thinking his granddaughter didn't want anything to do with him."

"And even sadder for Sophia." Fiona put a hand on his shoulder. "You did good. Are you planning on telling Sophia?"

"When I get back. It would be a moot point if the old man doesn't want to connect with her."

"Will you tell him about the book? He could validate Ross Robert and Ross MacLennan as being the same person."

"Finn's a grandson of Ross and Marjorie." Ian questioned why Mary never suggested he touch base with her father. "There might have been speculation back when he was a *bairn* about what happened to his grandfather. You know the *auld* ones. They spoke in whispers about such things."

"And the next several generations, as well." Fiona laughed. "Our grandparents said almost everything in whispers when we were around."

"*Aye.* They did. People like Granny Ulster are still doing it today." Ian carried the bottle of Scotch to the table. "It all comes back to the book she doesn't want anyone to see."

"Ross' story might be a touchy subject for Finn MacLennan." Fiona put a whisky glass on the table.

"If he brings it up, I'll tread lightly." Ian filled the glass. "From what I read so far, it's clear the Ulster clan is connected to Ross. Sophia could have relatives here."

"I don't think it really matters." Fiona shrugged. "Sophia's already fond of Tim and even his granny."

"Everyone likes the lad. It's his granny who takes some getting used to." He shook his head. "I know Sophia thinks of you and Alana as family"

"It's in your power to make her real family." She wiggled her brow. "I see the way you look at each other."

Ian swallowed hard. Was the chemistry between them so obvious?

"Your silence says a lot, brother. I might have to find another delivery boy as equally handsome to take the poor girl's mind off of you."

"I doubt she'll have time to pine for me. She has a lot to think about with her lease expiring."

Fiona filled his cup with whisky. "It's your decision. I'm sure you'll do the right thing."

He stared at the glass of whisky and asked himself the same question—was he doing the right thing?

Chapter 18

Sophia never remembered which way it went when Punxsutawney Phil saw his shadow.

On the other side of the counter, Tim and Alana argued the point. Would the groundhog emerge tomorrow and predict an early spring?

Sophia gathered their silly conversation was for her benefit. Her stomach was in knots all morning. The bidding on the land closed today.

"What do you think, Sophia?" Tim asked.

"About what?" she asked without looking up from the tray of heart-shaped cookies she rearranged for the third time.

"Do you think the groundhog will see his shadow?" Tim stooped and looked through the front of the glass.

"How's the display look from your side?" Arranging the display case with fresh baked cookies was usually her favorite part of her day. Today, it was just another busy activity to keep her mind off what was happening across the street. "Are there too many red cookies in the display? Maybe I should move some to the front window?"

Off to the side, her phone shimmied across the counter.

"Oops. I got it." Alana caught the phone at the edge.

"I hope it's from Megan." Sophia opened the text and stared at the phone.

"What's it say?" Alana drummed her fingers on the counter.

"My bid was submitted early this morning." She read the message a second time. "All the bidders have dropped out, except one."

"That's good news, boss." Alana came around the counter. "I'll finish the cookies. You take a seat by the window and watch who goes in and out of the building." She glanced at Tim. "Tim will join you. He's got eyes like a hawk. I'll bring you both some sipping chocolate and toast. You haven't eaten all morning."

"Toast?" Tim raised a brow.

His response was a little slow on the uptake. "Bring him a plate of cookies." Sophia laughed for the first time this morning. Comfort food was just what a certain doctor would have ordered.

"No problem, ladies. Toast sounds good."

Alana placed a plate of buttered toast and two cups of thick chocolate drink on the table.

"Drink," she ordered. "Chocolate is good for everything."

Sophia blew on her cup and took a sip. The thick, sweet liquid slid down her throat, providing a moment of solace. She stared out the window, avoiding City Hall, and watched the tourist in fancy ski outfits.

"They're here." Tim jumped from his seat. He pointed across the street. "That's the same black car they come in every day."

"That's the competition, all right." Sophia watched two men in expensive suits disappear beyond the brass doors. "Every day, it's the same scenario." She nibbled on a corner of her toast. "Just before bidding closes for the day, this land development group sends a different representative than the day before. Today's final bid has to be on the mayor's desk by noon." She checked the clock—eleven forty five.

"I'm sorry the town council treated you like this." Alana sighed.

"I heard the mayor had to break the tie with his vote." Tim frowned. "Boy, I'd like to know who voted against you."

"I have some idea." Alana glanced at Tim. "Council members I've known my entire life avoid me on the streets. The ones who voted in favor of Sophia's offer told me they were unable to convince the mayor to accept her first offer."

"I don't blame the mayor for wanting the best for the town. Everyone will benefit from the exuberant direction of the bidding." Sophia brushed toast crumbs onto her napkin. "The town council had no choice. Accepting the donation of *my land* from Mr. O'Neil's great-great-nephew was the right thing to do." *Could you dislike someone you never met?* "The bidding started within hours of hearing *my* prime piece of real estate was on the market." She still had a hard time digesting that the land could belong to someone else.

"You do know, except for a couple of council members, the town is on your side," Tim said. "No one wants you to close shop."

"I appreciate what they're doing." Sophia smiled. Even the disaster that was unfolding in front of her had a lighter side. "It's amazing what an organized group of gossips and eavesdroppers can accomplish. Every time a counter bid is placed, someone crosses the street, comes into my shop, and casually mentions what they overheard the mayor discussing."

"It's a dirty situation, but these guys don't play nice." Alana pointed in the direction of City Hall. "Look at what time they arrived today, just fifteen minutes before the bids close. I'd show them how things are done in this town, if I had a chance." She twisted a towel between her hands.

"Look they're leaving." Tim waved a hand in the direction of City Hall. "What'd you think? The visit was short."

"Too short." Alana nodded.

"We'll know soon enough," Sophia said with a confidence she wasn't really feeling.

The men climbed into their black SUV and drove away.

Within minutes, the bakery door opened. A cold draft of air woke them out of their despair.

Granny Ulster strolled through the door. "What's everyone doing sitting around with nothing to do?" She looked from Sophia to Alana, then her grandson. "I told you my water heater was making a strange noise again."

"I was just leaving, Granny."

"Will it be your usual—hot tea with warm milk?" Alana cleared the table.

"I've got this." Sophia walked behind the counter and turned on the kettle. She needed to get Granny settled so she would be free to speak with today's informer. "Would you like a shortbread with your tea?" She fiddled with the tie on her apron and glanced at the door.

"No for me tea today." Granny walked toward the

counter. "But I will take a dozen of the whisky shortbread to go." She watched Sophia box her order. "I've just come from City Hall. It's such a small building, don't you think so?"

"It's adequate." Sophia knew better than to push the conversation. Granny wasn't here to discuss the layout of City Hall. Was she today's informer?

"The mayor is so provincial. Don't you agree?" Granny gave Sophia a sideways glance. "Such an important man shouldn't keep his door open when he's discussing business."

"Does it matter?" Sophia shrugged. "Highland Falls residents can't keep anything secret." She didn't see the rhyme or reason to the old lady's idle chatter. If she was today's spy, why not just come out and tell her what she heard?

"It's difficult not to listen when you're standing directly in front of the open door."

"Of course not." Sophia winced and boxed a dozen shortbreads. The old lady's coy act was painfully played.

"Did you happen to notice two men in expensive suits going into the building?"

"My view's been obstructed by truck traffic," Sophia lied. Behind her, the kettle whistled.

"You know what?" Granny pointed toward the kettle. "I'll have a cup of tea and two cookies."

Is she torturing me on purpose? Sophia reached for a teapot. "Green or Ceylon?"

"You decide. Bring yourself a cup, too." Granny took a seat at the corner table.

Sophia poured the water over a tea ball filled with Ceylon leaves. The water turned a reddish golden orange. She placed the lid on the pot and carried it to the table. She let Granny fix their cups. "Is the tea to your liking?" From across the table, she waited for Granny to swallow. The gesture was reminiscent of Ian's Scotch drinking lesson. Maybe what they needed was a dram in their tea to get things moving.

"It'll do. I've had quite a morning." Granny placed her cup on the saucer. "I was standing at the desk, writing a check for my water bill. Darn pen wouldn't write, and Judy took forever to find another one. I couldn't help but notice two well-dressed young men walking into the mayor's office."

"And?" Sophia shifted in her seat.

"Patience, dear. Patience. You young kids have no staying power. Everything today has to have happened yesterday."

Patience. She did her best not to reach over and shake the information out of Granny. She took a sip of the warm tea and wrapped her hands around the teacup to avoid the temptation.

"As I was saying, those young men spoke to the mayor for a very short time." The old lady leaned forward. "They passed a paper across the desk, and said, 'This is Alpha Development's last offer, sir.' Such nice young men and so polite."

Perhaps they were polite, but they weren't nice people. They worked for the company that wanted to steal her land. She bounced her knee under the table. Was Granny ever going to finish telling her story?

"Do you know what the mayor said?" Granny looked at her watch. "I don't have time to tell you every detail. I heard him say the bid wasn't good enough. He had a better offer."

"Was it really their last offer?" Sophia was prepared to double her next bid. If what Granny heard was true, and the men representing the developer meant what they said, it could all be over. She'd own both the shop and the property. Her heart beat fast.

"Yes. Didn't you hear me, dear?"

Sophia nodded. *I hear you loud and clear.* She glanced at Alana and gave her double thumbs-up.

"Yes, yes." Alana threw her hands in the air and did a happy dance.

"Tell that silly girl to stop dancing like a fool, and bring us another pot of tea." Granny nodded in Alana's direction.

"I'll fill the kettle." Sophia walked toward the counter but was stopped short by a sudden rush of customers. Numerous cell phones went off at the same time. A jumble of tunes and beeps echoed around the shop. One-by-one, they turned to Sophia and clapped their hands in a round of applause.

"I can't believe it. In less than fifteen minutes, the whole town knows the good news."

"Small-town grapevine." Granny winked.

"I couldn't have succeeded without your help." She never experienced anything like it and acknowledged the well-wishers with a bow. All the attention threw her off balance. She felt her eyebrow twitch and stilled it with a finger. The one person she wanted to share the good news with was over three thousand miles away.

"Sit down." Granny pointed to the empty seat. "Let's finish our little chat."

Sophia didn't argue. She could celebrate later, but she might not get another chance to ask about Ross.

"Tell me, when is your handsome boyfriend

coming back? He's a bit nosy but does it with charm."

"Ian's questions are based on his academic research, not idle gossip." She wasn't always pleased with the results, but she wouldn't let anyone find fault with his research. "He just presented his findings at an important conference in Edinburgh."

"I heard he excelled at his dissertation and conference presentation." Granny sipped her tea. "Do you know when he'll be back?"

"He texted me the other night. He has some loose ends to tie up." Sophia pictured the tattoo on his forearm—*Forever Scotland*. She quickly dismissed any negative thoughts. She'd host an open house to celebrate their successes when he returned.

"Hmm. I assume you read the book Mr. Paisley located for your young man. The one written by Ross MacLennan's daughter." Granny put down her cup and folded her hands on the table. "You have a copy of the original book, don't you?"

"My copy was written by Ross *Robert's* daughter." How did she know Ian gave her a copy?

"Have you read it?" Granny asked.

"I thought you didn't want anyone to read it." Sophia shifted in her seat.

"You're kind to honor my wishes. I don't believe everyone in this town feels the same as you." Granny raised a brow. "You're not a very good liar. Don't think for a minute I believe that's why you didn't read it."

"You didn't let Tim or Ian read your copy." The day she decided she was done with Ian's research, she put the book in the top drawer of her dresser.

"You're different. The past doesn't haunt you."

"Maybe because I never knew much about it."

Sophia looked at the tartan. "I learned the truth about how Marjorie started the shop and passed it down to female descendants. I don't need to know any more." She waved an open palm in the air. "Marjorie's story was what encouraged me to stay and fight for what was rightfully mine."

"*Aye*, lassie. You put Marjorie's story to good use. Mary would be proud. You could do the same with what's written in my book."

"No. It's not my secret, it's yours."

"It's your decision."

Granny took her hand in a compassionate grip. Why was the old woman changing her tune? Had she just given her leave to read the book?

Later in the evening, encouraged by Granny's permission to read the book, Sophia removed it from her drawer. She placed a reissued edition on the kitchen table and glanced at the clock. "It's too late to call Edinburgh." If she phoned Ian, she would save hours of scanning through the book. If the author, Audrey Robert, was really Ross's daughter, it was best to leave it at that. Whether or not she was born out of wedlock had no impact on Sophia's life. Sophia suspected Aunt Mary never imagined Ian would search beyond Marjorie's story.

Her two-times great-grandmother moved on without her husband and created a legacy for her descendants. Finally at peace with the family history, she accepted the past for what it gave her. Let Granny keep her secrets. Ross's life after prison was over and buried. She looked from the clock to the phone. With the exception of a certain curious academic, the secret had no meaning to anyone alive today. "What would you like to say?" She placed a hand on the book and waited. Unlike the time she touched the plaid, she felt nothing but the feel of high-grade paper.

A gentle spring breeze blew through the open window. It kissed her cheek and rattled the pages. Audrey's words wouldn't change Sophia's current situation. She had bigger cookies to bake. Tomorrow, she would accompany Megan to City Hall. Together, they would present the mayor with a check. She left the book on the table and went to bed.

The hiss of the radiator jolted her awake. She had tossed and turned for what seemed like hours. No sense fighting it. A cup of chamomile tea might help. Her bare feet hit the cold floor as she scuffled for her slippers. While she waited for the water to boil, she opened the book. She would never know why she stopped on that particular page. Her judgment in the middle of the night wasn't as sound as it would be after a good night's sleep. Her eyes adjusted to the overhead light. The words came into focus.

My father, Ross Robert's real name was Ross Robert MacLennan. He loved my mother, Jane Ulster. Due to his complicated past, they never got married. I will explain the reasons later in this book.

"Jane Ulster." Her breath caught in her throat. "I know the reason," she whispered to the book. "He disappeared to protect his wife and children from the stigma of his prison sentence." She reached for the kettle and filled a mug with steamy water. The warm tea did little to relieve her anxiety. Her hand shook. She placed the mug on the table and stared at the page. The two words explained why Ross didn't go back to Marjorie. If Granny preferred to take this family secret to the grave than admit she married into a family with its own indiscretions—Sophia would let it be. She could never make her understand today's generation didn't view a child out of wedlock the same way. She turned the page.

This book is not a personal account of one life. It's a tribute to the men, like my father, who guided the tourists through the Adirondack Wilderness or North Woods as it was often called. Several routes took visitors to the woods. Only a few were suitable for parties with women. The trip to the first of the chain of lakes was more easily approached from the south end of the wilderness, but not without danger. Groups rode on horseback on a rough trail with perilous twists and turns. The hotel at the end of the line had been in my mother's family for many years.

It made sense. Ross disappeared into the wilderness in hope of starting a life far from anyone who could connect him to Marjorie and his sons. No reason existed to read on. Sophia discovered more than expected; she now knew one of Highland Falls' best-kept secrets. Only a couple of people knew her connection to the Ulster family. No worries. The secret wasn't hers to tell. Out of respect for Granny, Sophia would guard the secret until the old lady was willing to reveal what happened.

Chapter 19

Sophia looked around her little shop. "We did it, Marjorie. A MacLennan girl legally owns the land the shop is built on." Speaking out loud to her ancestors comforted her when she was alone. Never in a million years did she imagine the mystery of what happened to Ross would end this way. "No worries," she assured any ghosts listening. "The Ulster's secret is safe with me." The time had come to move on with the final touches for today's celebration. The day had been already postponed too long. She couldn't wait any longer for Ian to return. Today, she would show her gratitude to the people of Highland Falls.

"Morning, Sophia." Fiona struggled with a wildflower bouquet. "Am I the first?"

"Put it here." Sophia cleared off a nearby table. "It smells like your herb shed. I detect a subtle hint of lemon spice and vanilla." She inhaled deeply. "Thank you."

"They're not from me. Check the card," Fiona said. "I'm just the delivery girl."

Sophia glanced sideways and reached for the envelope hidden in between the spikes of thistles. She ripped open the envelope. "Ian. He ordered these all by himself?"

"I had nothing to do with it." Fiona waved an open palm. "He comes through when it's important." She sighed. "Don't worry. He'll be back. He always is."

Sophia blinked back tears and read the note. The Celtic blessing couldn't be from anyone else. She heard the posh lilt of his accent whispering in her ear.

May there always be work for your hands to do.
May your purse always hold a coin or two.
May the sun always shine upon your window pane.
May a rainbow be certain to follow each rain.
May the hand of a friend always be near to you and
May God fill your heart with gladness to cheer you.

Ian

Although the blessing was translated from Irish Celtic, she found the sentiment romantically Scottish. She handed the card to Fiona and dabbed her eyes with the corner of her apron.

"That's okay. I'm sure it wasn't meant for anyone but you." Fiona tucked the card into Sophia's apron pocket.

Their conversation was interrupted by the arrival of the judge and Lily Logan.

"How's your ankle?" Sophia nodded at the walking stick.

"He's fine but insists on using a cane." Lily waved a hand in the air. "He thinks it makes him look like a gentleman farmer."

"It's so nice of you to host this open house." The judge sat at a window table and hung his cane over the back of the chair.

"It's the least I can do to thank the town for helping me save my aunt's legacy." Sophia looked around the café. Every corner had a story to tell. She made Ian promise not to reveal everything at once. The time would come to learn all the secrets.

"Your aunt would be proud of you. We are." Lily wrapped her arms around her and hugged tightly. "Your success in outbidding the developers is definitely a reason to celebrate."

"Thank you." Sophia glanced out the window. She was an outsider when she stepped into the town's beloved bakery. Some people, like the Logans, were kind, while others were undecided about her ability to succeed. She wasn't the sort to pat herself on the back. She managed to convince even the naysayers she was here to stay. She turned her attention back to her guests. "How about some tea?"

"I'd love a cup." The judge took off his hat.

"Herbal tea or English Breakfast?" Alana approached with a pot in each hand and handed one to Sophia.

"We'll both have a cup of English Breakfast, please," Lily said.

"A lot of excitement is going on in this little town today." The judge looked out the window. You're not the only one with something to celebrate. An interesting discovery happened at the excavation site."

"Punxsutawney Phil not seeing his shadow turned out good for our town. Highland Falls experienced an early spring." Lily laughed. "Our old paddock changed overnight from a messy winter scene to a more workable environment."

So that's how the groundhog thing goes. Don't see your shadow and spring's around the corner. Sophia was happy for the crew at the dig site. She had a personal interest in the progress of their work. "Is the university crew there today? I haven't visited in a while. Last time I was there all I saw was a lot of dirt being tossed around."

"You haven't heard?" The judge raised a brow. "A recent discovery has drawn people from several disciplines. Before we drove here, I was talking to a professor who dabbles in problems left over by normal science. He referred to his field as extraordinary science."

"Did they find something on the site that's out of the ordinary?" Sophia placed the teapot on the table. "Crew members stopped by the other day, but no one mentioned a new discovery."

"Nothing's been released to the public yet. The discovery is just circulating within the academic community."

"I'm surprised no one mentioned it. The crew is always asking for details about the day Ian and I found the box." Sophia didn't mind sharing but wished Ian was here to tell his side. The crew would appreciate his excitement.

"What do you tell them?" Lily asked.

"I tell them how we brought the box to your house. We were all nervous when Ian opened it." Every time she retold the story, she felt the same chill. There wasn't much she'd forgotten, but a lot she excluded. How could she explain how touching the brooch brought back memories of her parents or that she found comfort in Lily's stories about her mother and aunt? Those were private memories.

"Lots of strange things happen out there." The judge shook his head. "You never know what you'll see from one day to the next. The crew hopes to avoid a slew of curious tourists who could compromise the site."

"Of course. I respect their decision." If she learned anything from Ian, she learned you couldn't rush a research project.

"I don't think they'd mind you visiting." Lily glanced sideways at her husband. "Don't you agree some of Sophia's delicious shortbread would be a perfect touch to their celebration?"

"I can't think of a better way to celebrate." Judge Logan nodded.

"Now?" Sophia stepped back with her mouth open. "Today's not good. Tomorrow would be better."

"I'm sure the team would be happy to see you." Alana handed her a large box of cookies.

"Everyone in town is happy for you, but don't believe for a minute they're not here for free cookies and tea." Fiona tossed her a sweater.

"It's so early." Sophia looked at the clock. "The party just started."

"We'll tell everyone something came up, and you'll be back soon." Fiona glanced at the little group seated around the table.

"She's right. We've got this, boss." Alana placed her hands on her hips.

Her assistant's smile was almost convincing.

"You should go, dear," Lily said. "It's as much your discovery as it is theirs."

"If I didn't know better, I would think you're all up to something." Did the judge just wink? After weeks of negotiation, Sophia didn't have the strength to argue. In all honesty, it was time for a break. She had started baking before sunrise. "Okay, maybe just a short visit." She untied her apron and tossed it over the back of a chair.

"Good idea." Alana handed Sophia the keys to the roadster. "Get going." With a gentle nudge, she pushed her out the door.

Sophia visited the paddock twice since Ian left. One time was out of curiosity, and the other was when the Logans invited her to join them berry picking. She stopped on the outside of town to adjust her rearview mirror. An Adirondack red stag with the largest antler span she ever saw looked back. Locals bragged how their red stags were the largest on the planet. Now she knew it was true. "Good morning," she whispered. Such a sighting was a sign of something good. When she looked again, the stag was gone.

The dig site was just around the next bend. Festivities were in full swing. Members of the crew gathered around the open tailgate of a truck parked along the paddock. She recognized many of the graduate students who stopped by her shop. Today belonged to them. She parked off the road.

"Hey, Sophia." One of the grad students waved a bottle of whisky. "Come join us."

"I heard you made a big discovery." She crossed the road and placed the box of shortbread on the open tailgate.

"We did." The grad student with the whisky poured a glass. "Professor Adams has uncovered the first bone." He pointed to a tall, gray-haired man.

"Bones?" Sophia shuddered. "Are they human or animal?" A chill ran down her spine. The impact of the discovery hit her full force. The professor, her favorite member of the team, approached the open tailgate. He had a fondness for shortbread and an academic personality similar to Ian's.

"Definitely human," the professor said. "The bones will tell us so much once they're sorted and cleaned." He looked over the rim of his glasses. "Is that full of your shortbread?"

"I came to help you celebrate." Sophia untied the bakery string. "Do you mind if I take a look at what you found?"

"Not at all." He walked her to the gate. "A man is out here who can explain it. He's a combination of a forensic doctor and a genealogist." He winked.

"A forensic genealogist?" Sophia's heart beat faster. She took small, cautious steps toward the gate. The paddock looked different from the day she and Ian examined the cornerstones. The horses were gone. Early in the digging, the judge moved them away from the commotion. She opened the gate but hesitated before moving forward. Bursts of bright spring flowers and patches of grass covered the field. Yellow caution tape wrapped around the perimeter of the dig site.

She couldn't miss the man standing at the rim. Even at distance, she recognized familiarity of the man's serious intent and confident stance. "Ian," she whispered to the wind. A flat cap hid most of his red hair. His face was covered with more than his usual stubble. *Had he grown a beard?* Two months had passed since he left. To keep her sanity, she stopped counting the days. Would he be happy to see her? A gust of wind pushed her forward. She made her way toward Ian and stopped a safe distance from the hole.

"Hi." He turned and smiled.

Was the smile for her or what he saw in the hole? *Only one way to find out.* She edged closer and glanced in. The earthy smell of overturned dirt mixed with the crisp scents of spring. "What's in the hole?" These weren't the words she thought she would say the first time she saw him.

"Bones." He circled the pit.

Was he expecting her? From what she could see, he didn't appear at all surprised.

"Take a look." With a hand on her elbow, he guided her precariously close to the edge.

His touch, no more than a baby's breath, sent a shudder to her toes. "Whose bones?" she asked in a whisper.

"The answer to that question will take time. All my resources will be at the crew's disposal for as long as they need." He slipped an arm around her waist and pulled her close. "Watch your step."

She was happy for Ian. He would never miss the opportunity to see the bones before they were removed. The discovery validated his desire to combine his knowledge of forensic medicine with his research on ancient clans. "When did you get back?" She couldn't deny the delight she saw in his face as he walked around the hole. Did he return to Highland Falls to see her or the bones? Her excitement dipped.

"I landed at JFK early this morning. I would have arrived here sooner, but my connecting flight to Albany was cancelled. I didn't know when I'd get another." He looked into the hole and smiled. "I couldn't wait. I rented a car and drove here."

"You drove all that way after a long international flight just to see some old bones?" At the bottom of the pit, she saw bones, dirt, and a forgotten shovel.

"Not the bones." He guided her back a few steps

and swung her into his arms.

"You must be exhausted." She searched his face for signs of fatigue.

"Not any longer." He held her face in his hands and gazed into her eyes. "I have so much to tell you."

His breath stirred her hair. "I thought you were never coming back." She bit her bottom lip. The words didn't sound so overwhelming when she said them out loud. "Why didn't you let me know?"

"I wanted to surprise you. How did you know I was here?"

"The Logans came into my shop and ordered cookies for the crew." She gazed at Ian's deep-blue eyes. All doubts melted away. "The judge said he saw a man out here who studies extraordinary science." She glanced around the field. "Did you see him?"

"Dig sites are like UFO sightings. They attract all sorts of academics." He brushed a stray hair from her cheek.

"What about the Logans? Did you see them before they came into town?"

"They were leaving the site when I got here. The extraordinary scientist must have left before I arrived." He took her hand and pressed a kiss to her palm. "I'll have to thank them for sending you."

"They were pretty insistent. So were Fiona and Alana." Sophia raised a brow. "I thought there was something funny about their urgency. Did they know you were back?" Alana grew up in Highland Falls. She knew how to keep secrets. This secret was different. It must have taken all of her assistant's restraint to keep the secret that Hot Scot was back.

"*Aye*, lass. They did." He smiled again. "I can tell

by that *wee* tilt of your brow they kept their word."

"Why didn't you come into town?"

"Too much is going on in your shop today. Congratulations." With one hand still clutched around her waist, he waved his free hand in the air. "More private out here."

"I agree. There's never any privacy in the shop." She glanced into the hole. "Why do I get an eerie feeling we're still not alone? Looks like you've won the trifecta, bones, dead people, and a big hole full of secrets."

"More than that. Things worked out with my connections in Edinburgh. Before I left, Mr. Paisley and I talked about opening a satellite genealogy division here in Highland Falls." He gestured to the field. "All this could be our classroom."

Was this the important event that her stag sighting prepared her for? "Would you move here?" Her heart beat fast at the thought that he would be living so close.

"I plan on it. Fiona found a charming cottage not too far from town."

"Fiona never mentioned she was looking at local real estate."

"I wanted to surprise you." He placed a finger under her chin, tilted her face, and kissed her.

"I'm surprised," she whispered against his lips, forgetting all those weeks without him.

"The cottage needs some work." He nibbled on her earlobe. "We could work on it together."

"I'd like that." She snuggled close. "I know the cottage." She pictured a gaggle of little redheads running in and out the front door. "What delayed your return?"

"I was *verrry* busy." He smiled.

She studied his face. An artful smile aroused her curiosity. "Doing what?" Content in his arms, she wasn't sure she needed an answer. Sooner or later, she'd find out what he did after the conference. Like the bones, eventually everything came to the surface.

"I visited your grandfather," he said.

"Finn...?" An uncanny feeling settled in her stomach. "How...is he?"

"Amazing for a man his age." Ian placed a tender kiss on her forehead and released her.

"I told him I tried my best to persuade you to come to Scotland."

"I regretted the decision the moment after you left." She put a hand over his heart. "But I had to stay."

"I know." He took a deep breath and nodded. "Finn wasn't at all surprised by your decision. After all, you've got MacLennan blood running through your veins."

"Your words or his?" she asked.

"He's proud of you for taking on the fight. So am I. He knew every detail about you growing up. Your father sent him letters with your photo. He made him promise not to write back. He tried to get in touch with you when your father died. His letters came back unanswered."

Sophia kicked at the dirt. "Mother Malevolent never gave me his letters." She felt a moment of pity for the woman.

"She's not important. Just hearing about you was enough for Finn." He reached into the pocket of his jacket and handed her a small package. "He sent you a gift."

Sophia stared at the plain brown paper. For so long, she thought no one cared. In her hand was proof she had a loving grandfather. Her stepmother was no longer a thought. She ripped open the paper. Rays from the sun illuminated the brooch in her hand. She brushed her fingers over the raised inscription. "This is for the Valor of my Ancestors," she whispered. Peace and fulfillment overwhelmed her. "The motto is so significant after all I've been through."

"Your perseverance and diligence kept the shop where it belongs. I wish I had seen the faces of the firm's lawyers bidding against you."

"According to Granny, they left in quite a huff." She had so much more she needed to say. "Keeping my family legacy alive wasn't the only thing keeping me busy." She rushed the words. "I read the important parts in Granny's book."

"And—?" He raised a brow.

"I know why she kept the book a secret. I learned my great-great-grandfather, Ross, was quite an adventurer." She decided to put an end to the unanswered questions about her descendants. Maybe someday she would want to know more, but not now. At the moment, the book's secret was meaningless compared to the possibilities of a future with Ian.

"Are you okay with what you discovered?"

"It's an Ulster secret, too. It doesn't matter if the truth is ever revealed." The loud sound of honking car horns distracted her. "What's going on?" She turned toward the far end of the field and watched a caravan of vehicles roll to a stop.

Alana and Tim stepped from the pink-and-white bakery van.

The mayor and Judy arrived together.

The Logans pulled in behind them.

Fiona parked across the road.

Mr. Gordon stepped from his car and reached in the back seat for his pipes.

"Looks like the party is here." Ian glanced toward the road.

"Hey, you two, come on over," Tim shouted above the ruckus.

"We should join them." Perfectly happy standing by the dusty site with Ian, she made no effort to move.

"*Aye*, lass. We just lost the privacy I was striving for. If you're okay with standing here a little longer, I'll tell you more about my meeting with your grandfather."

"They can wait." She was eager to hear what he had to say. She dismissed the newcomers with a wave.

"Your grandfather asked me all about you. I should have brought a recent photo." He brushed a knuckle across her cheek.

"What did you say?" Sophia knew how she would answer the question if asked what she loved about Ian. His confidence, compassion, and sexy intelligence drew her to him from the beginning. Add his charming accent and ginger hair, she found the perfect man.

"I told him how you greeted me with a rolling pin in your hand the first time we met, but your temper was balanced by the sweet scent of your delicious cookies. He laughed when I told him your brow tilted just like your ancestor Marjorie."

Sophia purposely wrinkled her brow.

"He said he would fall in love with you if he wasn't already your grandfather. He gave me another gift and suggested I put it to good use." Ian removed a worn, velvet ring box from his pocket. "This belonged to your Grandmother Sophia." He sank down onto one knee. "So what do you think?"

"Is this a proposal, Professor Campbell?" Her heart pounded hard. "Get out of the dirt." She tugged his elbow.

"I'm not very good at impromptu situations." He stood and placed the ring in her palm. "Will you marry me, Sophia MacLennan Porter?" He closed his fingers around her hand.

The answer stuck in her throat, but she managed a definite nod. The ring felt warm in her palm. She slipped it on the tip of her index finger. "It looks like my grandmother's fingers were very slim."

"We can have it sized to fit, but it might damage the engraving. You can wear it around your neck until we find a more suitable band."

"You always have a practical solution to the problem." She slipped the ring off her fingertip and held it up to the light. The etching on the inner circle was difficult to read. "I can't make out the engraving." She handed the ring to Ian. "It looks like two names.

The sun hid behind a cloud.

"It's a traditional hand-engraved sentiment." He waited for the sun to reappear and read the simple inscription. "Sophia and Finn."

"*My* grandparents." She leaned closer. The old-world look to the letters, and knowing she had a family that cared, warmed her heart. "We could continue the tradition. I'd like our rings to say Sophia and Ian. How does that sound, professor?"

"The correct names would make it far easier for prospective genealogists to figure out who we are." He slipped the ring into his pocket.

"Remember the first time we came here?" She glanced past the site in the direction of the cornerstones. "Everything is so different."

"The suggestion was yours." He laughed. "You were a reluctant assistant."

A warm breeze blew across the hole full of dirt, bones, and MacLennan history.

"You were very persuasive." Sophia grabbed hold of his hand and looked into the pit. "Do you believe Marjorie and Ross connected us for a purpose other than to tell their story?" Could he, a man, who based everything on fact, believe in a supernatural power?

"I couldn't completely ignore the theory." He edged her back and turned her toward him. "I know one thing that's a reality."

"What's that?" Her heart beat fast.

"Whatever power brought us together is not important." He brushed a kiss across her lips. "I love you and want to spend the rest of my life waking up next to you."

A word about the author...

Zelda Benjamin has always had a passion for storytelling. A former pediatric ER nurse, she now spends her free time baking and traveling with family when traveling is safe. Combining her passions has led to many memorable experiences, whether it's the food, the culture, or authentic lifestyles.

You can find recipes and travel tips on her blog http://lovebychocolate.blogspot.com

Visit her author page for more information about her books https://www.amazon.com/Zelda-Benjamin/e/B001JS8IPG%3Fref=dbs_a_mng_rwt_scns _share

http://www.zeldabenjamin.com